Cole stepped closer and put
his mouth to Olivia's ear.

"Admit it, you're just a big softie."

"Am not."

He nipped her ear, making her quiver. "I like watching you with the kids," he said. "You gave them costumes from your trunk, the one you so carefully keep separate from your usual stock because the things in there mean something to you."

She sucked in a breath. "How do you know?"

"Because you almost took my finger off when I touched it the other night."

"Am I that transparent?"

"No," he said. "You're actually hard as hell to read. You don't give away much. I just happen to know you now."

"You think you know me? Just because we've done… it," she said, "doesn't mean—"

"We discussed your sexual vocabulary. 'It' is not on the list of acceptable descriptions for what we did."

"Fine, we had wild monkey sex that ruined me for all other men. Happy?"

"Getting there." He moved in close. Real close…

Praise for Jill Shalvis and Her Novels

Once in a Lifetime

"Top Pick! 4½ stars! Shalvis never disappoints with her witty, comical and überromantic reads...should be on every reader's TBR list. Fans of contemporary romance will fall in love with Aubrey and Ben and find their sexual tension electrifying...Sweet and spicy—what more could you ask for?"

—*RT Book Reviews*

"As Aubrey grows stronger and more certain, readers will cheer for her—and for the love she deserves."

—*Washington Post*

"Nine books into this series and I still look forward to each one...There is no stress or that guessing game of will I or won't I like it when I open these books...The first three Lucky Harbor books will always be my favorite but *Once in a Lifetime* gave those books a run for their money."

—**FictionVixen.com**

"*Once in a Lifetime* is aww-inducing, entertaining, and all-in-all quite the charming love story. I love the characters, from the lovebirds to the regulars. I love the setting and wish I lived in a place like Lucky Harbor."

—**DreysLibrary.com**

It Had to Be You

"Engaging writing, characters that walk straight into your heart, and a town you can't wait to revisit make this touching, hilarious tale another heart-warmer worthy of Shalvis's popular series."

—Library Journal

"Four stars! A winner...Readers will laugh out loud as they rush to turn the pages."

—RT Book Reviews

"Ms. Shalvis has a gift for writing down-to-earth yet quirky heroines and swoonworthy, honorable heroes."

—HeroesandHeartbreakers.com

"A sweet and sexy romance to warm the heart, all wrapped in warm fuzzies and humor. If you love contemporary romance, you'll have to read Jill Shalvis."

—DreysLibrary.com

Forever and a Day

"4½ stars! Top Pick! Shalvis once again racks up a hit... laughter is served in doses as generous as the chocolate the heroine relies on to get through the day. Readers will treasure each turn of the page and be sorry when this one is over."

—RT Book Reviews

"[Shalvis] has quickly become one of my go-to authors of contemporary romance. Her writing is smart, fun, and sexy, and her books never fail to leave a smile on my face long after I've closed the last page...Jill Shalvis is an author not to be missed!"

—TheRomanceDish.com

"Jill Shalvis is such a talented author that she brings to life characters who make you laugh, cry, and are a joy to read."

—RomRevToday.com

At Last

"Full of laughter, snark, and a super-hot attraction between the main characters. Shalvis has painted a wonderful world, full of entertaining supporting characters and beautiful scenery."

—RT Book Reviews

"A sexy, romantic read...What I love about Jill Shalvis's books is that she writes sexy, adorable heroes...the sexual tension is out of this world. And of course, in true Shalvis fashion, she expertly mixes in humor that has you laughing out loud."

—HeroesandHeartbreakers.com

"A sexy, fun tale from the creative mind of Jill Shalvis...*At Last* will have you laughing, smiling, and sniffling... Another stellar read I highly recommend."

—RomRevToday.com

Lucky in Love

"Shalvis pens a tale rife with the three H's of romance: heat, heart, and humor. *Lucky in Love* is a down-to-the-toes charmer...It doesn't matter if you're chuckling or reaching for an iced drink to cool down the heat her characters generate—Shalvis doesn't disappoint."

—RT Book Reviews

"I always enjoy reading a Jill Shalvis book. She's a consistently elegant, bold, clever writer...Very witty—I laughed out loud countless times reading *Lucky in Love*...[It] is also one of the hottest books I've read by Ms. Shalvis. Mallory and Ty burn up the sheets (and the pages) with regularity and these scenes are sizzling."

—All About Romance (LikesBooks.com)

"Whenever I'm looking for a romance to chase away the worries of life, all I have to do is pick up a Jill Shalvis book. Once again she has worked her magic with the totally entertaining *Lucky in Love*."

—RomRevToday.com

Head Over Heels

"[A] winning roller-coaster ride…[a] touching, character-rich, laughter-laced, knockout sizzler."

—*Library Journal* (starred review)

"Healthy doses of humor, lust, and love work their magic as Shalvis tells Chloe's story…Wit, smoking-hot passion, and endearing tenderness…a big winner."

—*Publishers Weekly*

"The Lucky Harbor series has become one of my favorite contemporary series, and *Head Over Heels* didn't disappoint…such a fun, sexy book…I think this one can be read as a stand-alone book, but I encourage you to try the first two in the series, where you meet all the characters of this really fun town."

—USAToday.com

The Sweetest Thing

"A Perfect 10! Once again Jill Shalvis provides readers with a sexy, funny, hot tale."

—RomRevToday.com

"Witty, fun, and the characters are fabulous."
—**FreshFiction.com**

"It is fabulous revisiting Lucky Harbor! I have been on tenterhooks waiting for Tara and Ford's story, and yet again, Jill Shalvis does not disappoint…A rollicking good time."
—**RomanceJunkiesReviews.com**

Simply Irresistible

"Hot, sweet, fun, and romantic! Pure pleasure!"
—**Robyn Carr,** *New York Times* **bestselling author**

"This often hilarious novel has a few serious surprises, resulting in a delightfully satisfying story."
—**LibraryJournal.com**

"Heartwarming and sexy…an abundance of chemistry, smoldering romance, and hilarious sisterly antics."
—*Publishers Weekly*

He's So Fine

Also by Jill Shalvis

The Lucky Harbor Series

Simply Irresistible
The Sweetest Thing
Heating Up the Kitchen (cookbook)
Christmas in Lucky Harbor (omnibus)
Small Town Christmas (anthology)
Head Over Heels
Lucky in Love
At Last
Forever and a Day
"Under the Mistletoe" (short story)
It Had to Be You
Always on My Mind
A Christmas to Remember (anthology)
Once in a Lifetime
Lucky Harbor (omnibus)
It's in His Kiss

Other Novels

Blue Flame
White Heat
Seeing Red
Her Sexiest Mistake

He's So Fine

Jill Shalvis

GRAND CENTRAL
PUBLISHING

NEW YORK   BOSTON

Copyright © 2014 by Jill Shalvis
Excerpt from *One in a Million* copyright © 2014 by Jill Shalvis

Grand Central Publishing
Hachette Book Group
237 Park Avenue
New York, NY 10017

www.HachetteBookGroup.com

Printed in the United States of America

OPM

First edition: September 2014
10 9 8 7 6 5 4 3 2 1

Grand Central Publishing is a division of Hachette Book Group, Inc.
The Grand Central Publishing name and logo is a trademark of Hachette Book Group, Inc.

The Hachette Speakers Bureau provides a wide range of authors for speaking events. To find out more, go to www.hachettespeakersbureau.com or call (866) 376-6591.

The publisher is not responsible for websites (or their content) that are not owned by the publisher.

To Laura and Julie and HelenKay,
for loving me through the writing
of this one despite the fact that
I wasn't always lovable :)

He's So Fine

Chapter 1

♥

For a guy balancing his weight between the stern of his boat and the dock, thinking about sex instead of what he was doing was a real bonehead move. Cole Donovan was precariously perched on the balls of his feet above some seriously choppy, icy water. So concentrating would've been the smart move.

But he had no smarts left, which was what happened when you hadn't had a good night's sleep in far too long—your brain wandered into areas it shouldn't.

Sex being one of those areas.

He shook his head to clear it. It was way too early for those kinds of thoughts. Not quite dawn, and the sky was a brilliant kaleidoscope of purples and blues and reds. Cole worked with a flashlight between his teeth, his fingers threading new electrical wire through the running lights on the stern. He only had a couple hours before a group of eight was coming through for a tour of the area.

That's what Cole and his two partners and best friends

did—they hired out themselves and their fifty-foot Wright Sport boat, chartering deep-sea fishing, whale watching, scuba diving…if it could be done, they did it. Sam was their financial guy and boatbuilder. Tanner was their scuba diving instructor and communications expert. Cole was the captain, chief navigator, mechanic, and—lucky him—the face of Lucky Harbor Charters, mostly because neither Sam nor Tanner was exactly a service-oriented person.

They'd had a warm Indian summer here in the Pacific Northwest, but October had roared in as if Mother Nature was pissed off at the world, and maybe in need of a Xanax to boot. But business was still good. Or it had been, until last night. He and Tanner had taken a group of frat boys out, and one of the idiots had managed to kick in the lights running along the stern, destroying not only the casing but also the electrical.

Cole could fix it—there was little he couldn't fix. But as he got down to it, a harsh wind slapped him in the face, threatening his balance. He kicked off the dock so that he was balanced entirely on the edge of the stern. Still not a position for the faint of heart, but after five years on oil rigs and two more running Lucky Harbor Charters, Cole felt more at ease on the water than just about anywhere else.

He could smell the salt on the air and hear the swells smacking up against the dock moorings. The wind hit him again, and he shivered to the bone. Last week, he'd been out here working in board shorts and nothing else, the sun warming his back. Today he was in a knit cap, thick sweatshirt, cargo pants, and boots, and he was wishing for gloves like a little girl. He shoved his flashlight into his pocket, brought his hands to his mouth, and blew on his fingers for a moment before reaching for the wires again.

Just as they connected, there was a sizzle and a flash, and he jerked, losing his footing. The next thing he knew, he was airborne, weightless for a single heartbeat...

And then he hit the icy water, plunging deep, the contact stealing the air from his lungs. Stunned, he fought the swells, his heavy clothes, himself, eyes open as he searched for the flames that surely went along with the explosion.

Jesus, not another fire. That was his only thought as panic gripped him hard. He opened his mouth and—

Swallowed a lungful of seawater.

This cleared his head. He *wasn't* on the oil rig in the gulf. He *wasn't* in the explosion that had killed Gil, and nearly Tanner as well. He was in Lucky Harbor.

He kicked hard, breaking the surface, gasping as he searched for the boat, a part of him still not wholly convinced. But there. She was there, only a few feet away.

No flames, not a single lick. Just the cold-ass swells of the Pacific Northwest.

Treading water, Cole shook his head. A damn flashback, which he hadn't had in over a year—

"Omigod, I see you!" a female voice called out. "Just hang on, I'm coming!" This was accompanied by hurried footsteps clapping on the dock. "Help!" she yelled as she ran. "Help, there's a man in the water! Sir, sir, can you hear me? I'm coming. *Sir?*"

If she called him "sir" one more time, he was going to drown himself. His dad had been a *sir*. The old guy who ran the gas pumps on the corner of Main and First was a *sir*. Cole wasn't a damn *sir*. He was opening his mouth to tell her so, and also that he was fine, not in any danger at all, when she took a flying leap off the dock.

And landed right on top of him.

The icy water closed over both of their heads, and as another swell hit, they became a tangle of limbs and water-laden clothing. He fought free and once again broke the surface, whipping his head around to look for the woman.

No sign of her.

Shit. Gasping in a deep breath, he dove back down and found her doing what he'd been doing only a moment before—fighting the water and her clothes, and herself. Her own worst enemy, she was losing the battle and sinking fast. Grasping the back of her sweater, Cole hauled her up, kicking hard to get them both to the surface.

She sucked in some air and immediately started coughing, reaching out blindly for him and managing to get a handful of his junk.

"Maybe we could get to shore first," he said wryly.

Holding on to him with both arms and legs like a monkey clinging to a tree, she squeezed him tight. "I've g-g-got y-y-you," she stuttered through already chattering teeth, then climbed on top of his head, sending him under again.

He managed to yank her off him and get her head above water. "Hey—"

"D-don't panic," she told him earnestly. "It's g-g-gonna be o-o-okay."

She actually thought she was saving him. If the situation weren't so deadly, Cole might have thought some of this was funny. But she was turning into a Popsicle before his very eyes, and so was he. "Listen, just relax—"

"H-hang on to m-me," she said, and…dunked him again.

For the love of—. "*Stop* trying to save me," he told her. "I'm begging you."

Her hair was in her face, and behind the strands plastered to her skin, her eyes widened. "Oh, my God. You're trying to commit suicide."

"What? *No*." The situation was ridiculous, and he was frustrated and effing cold, but damn, it was hard not to be charmed by the fact that she was trying to save him, even as she was going down for the count herself. "I'm trying to keep you from killing me."

The flashback to the rig fire long gone, Cole treaded water to keep them afloat as he assessed their options. There were two.

Shore or boat.

They were at the stern of the boat, much closer to the swimming platform than to the shore. And in any case, there was no way his "rescuer" could swim the distance. Though Cole was a world-class swimmer himself, he was already frozen to the bone, and so was she. They needed out of the water…fast.

With a few strokes, he got them to the stern of the boat, where he hoisted her up to the platform, pulling himself up after her.

She lay right where he'd dumped her, gulping in air, that long, dark hair everywhere. Leaning over her, he shoved the wet strands from her face to better see her and realized with a jolt that he recognized her. She lived in one of the warehouse apartments across from Lucky Harbor Charters.

Her name was Olivia Something-or-Other.

All he knew about her was that she hung out with Sam's fiancée, Becca; she ran some sort of shop downtown; she dressed in a way that said both "hands off" and "hot mama"; and he'd caught her watching him and the guys surfing on more than one occasion.

"Y-y-you're bleeding," she said from flat on her back, staring up at him.

Cole brought his fingers to the sting on his temple, and his fingers indeed came away red with his own blood. Perfect. Just a cut though, no less than he deserved after that stupid stunt of shocking the shit out of himself with the wiring and then tumbling into the water. "I'm fine." It was her he was worried about. Her jeans and sweater were plastered to her. She was missing a boot. And she was shivering violently enough to rattle the teeth right out of her head. "You're *not* fine," he said.

"Just c-c-cold."

No shit. "What the hell were you thinking?" he asked, "Jumping in after me like that?"

Her eyes flashed, and he discovered they were the exact same color as her hair—deep, dark chocolate.

"I th-th-thought you were d-d-drowning!" she said through chattering teeth.

Cole shook his head. "I didn't almost drown until you jumped on top of me."

"What h-h-happened?"

"I was working on the electrical wiring and got shocked and fell in."

"S-s-see? You needed help!"

He absolutely did not. But arguing with her would get them nowhere, except maybe dead. "Come on, the plan is to get you home and warmed up." Rising to his feet, he reached down and pulled her up with him, holding on to her when she wobbled. "Are you—"

"I'm f-f-fine," she said, and stepped back to look down at herself. "I l-l-lost my favorite b-b-boot rescuing y-y-you."

She called that a rescue? "Can you even swim?"

"Y-y-yes!" She crossed her arms over her chest. "A l-l-little bit."

He stared at her in disbelief. "A *little bit*? Seriously? You risked your life on that?"

"You were in t-t-trouble!"

Right. They could argue about that later. "Time to get you home, Supergirl."

"B-b-but my b-b-boot."

"We'll rescue the boot later."

"We w-w-will?"

No. Her boot was on the ocean floor and DOA. "Later," he said again, and grabbing her hand, he pulled her across the platform, through the stern. He needed to get her off the boat.

She dug her heels in, one in just a sock, one booted.

"What?" he asked.

Still shivering wildly, she looked at him with misery. "I d-d-dropped my ph-ph-phone on the dock."

"Okay, we'll grab it."

"Y-y-yes, but I d-d-didn't drop my keys."

"That's good," he said, wondering if she'd hit her head.

"Y-y-you don't get it. I th-th-think I lost my k-k-keys in the w-w-water."

Well, shit. No keys, no getting her inside her place. This wasn't good. Nor was her color. She was waxen, pale. They couldn't delay getting her out of the elements and warm. "Okay, plan B," he said. "We warm you here on the boat." Again he started to tug her along, needing to get her inside and belowdecks, but she stumbled against him like her limbs weren't working.

Plan C, he thought grimly, and swung her up into his arms.

She clutched at him. "N-n-not necessary—"

Ignoring her, he got them both into the small galley, where he set her down on the bench at the table. Keeping his hands on her arms, he crouched in front of her to look into her eyes. "You still with me? You okay?"

"Y-y-y—" Giving up, she dropped her head to his chest.

"Not okay," he muttered, and stroked a hand down the back of her head and along her trembling frame.

Truth was, he wasn't much better off. His head was still bleeding, and his shoulder was throbbing. He had nothing on her, though. She was violently trembling against him. Easing her back, he got busy. First he cranked the heater, then he opened their linens storage box, pulling out towels and blankets, which he tossed in a stack at her side. "Okay," he said. "Strip."

Chapter 2

♥

Olivia's head jerked up, and her dark eyes met Cole's. "Wh-wh-what?"

Not good, he thought. She wasn't tracking. "Your clothes are keeping you cold," he explained as gently as he could. "So you gotta lose 'em. Towel dry and then we'll wrap you in blankets." He kicked off his boots and pulled off his water-laden sweatshirt, which hit the floor like a fifty-pound weight. "I've got spare clothes here. I'll get you something to wear." His T-shirt went next. Another *thunk*.

Not moving, she stared at his chest. "You're c-c-crazy if you think I'm g-g-going to s-s-strip—"

"That," he said, "or I call nine-one-one. Nonnegotiable, Olivia."

She blinked. "You kn-kn-know my name?"

"Yeah. You're the woman who watches me and the guys surf while pretending to talk to Becca. Get moving, Supergirl."

"I d-d-don't watch," she said, her gaze still lingering on his chest.

He had to laugh. "Okay, fine. You don't watch us." And he was the Tooth Fairy.

"And I'm f-f-fine," she said with a shiver that nearly threw her off the bench.

"You're blue, is what you are. You could pass for a Smurf."

She flashed those dark eyes at him. Clearly she had plenty on her mind, but she was shaking too hard to let him have it. Lucky him.

"Look," he said. "I'll close my eyes, okay? And it's not like we're going to do the stupid chick flick thing where we have to get into bed together to warm each other up."

"G-g-good, 'cause if you tried it, you'd be w-w-walking funny tomorrow."

If she could toss out threats like that, she probably wasn't in immediate danger of dying from hypothermia. But caution and safety first, as he'd learned the hard way over the years. "You're still shaking badly," he said. He grabbed a huge beach towel and shook it out, holding it up between them.

Instead of jumping up to follow his unspoken command, she narrowed her eyes.

But she wasn't the only one who could play tough-as-hell. "Strip," he said again, losing the gentle voice and going with the one he'd used as chief positioning operator and navigator, directing crews on the rigs. "Or I'll do it for you."

In truth, this was an empty threat, but the Boss Voice got through to her. She stood up, glaring at him before ducking behind the towel.

There was some movement, some rustling, which he took as a good sign. "We'll get you dry," he said, staring up at the ceiling to avoid catching a peek at her. "And then I'll find you a pair of sweats and help you break into your place, since you lost your keys trying to kill me—er, save me."

Her head reappeared for the sole purpose of delivering a pretty impressive eye roll, then she vanished behind the towel again. When he heard the heavy, wet thud of her clothes hitting the floor, he leaned forward and wrapped the towel around her body as best he could. His fingers inadvertently brushed the soft, wet skin of her shoulders and back, and he had to force himself not to think about the fact that she'd dropped her sweater and jeans. He was about to do the strip routine himself, and he didn't want to be sporting wood while he was at it. "Dry off," he said, and stepped back from her.

She nodded but didn't move.

"Olivia?" he asked.

Her face was a mask of misery. "M-m-my arms won't w-w-work."

Shit. He quickly and gently pushed her back down to the bench, sat at her side, and began to pile blankets over the top of them both.

"W-what are you d-doing?"

"Sharing my body heat," he said.

"I c-c-can't feel any h-h-heat."

"You will." Beneath the blankets, he reached for the towel she still had wrapped around her. "Don't freak," he warned. "I'm just going to remove the wet towel and pull you into me."

She opened her mouth, but using her sluggishness to

his benefit, Cole quickly stripped the towel away from her, wrapping his arms around her, pulling her into him as two things happened simultaneously. One, she squeaked. Probably trying to formulate her next threat.

And two—holy shit—he realized she was completely, totally, one hundred percent naked beneath the layer of blankets.

And *pissed*. "Y-y-your pants!" she gasped. "Th-th-they're c-c-cold!"

"Sorry, but I'm trying to do the right thing here," he said through clenched teeth. He couldn't see a thing below her neck, but he could sure as hell feel her. His hands were on her hip and low on her back, respectively, not touching anything he shouldn't be, but damn she was soft, and at the feel of her, his brain clicked off. Just completely flatlined.

"I'm n-n-naked," she snapped.

And oh, how well he knew it. He was pretty sure her nipples were boring holes in his chest. Just thinking about it had him warming up considerably. In fact, he might be starting to sweat. It'd been a while, but he was pretty sure he remembered nipples being one of his favorite parts of a woman's body—

She gave him a shove.

"Sorry," he said. "But you don't want me to go away. I'm the one making you warm."

"N-n-not what I m-m-mean," she said. "Y-y-you have to be n-n-naked too!"

He stared at her. "That's a *really* bad idea."

"You w-w-want me to freak out?" she asked. "No? Then s-s-strip, Donovan."

Bossy thing, wasn't she.

"N-n-now," she added, eyes sparking.

Yeah, bossy. And he liked it. "Whatever you say." Still covered by the blankets, he shucked out of his pants—feeling more than just a twinge of pain in his shoulder now, something he ignored—and kicked the material away. "Better?"

"Are y-y-you…smiling?" she asked in disbelief.

He didn't even try to hide it. "A beautiful woman just ordered me to strip," he said. "But not because she wants my body. It's funny, so yeah, I'm smiling."

"Oh p-p-please," she scoffed, and surprised the hell out of him by leaning in and carefully dabbing at the cut on his temple with the edge of a towel. "I've s-s-seen you *and* your partners," she said, eyeing the cut and apparently deciding he was going to live. "You're all l-l-listed on Lucky Harbor's Tumblr as some of the hottest guys in t-t-town," she said in a tone that didn't suggest she was all that impressed by the dubious title. "I know you've got to have game."

Seemed he wasn't the only one warming up—her teeth were rattling less and less.

"You could probably turn a woman's head with a single crook of your finger," she muttered, rolling the towel to get to a clean spot to press against his temple.

He didn't just smile now, he out-and-out laughed.

"What's so funny now?"

"I was the runt all the way through high school. Small and skinny, and sickly too, even ending up in the hospital annually for strep and pneumonia. I've never crooked my finger at a woman in my life, though that's definitely a skill I wouldn't mind acquiring." Luckily, in his senior year, he'd finally had his tonsils removed, and in the next year he'd grown eight full inches and gained fifty pounds of muscle, which had come in handy when he'd been working on the oil rigs. Unfortunately, there hadn't been a lot of women on those rigs.

In fact, there'd been a total of three.

Given the odds—eighty-five guys to three women—Cole had done pretty well for himself, considering. But that was then.

He, Sam, and Tanner had come back to Lucky Harbor after the rig fire, having lost Gil. And in the time since losing his best friend, and then his father last year as well, he hadn't had much game at all.

Correction. He'd had *no* game. "If I could turn a woman's head that easily," he said, "you'd be doing something other than dabbing the cut on my forehead."

She went still for a beat, her eyes wide on his. He had no idea what was in her head, but he knew what was in his—the feel of the soft, curvy body practically in his lap.

And he nearly choked when she lifted the blanket and took a peek at him. "What the hell—"

She raised her gaze to his. "You left your underwear on."

"Yes," he said.

"But you told me to strip, and I did."

"I didn't say strip *everything*," he said. "It never occurred to me that you'd lose the undies. Hot as they are."

They both stared at the black lace lying innocuously on the floor. She flushed and lifted her chin. "Well, there's only one thing to do now," she said.

"What?"

"You have to do the same."

"Excuse me?" he asked.

"Drop the boxers."

He stared at her. "Tell me the truth. You hit your head, too, right?"

"No. And I'm not kidding," she said, jabbing him in the chest with a finger. "Lose 'em, or a freakout of *epic* proportions will commence in three. Two. One—"

"Jesus, hang on." He worked at shedding his boxers, doing his best to keep covered by the blanket. "I can't believe you looked after I promised not to look at you—"

"Yes, well, one of us isn't a gentleman, now are we?" she asked.

A short laugh escaped him, which he cut off when she—holy shit—lifted the blanket and peeked again.

Grabbing the blankets like a virgin at a frat sleepover, he swore. "Jesus, woman!"

"Just making sure," she said.

"Sure of what?"

Looking pretty damn pleased with herself, she laughed.

And damn, she had a smile on her. Mischievous and full of secrets, but still contagious. "Okay," he said. "I like that look on your face much better than the abject misery you were wearing, but didn't anyone ever tell you not to look at a naked man and laugh?"

She just laughed again, the sound soft and musical and somehow both sexy and sweet at the same time.

He sighed. "At least you're warming up."

"A little," she allowed.

"Maybe I should peek to make sure." Teasing, he made to lift the blankets.

With a squeak, she fisted them tight to her chest. "Don't you dare!"

"Uh-huh. What's good for the goose and all that." All

he could see of her over the pile of blankets was her face, those fathomless eyes, and all that wet, dark hair. She smelled like ocean and sexy woman—his favorite scent— and he was suddenly struck by how beautiful she was.

Oh shit, Donovan, don't go there…

"Cole?"

He had to clear his throat twice to answer. "Yeah?"

"I really need my phone—it's on the dock where I dropped it. Hopefully. But I'm still cold."

Still staring into her eyes, he pulled her tighter into him, and at the feel of her soft curves, his body gave up the valiant fight and tightened.

Some parts more than others.

He immediately began to work complicated calculus problems in his head, trying to remember the definition of the derivative of the function—

She pressed her icy feet against his calves, and he yelped like one of his sisters.

She laughed again, and he immediately lost track of calculus. All he could feel was her frozen limbs. Rubbing her arms to warm her up, he forced himself not to think about what she might look like under the blanket.

He failed miserably, which meant he was hard as a rock and buck-ass nekkid. And worse, she had to feel it pressing into her hip. He tried to pull back, but she made a soft, disagreeable sound and tightened her grip on him.

"You're not warm yet?" he asked in a voice so low as to be almost inaudible.

He couldn't help it. He didn't have enough blood to run both heads. And on top of that, their bodies were melded together in a way that had him heated up and aching to lay her flat on her back on the bench and—

"You're really warm," she whispered.

Try hot as hell, babe. "I'll go get your phone," he said valiantly. "And something hot for you to drink." *Coffee, tea...me.*

"Uh..." She shifted, bumping a bare thigh right into his erection.

He hissed out a breath as his hips gave an entirely instinctive roll to get closer. *Christ.* And there, perfect, now she was back to staring at him.

"You're..." She broke off. "Um."

"Yeah." He was "um" all right. "Involuntary reaction," he promised. "Just ignore it."

"But—"

"Seriously. Don't give it another thought." He went to shrug and had to bite back a grimace thanks to the pain in his shoulder. "Drink?" he asked again.

She bit her lower lip and nodded. "Tea, please."

Tea for her, and never mind that it was the crack of dawn, he'd take a vodka, straight up. He grabbed a towel for coverage and worked at not further revealing himself, which involved gymnastics that should have won him a medal.

Olivia was smiling by the time he got all wrapped up. "I've already seen it all," she reminded him.

"I really wish you'd stop smiling when you say that." Shaking his head when her smile only widened, he moved up the stairs to go retrieve her phone for her, the irony that she was now amused instead of disgruntled—and he was disgruntled instead of amused—not escaping him.

Chapter 3

♥

Olivia watched Cole go, nothing but a towel low on his hips, the muscles in his back all taut and delineated—and perfect. He moved like an athlete, with easy, economical, and innately testosterone-fueled grace—

Her smile faded as he rolled a broad shoulder, his other hand settling on it to rub absently as if it ached.

He'd been hurt. Which meant she wasn't the only one of them good at deflecting attention away from herself.

Not that this surprised her. There was a sharp intelligence in Cole's eyes, which went along with his healthy survival instinct.

Damn. She still couldn't believe what had just happened. She'd been out for an early walk on the dock when she'd seen a guy in a knit cap, sweatshirt, and cargo pants hit the water and go under. And yeah, she'd mistakenly assumed he'd needed help and had jumped in after him to try to save him. So what? It meant that she still had a heart, that she could indeed care about someone other than herself.

And that was a good thing. A relief, to be honest. But she was feeling pretty damn naked about now.

Oh, that's right. She *was* naked.

At least Cole was in the same boat. His wet clothes were still lying at her feet, mixed in with hers, which gave the situation an air of intimacy that she could have done without.

As if being bare as on the day she'd been born didn't do that all on its own.

She nudged the clothes with a foot and curled in on herself a little. Having spent her formative years on a TV set where assistants and dressers had tugged and pulled at her nonstop, she'd long ago lost her modesty in urgent situations. Cole had said strip, and she'd done so.

But at the memory of his shock when he'd realized she'd stripped to her birthday suit, her face flamed all over again.

Cole came back in less than a minute, handing over her phone.

"Thanks," she said, and thumbed the screen to activate it. Four missed texts, three from her mom, and though they hadn't actually spoken in weeks, her mom got right to the point.

TV Land called. Again. They need your commitment to do the retrospective show, and there's talk of a spin-off series where they'd want your voice-over!!!

And then, time-stamped only two minutes later:

Hello??? Sharlyn?? This is the big break we've been
waiting for…

First, Olivia really hated it when her mom called her
Sharlyn. She knew Olivia had changed it years ago. And
second—*we*? No. It was the break *her mother* had been
waiting for. Olivia didn't want a break. She'd had her
one and only break when *Not Again, Hailey!* had been
canceled shortly after her sixteenth birthday. Yes, she'd
gone on to have a meltdown of epic proportions. Britney
Spears and Miley Cyrus had nothing on her; hence the
name change from Sharlyn Peterson to Olivia Bentley.

She'd come out on the other side a long time ago and
now lived a normal life. Or at least as normal a life as she
could have ever wished for.

And she loved it.

She loved it so much she was willing to lie to everyone
she met to keep it.

And had.

The third text wasn't any more a surprise than the first
two.

Remember I spent my 17th bday in the bathroom @
my high school graduation kegger party having you
Sharlyn—you owe me.

No, her mother hadn't exactly been the classic mom-
manager, but it wasn't as if being a teenage mom from
a farm in Kentucky had exactly prepared her for Hollywood.

The fourth and last text was from Jolyn, Olivia's older
sister by eleven months.

Fair warning, she wants her boobs done again.

"What's wrong?"

Olivia jumped and set her phone down on the bench away from her.

Cole studied her for a beat, and she took the opportunity to do the same. He had glossy brown hair gone wild thanks to their impromptu swim. He was also sporting at least two days' worth of scruff on a square jaw, and his ready smile was devastatingly contagious. And then there were his eyes, ocean blue and deep and…mesmerizing. They held as many secrets as hers did.

Clearing her throat, she shook her head. "Nothing's wrong," she said. *Or everything, take your pick.*

"Nothing's why you're frowning at your phone like you wish it'd gone into the drink along with your keys?" he asked with a healthy dose of *get real* in his tone.

Olivia shrugged and pulled the blanket in tighter around herself with a shiver.

Swearing softly, he covered her with two more blankets, pressing the wool closer against her, his hands thorough but carefully respectful.

And damn, she missed his body heat.

Apparently not versed in reading a woman's mind, Cole moved to the stove in the kitchen. *Galley*, Olivia corrected. On a boat, it was called a galley. And it was a damn fine one, too. In fact, the entire boat was nice. Beautiful wood accents and cabinetry, state-of-the-art interior and electronics. It was huge, and extremely well taken care of.

"What were you doing on the dock so early?" he asked.

"Just walking."

"At five thirty in the morning?" he asked.

"Best time to go." She'd moved to Lucky Harbor about a year ago and had taken over the vintage shop from a proprietor who'd run it into the ground. Olivia had wanted to come here since she'd been a child and her on-set tutor, Mrs. Henderson, had told her about growing up in idyllic, quirky, beautiful Lucky Harbor. Olivia had turned Unique Boutique around, babying the place back to life. It was a love affair for her, making the old valuable in a new way, and for the first time in her life, she was proud of her occupation.

She didn't open up for business until ten, but her body's inner clock had never gotten the message and was set for Annoyingly Early. Having spent a good number of years in Los Angeles, she never got tired of taking in the gorgeous landscape that was Lucky Harbor. The place was cradled between the Olympic Mountains and the gorgeous Pacific Northwest rocky coast, and she loved walking here. "It's peaceful," she said. "Safe."

"Not so much on the dock this morning."

"No," she agreed, taking in the way he smiled and how it caused her to as well.

"You took jumping my bones to a whole new level," Cole said.

Before this morning, she'd never had the occasion to speak to him directly, nor had she ever given him much thought. He was just a guy she occasionally caught glimpses of, in his company T-shirt and his low-slung cargo shorts with all the pockets, usually with tools sticking out of them.

Liar, the devil on her left shoulder said. *He's big and*

built, and when you watch him work on the boat in those shorts where all his goodies aren't necessarily relegated to his pockets, you give him plenty of thought...

It's okay, the angel on her right shoulder said. *He's a really great guy. All techno-geek with some alpha mixed in. It's natural to think about him.*

Naked? the devil asked. *Can we think about him naked?*

"If it helps, I think my rescuing days are over," Olivia told him, shoving aside her inner voices.

"Nah. You'd jump in again if you had to," he said, sounding confident.

"What makes you so sure?"

"Because you took a flying leap for me, a perfect stranger," he said. "Without even thinking about it." He was staring into the pot of water like it couldn't boil fast enough for him, and a whole new layer of emotion hit her.

Embarrassment.

Olivia had a lot of experience with not being wanted. Too much. Suddenly antsy to go, to get away from the boat and that horrible feeling of déjà vu, she started to get up.

But Cole's gaze lifted and pinned her in place with the bluest eyes she'd ever seen. "Stay still a few more minutes," he said.

"It's you who has a bump on your head," she said.

"Trust me, I've had a lot worse."

"And your shoulder?"

He ignored this. "Can you feel your fingers and toes?"

With him studying her carefully, she could feel every single inch, thank you very much, not to mention certain erogenous zones. "I can feel irritation at your bossiness," she said. "Does that count?"

He grinned. "That's a good start."

She didn't bother to roll her eyes. "You seem pretty at ease with a woman's irritation," she noted, curious about him, which was unusual in itself. Since moving to Lucky Harbor, she'd done a lot of keeping to herself, and other than making a habit of staring at Cole every chance she got, very little noticing of the opposite sex.

"A woman's irritation doesn't scare me much," he said. "I've got three sisters. I grew up in the House of Estrogen." He shrugged a broad, bare shoulder. "I'm good at inspiring whole new levels of irritation."

She couldn't imagine that to be true. He was easygoing and laid-back, and he had a way about him that inspired confidence. Or at least the sense that with him around, everything was going to be okay.

"How about you?" he asked. "You have family around who are a pain in your ass, too?"

She nearly let out a laugh, but it'd have been a manic one so she kept it to herself. Besides, his statement had been made with a small, affectionate smile. He clearly loved his family, pain in the ass or no. Explaining her situation would be like trying to describe life on Mars. Easier to simplify. "No," she said. "No family around at all."

Which, for a big, fat lie, was pretty much also the truth.

His smile vanished, and she looked away before she could catch any sort of sympathy in his gaze. She didn't want that. She didn't deserve that.

"I'm sorry," he said. "That sucks."

Look at that, she needed to give herself a pedicure.

Her pale purple toenails—complete with a few randomly placed white daisies—were peeking out from the blanket, and were chipped. The silver ring on her left second toe sparkled, though. Her agent had given it to her on her fifteenth birthday, only one year before *Not Again, Hailey!* had been canceled and everyone in Olivia's—Sharlyn's—life had deserted her. She pulled the blanket in tighter, suddenly feeling *very* naked. "You mentioned some spare clothes?"

"Yep." Cole poured hot water from a pan into a mug. "How do you take your tea?"

"Laced."

He smiled approvingly and bent low to a cabinet, coming up with a bottle of brandy. He doctored up her tea and brought it to her. "Hang tight." He vanished through a door and came back a moment later. "Try these," he said, dumping some clothing in her lap.

He still wore only the towel wrapped low on his hips. He had to be cold, but was seeing to her well-being first with the tea and clothing. It'd been a long time since anyone had catered to her needs before their own. A really long time. And even then it'd been because something was expected of her.

Not Cole. Not appearing to expect a damn thing, he hunkered down before her, hands on the bench on either side of her hips as he looked at her—not at her body, but right into her eyes. "Can you move your limbs now?" he asked. "Or are you still stiff with cold?"

She stared at him as she felt her hardened heart roll over in her chest and expose its tender underbelly, shocked at the way her throat tightened so that she couldn't speak.

If she lost it now, she told herself, she'd…make herself run every morning for a week.

She hated to run. She put it just behind a root canal in the list of things she hated. A root canal without drugs.

But her body apparently didn't care, because along with the tight throat her eyes burned. *Well, crap.*

Chapter 4

O livia?"

She did her best to give Cole a reassuring I'm-peachy-perfect-all-is-well smile, but she had to settle for baring her teeth because she was an inch from breaking down and she had no idea why. Oh, wait, it was because a man had just put her well-being before his own. That's how pathetic she was. She attempted another I'm-peachy smile, just for practice.

Clearly not buying what she was selling, Cole put a hand to her foot, gently squeezing as if testing her skin temperature. "Better," he said, and pulled a pair of thick socks from the pile of clothes he'd handed her. While she stared at him crouched at her side, he bent his head to the task and put the socks on her feet for her.

As he slid the socks up her calves, she had a moment of panic.

Had she shaved her legs? And when? Two days ago, yes? No? *God, please yes.*

"Unfortunately," he said, clueless to her internal debate, "my spare clothing stash doesn't extend to a pair of really hot boots like the ones you were wearing, so we're going to have to improvise." He lifted a pair of running shoes for her inspection. "Best I can do."

"No, they're great, thank you," she said, but she had to take a girl moment to mourn the boots. They'd been with her since her Hollywood days. She'd gotten them from her favorite set dresser, and once upon a time they'd meant the world to her. But that world no longer existed for her, and she was nothing if not pragmatic. She refused to waste any real time grieving something as ridiculously sentimental as a pair of boots.

Most likely not holding a boot funeral in his mind, Cole rose lithely, his entire body moving upward through her line of sight like a really great movie. Wide shoulders. Hard chest. And then mouthwatering abs that made her own stomach quiver a little bit.

Or a lot.

Now the towel was almost indecently low on his hips, and she stared at those cut muscles on his sides. She had no idea what they were actually called. "Muscles that make women stupid"?

At his soft laugh, her gaze jerked up to his face. "I'm just worried about your shoulder."

"Is that why you were staring at my abs?"

"Uh—" She broke off when he snorted and before she could come up with an excuse, he vanished into the other room again. Probably to give her privacy to dress. Standing up, she was happy to put that awkward, embarrassing moment behind her, and happier still to find that her limbs were indeed working again. She dropped the blankets and considered her options. A pair of sweat bottoms that were about a foot too long for her, and no underwear. Shrugging, she slid the sweats on.

Commando.

She rolled the excess material at her waist and cuffed them at her feet. Cole had provided a T-shirt advertising some dive shop in the Turks and Caicos and a thick Navy sweatshirt. Both smelled delicious as she pulled them on, like some sort of fresh, clean detergent, but there was also a hint of something she couldn't put her finger on. Whatever it was made her want to bury her face in the material and inhale for about a month. She was doing just that when he walked back into the room.

He arched a brow.

"I like the smell of your detergent," she said.

He smirked, and she barely resisted smacking herself in the forehead for being so lame.

Cole had pulled on another pair of cargo pants and a long sleeved T-shirt. He was still barefoot, his hair standing up on end like he hadn't even bothered to brush his fingers over it after pulling on the shirt. He eyed her wearing what she presumed were his clothes and smiled, sexy as all get out.

"I feel like we're going steady now," he said.

He had no problem talking about his feelings, joking or not. She wasn't anywhere close to as comfortable with her own emotions, and she drew an unsteady breath rather than admit she felt the odd sense of intimacy as well. "It takes more than clothes sharing to get me to go steady," she said.

"You did see me naked," he reminded her with a smile.

Yes, and the image of his naked body was burned in

her brain in the best possible way, not that she was about to admit that either. It was much smarter, and much easier, to give him a smart-ass smile in return.

He groaned and shook his head. "Giving me a complex," he said, but she knew he was just playing, because something warm had come into his eyes.

Uh-oh.

"You should know something," he said.

"What?"

"I peeked too."

She had long years of acting more hours a day than she'd actually lived her life, and from this, she'd developed a healthy cynicism. Nothing much surprised her or caught her off guard.

But Cole did both.

He grinned at the look on her face. "You're cute," he said.

Okay, back on familiar ground. She'd heard this. A lot. Child stars were inevitably "cute."

Until they weren't.

But she wasn't a little kid anymore, and nothing about the responses he effortlessly coaxed from her made her feel juvenile. Before she could respond, the boat shifted as if someone had come on board, and then there were male voices.

Two someones.

"Fuck me," Cole said conversationally. "Listen, you might want to brace yourself—"

Four feet and then four long legs appeared on the stairs. Cole turned to face them and Olivia started snatching up her clothing before sinking to the bench again, out of immediate view.

"What's up?" one of the men said to Cole. "You were supposed to call me—" There was a pause and the sound of exaggerated sniffing. "You smell like a woman. A really great-smelling woman, which can't be. You haven't gotten laid since the Ice Age. What gives?"

"Nothing," Cole said, standing in a way that clearly told her he was purposely blocking her from view. "You two go get a booth at Eat Me; I'll meet you there for breakfast."

"No can do," the other guy said. "We've got clients coming— Why is there a pair of black panties on the floor?"

From her perch on the bench, Olivia cringed. *Whoops.*

Cole sighed. Or at least Olivia assumed it was Cole. She was doing her best to be invisible.

"Either you're making a lifestyle change," the first guy said, "or you've had a woman in here."

"It's got to be the lifestyle change," the other guy said, "because we have the no-booty-call-on-the-boat policy, and the one who breaks it has to work a week in the buff as the walk of shame."

Horrified, Olivia stood up, and still holding her clothes—minus her panties—she took a few steps forward, wanting to clear the air about this being a booty call.

As she suspected, the two men were Sam and Tanner, Cole's partners. She'd interacted with Sam on a few occasions, since he was engaged to Olivia's friend and next-door neighbor Becca. Tanner she'd seen but not spoken to. He had dark hair, dark eyes, and a way of holding his body that suggested he'd had a dark life as well.

Tanner's gaze locked on Olivia, took in her appearance, and then reached out and gave Cole a shove.

"It's not what it looks like," Olivia said quickly. "He fell into the water, and I jumped in to help—"

Tanner shot Cole a look of disbelief. "You had to be *rescued*?"

"Oh, no," Olivia interjected. "He was fine. I just didn't know it, so I—"

Tanner finally grinned. "Yeah," he said to Cole. "You had to be rescued."

"Really," Olivia said, "he didn't. He wasn't drowning at all. He just fell into the water, and it was really cold and—"

"He *fell* into the water," Sam repeated, as if this didn't compute. "And it was cold."

Cole grimaced and ran a hand down his face. "It *is* cold."

For some reason, this made Tanner grin.

"Yes, very cold," Olivia said, feeling the urge to come to Cole's defense. "I thought he was in trouble, so I jumped in to help, and then our clothes were all wet so…" She trailed off and realized from the look on Cole's face that she'd only made things worse. So she shut up and bit her lower lip as Cole turned back to Tanner and Sam.

"*Out*," he said.

"But I want to hear more about you getting scared," Tanner said.

"Out. *Now*."

"No, it's okay. I'll go," Olivia said, and still gripping her clothes, she shoved her feet into Cole's athletic shoes. They were huge on her, and she had to work at not tripping as she moved past the guys, walking like a clown to keep the shoes on. "I've got to get moving anyway. I'm late—"

Cole caught her arm and very gently drew her around. The scowl that had appeared along with Sam and Tanner smoothed out as he ducked down a little to look into her eyes. "Give me a sec," he said. "And I'll walk you—"

"Not necessary." She pulled free. "I'm…late," she repeated.

Olivia wasn't exactly sure what was wrong with her. She knew she was being rude as hell, but she had this overwhelming desire to get the hell out, to get away from Cole's warm baby blues and his yummy man smell and the way his voice sounded like smooth whiskey.

She didn't even know what smooth whiskey was supposed to sound like.

"You look familiar," Tanner said.

She shifted her wet things to one arm and put a hand to her still damp hair, wondering how bad she must look if he wasn't sure. "We've seen each other around," she said.

"No, I know that," he said. "You watch us surf."

She did her best not to turn red. "I…" Well, hell. "Yeah," she said on a sigh. "That's me."

"But that's not it," he said with a slow headshake. "It's something else…You ever model or act or anything like that?"

Her heart picked up speed. This sometimes happened, people almost-but-not-quite recognized her from *Not Again, Hailey!* Luckily, enough time had passed that it rarely happened anymore, and it'd never happened here in Lucky Harbor. This was a good thing, as she was happy living anonymously. Not in the shadow of Sharlyn's wild and crazy charades, but as Olivia Bentley, sole proprietor. Law-abiding citizen. "I get that a lot," she said as casually as she could. "I have that kind of face, I guess."

Tanner smiled easily. "My mistake," he said.

She nodded and told herself to *breathe, idiot, breathe*.

Cole's eyes were on hers, steady and sure in a way she admired, since she wasn't feeling either at the moment. "You're locked out of your place," he reminded her, bending to pick up her sole boot. "I can—"

"No worries," she said quickly. "I've got a hide-a-key." Another big fat lie, but one of her dubious skills, on top of knowing a little bit about everything, was that she was a really good liar.

Taking the stairs with the big, built, intimidating Sam and Tanner still standing at the base of them wasn't easy, but Olivia was nothing if not an actress from birth. She lifted her chin, kept hold of her smile, blanked out her expression, and...

Hightailed it out of there.

Once on the dock, she ran down the length of it like the devil himself was on her heels. She tried to banish the image of Cole from her mind—standing in his bare feet with his tousled brown hair and those warm eyes that were somehow both sharp and soft at the same time, holding her boot, looking for all the world like Prince Charming with the glass slipper.

Good thing she knew better than anyone that fairy tales didn't exist.

Never had.

Never would.

Chapter 5

♥

Cole turned from the stairs to find Sam eyeballing the boat interior and Tanner eyeballing him. "Keep looking at me like that," Cole told him, "and you'd better be buying me dinner afterward."

"You fell in?" The words were heavy on the doubt, which made sense given the three of them were as sure-footed at sea as a Navy SEAL, even if only Tanner had actually been one.

Cole thought of the stupid spark when he'd been rewiring the running lights, the one that had given him the flashback that had started this whole adventure, and how badly he didn't want to admit that. Far less humiliating to let them think he'd been clumsy in front of the pretty woman. "Yeah. I fell in."

"And then you convinced her to get naked," Tanner said, and shook his head, impressed. "Fast work for a guy who usually moves like he's been dipped in cement."

"It's called hypothermia," Cole said. "I was trying to make sure we didn't get hypothermic."

"Is that what the kids are calling it these days?" Tanner asked drily.

"She thought she was saving me," he repeated.

She'd certainly woken him up. He'd been walking around in a fog lately, a fact he hadn't even fully realized until Olivia had plunged into the water on top of his head and nearly drowned them both.

Getting her out of the water and dealing with the aftermath, sitting and talking beneath the blankets, looking into her dark chocolate gaze and seeing all sorts of secrets there to be mined…he'd felt more alive than he had in a damn long time.

Even if his head was aching like a son of a bitch. And so was his shoulder, now that he thought about it.

"You could've just picked up the phone to get a date," Tanner said. "It'd have been a hell of a lot easier."

"Yeah?" Cole asked. "And that's worked so well for you? When was the last time you got laid?"

"Hey, I don't kiss and tell," Tanner said.

Sam snorted, and Cole turned to him. "You don't get to talk. You just went through a damn long drought yourself."

"Maybe," Sam said. "But now I sleep with Becca. Nightly."

"No one likes a bragger," Tanner said.

"I'm just saying," Sam said, looking smug, even though only a few months ago he'd let his past mess with his head so thoroughly he'd nearly thrown his shot with Becca right out the window.

Ignoring them both, Cole caught a flash of something

on the floor. The tiny scrap of black silk that had been masquerading as Olivia's panties.

Feeling both Tanner's and Sam's gazes boring holes into his back, he scooped them up and shoved them into his pocket.

Tanner opened his mouth, but Cole gave him a do-it-and-die look, and Tanner shut it again. Good to know that once in a while the guy did use his brain.

"We good to go with the running lights?" Sam asked, clearly changing the subject on purpose.

"No." Cole was still holding Olivia's boot. Setting it aside, he thought he wouldn't have minded seeing her long legs in nothing but those boots, doing anything other than running to his rescue. "I didn't get a chance to finish the wiring."

Tanner made a show of glancing at the diver's watch on his wrist.

"Shut up," Cole said.

"Didn't say a word."

"Didn't have to," Cole said. "I'm well aware we have clients arriving in less than half an hour."

"If you know that, then why were you messing around in the water with our pretty neighbor? And Christ, even I know it's too cold to mess around in that water, no matter how pretty the girl is."

Cole let out a long breath. "The water part was unintentional, believe me."

"I'll call our clients and buy us an extra hour or two," Tanner said, and pulled out his cell.

"They can wait," Sam said, eyes on Cole. "Tell us what happened."

"Nothing," Cole said.

Sam and Tanner exchanged a look.

"Seriously," Cole said. "Nothing."

"Yeah, see, you keep saying that," Sam said. "We're still not buying."

This was the problem with partnering with the two guys who not only had known you longer than just about anyone else, but also knew you better than you knew yourself.

They'd been together in some form or another since high school. Back in those days, Sam had been the wild one, reined in only by his foster mom—who happened to be Cole's birth mom—but even Amelia could only do so much.

Tanner had been a juvenile delinquent in the making, and little had reined him in either, until at age seventeen he'd gotten a girl pregnant—which had so completely turned his ass around that he'd made Cole dizzy with how fast he'd both grown up and manned up. Or maybe the navy had done that.

Cole was the only one who hadn't needed reining in. He'd always been the calm one, the peacemaker. Not to say that he was completely easygoing, because he wasn't. He knew that. He had expectations of the people he loved, and one of them was that they stay alive.

Which had made it all the harder when tragedy had struck and they'd lost Gil. None of them had been the same since. Cole knew it. And Sam and Tanner knew it, too.

It was the only reason he shook his head and came clean with the truth. "It wasn't quite light yet, and I was balanced on the railing, reworking the wiring. That asshole yesterday shredded it but good. And then something sparked…" He closed his eyes, remembering. "And I blanked out a moment, and that was all she wrote. In my head, I saw flames; I jerked and lost my balance." He opened his eyes and met Sam's and Tanner's gazes. "Right into the fucking water, making me a bigger idiot than yesterday's frat boy."

Sam didn't say anything. He didn't have to. His grim expression said it all. "A flashback."

"It was only for a second. I came out of it, and I was in the water."

Sam blew out a sigh and shoved his hands through his hair.

Tanner hadn't moved.

Cole turned away, frustrated. He had no business still being so fucked up.

Two years. It'd been two years, and he was still mad as hell on the inside.

Furious.

And so effing tired of hiding it. "It wasn't a big deal," he said. "But after I went in, Olivia saw me and thought I was hurt, so she came in after me."

"Clue in," Tanner said, finally speaking. "You are hurt." He pushed Cole to the bench and retrieved their first-aid kit from its storage spot.

Cole lifted his arm to touch his head, but stilled when a bolt of pain sliced through his shoulder at the movement.

Tanner moved close. He was limping this morning. It was the cold. That always bothered his leg. They'd made enough money in the past two years chartering that they could close on the cold days, but Tanner wouldn't allow it. Neither Cole nor Sam could say a damn word to him about it without getting his head bitten off.

Cole was at least smart enough to say nothing when Tanner dropped to his knees in front of him with a wince of his own and prodded at the cut over Cole's eyebrow.

"It's not bad," Tanner finally said.

"Told you—" Cole's eyes flew open when he realized Tanner was cutting off his shirt. "What the hell—"

"Hold still," Sam said, and crouched in front of him as well, the two of them looking at his shoulder with twin frowns as Tanner peeled the shreds of the shirt away.

"Can you lift your arm?" Sam asked.

"Yeah," Cole said. "Of course I can—"

The words caught in his throat as he tried to do just that and got halfway before the stab of pain nailed him again. "Oh, shit," he said, starting to sweat.

"But you're not hurt, right?" Tanner asked.

"Fuck. You."

Tanner snorted. "No thanks. I've seen you naked and cold, too." He rose and went to the freezer. A minute later he was back with an ice pack, which he tossed to Cole, smacking him in the face.

"Hey."

"Oh, sorry," Tanner said. "Was that a stupid thing to do? As stupid as, say, hoisting a woman out of the water and onto the deck platform when you've been told by your doctor to knock that shit off if you want to avoid surgery for the rotator cuff tear? Jesus. You and your damn hero complex."

This pissed Cole off because Tanner had a hero complex the size of his own big, fat head. The guy was currently playing hero to a long list of people who depended on him: his mother, his ex, his son…"So I should've what," Cole asked, "let her drown?"

Tanner pulled a sling from the first-aid box and put it on Cole. "Look familiar?"

Cole stared at the thing he'd worn for months after the rig fire. "Shit."

Tanner rose. "I'm going to go file today's float plan," he said, "which is changing. I'll captain this one, and you—" He pointed at Cole. "You're off duty."

Cole ignored this. As a male, he was allowed selective deafness. "I've got the float plan done already."

"*Off. Duty*," Tanner repeated, and didn't move a single inch when Cole rose to his feet, putting them nose to nose.

"He's going to make this harder than it needs to be," Tanner muttered to Sam.

"Fuck you," Cole said.

Tanner lifted a hand, palm out, as if to say *See?*

"This is bullshit," Cole said. "I'm fine."

"You really think you can run this boat today, or even at any point for the rest of the week?" Tanner challenged.

"Watch me." Cole rolled his shoulder, felt the wave of pain nearly steal his breath, and had no additional comment. He turned away, but Tanner ducked in front of him and forced eye contact.

"Yeah, hi," Tanner said, waving at him like a prom queen. "I'm going to watch you all right. I'm going to watch you do jackshit for the next three to four days, minimum. Now repeat that back for me."

Cole narrowed his eyes.

Tanner smiled. A badass, try-me smile. "Try again."

Cole opened his mouth, most definitely not to try again and possibly to tell Tanner where to shove it, but Sam took over. He put his hand on Cole's good shoulder, wisely stepping between them since they'd all at one time or another been known to swing first and ask questions later. "Look at it this way," Sam said. "You get a few days to sit around and watch Oprah and eat bonbons while we have to work our asses off."

"Oprah doesn't have a show anymore," Cole said. "And what the hell are bonbons, anyway?"

Sam shrugged. "Hell if I know."

"A chocolate," Tanner said. "Ladies used to eat them in the eighteen hundreds or some such shit." He seemed to realize that both Sam and Cole were staring at him and he shrugged. "Hey," he said defensively, "blame Cara."

Cara was one of Cole's three sisters, and she'd always had a thing for the bad boy, any bad boy. Saying Tanner qualified for that category was like saying the sun was a tad bit warm at its surface.

But Tanner took one look at Cole's face and lifted his hands. "It's not what you think," he said. "It's from the fancy fact-a-day calendar she gave me last Christmas. It was today's fact."

Cole shook his head and shoved past the two idiots he was tethered to by stupid loyalty.

"Where are you going?" Sam asked his back.

"If I'm off, I'm off," he said.

"He's butt-hurt," Tanner said. "Needs a good pout."

"I'm not butt-hurt," Cole said. But shit. He totally was.

"Look," Sam said, stopping him. "You're injured, you're off. It's nothing personal. It could've just as easily been one of us."

"I'm not that hurt."

"You want to risk a client's life on it?" Sam asked. "Come on, man. You know damn well you sometimes have unrealistic expectations of people, and this time it's about yourself. You're down for the count. Go home. Rest. That's all. It's easy enough, but if it's not, we'll be happy to hogtie you to your couch. Just say the word."

Tanner smiled evilly, clearly on board with that.

Shoving free of them both, Cole headed up to the dock.

"You're a jackass," he heard Sam say to Tanner.

"Who? Me?"

Ignoring them both, Cole kept going. He realized he was disproportionately pissed off, but it'd been that stupid, frustrating flashback.

He felt…itchy.

Unsettled.

Angry.

And he didn't want to think about any of it. Not what had happened, not his reaction.

And most definitely not *why*.

What he did want was to go check on Olivia and make sure she'd gotten into her place and warmed up.

The sun was just rising over the top of the mountain peaks when he hit the dock. This did not mean the day was warm.

It wasn't.

The temp was forty-five degrees, maybe, and as the salty breeze blew over Cole's still bare chest, he refused to shiver, or go back for a sweatshirt, not to mention shoes. Hell no. Instead he went to the street where he'd parked his truck.

He was pulling out his spare duffel, which had a stash of clothes, when he heard a soft intake of breath followed immediately by the unmistakable click of a camera lens.

He whirled around and found the devil in the form of a barely five-foot-tall old woman named Lucille.

Lucille ran the local geriatric band of merry bluehairs and the gossip train with equal aplomb, and rumor had it that her internal elevator didn't serve all her floors. Today her rheumy eyes were sharp as a tack, her lips hooker red. This somehow worked with her capri yoga pants and snug athletic top, neither of which hid the fact that gravity hadn't been especially kind to her.

"What are you up to?" he asked her suspiciously.

He had good reason for the suspicion. A few weeks back she'd managed to catch him and Tanner stripping down behind their warehouse after surfing. Instead of apologizing, or, say, leaving, she'd stood there gumming her dentures while trying to talk them into posing for a "tasteful" nude show at her art gallery.

The woman needed her hormone levels checked.

"I'm just out for a walk," Lucille said innocently.

Innocent, his ass.

"My doctor says I've gotta put in a few thousand steps a day minimum." She waved her cell phone. "It's an app."

"Good," he said, "because for a minute there I thought you were taking a picture."

"Of you shirtless?" she asked guilelessly. "On the open street that's free public domain? Would I do that?"

"Yes," he said. "And then you'd put it up on Pinterest or anywhere you're not banned."

"Tumblr," she said. "I'm at Tumblr now. They don't have a stick up their ass about *tasteful* art the way Facebook does."

"Uh-huh," he said, and awkwardly—and painfully—yanked a sweatshirt over his head. Then he shoved his feet into another pair of running shoes. It was bad enough that he'd just gotten himself three to four days of leave for being a pussy. He didn't need to extend the leave by getting sick on top of it.

"Going running or something?" Lucille asked.

He just gave her a long look.

She raised a hand in supplication. As if. "Fine," she said. "None of my business. Moving on. But remember, call me if you and your fellow hotties change your minds about a show at my gallery. You and Tanner are the last hot single guys in town. That warrants a show, you know. It's practically a public service."

"I'll keep it in mind."

Chapter 6

♥

After leaving the boat, Olivia went straight for the old warehouse that was her current home, moving fast. She had a feeling that Cole was going to come after her in some misguided attempt to help her get into her place without a key, and she didn't want that.

Correction. She wasn't ready for that.

And she couldn't even explain why; not to him, not to herself.

Halfway there a call had her phone vibrating in her pocket.

Her mother.

Hard to say why Olivia answered. Maybe she was just sick of the badgering about doing a retro show and wanted to get the fight over with. But there was also the daughter in her that needed to be sure everything was okay, especially since there'd been plenty of times when things hadn't been. Such as last year when Tamilyn had wrapped her car around a pole after one too many drinks.

She'd walked away from that accident with a DUI and a leg cast, which had given Tamilyn yet another excuse to play the victim. But Olivia had been in touch with the doctors herself and knew that no matter what Tamilyn wanted people to believe, she was fully recovered. "Hi, Mom."

"Finally, Sharlyn. My leg's killing me and you're taking your damn time picking up the phone. You've gotten my texts?"

"Olivia," she said, as she'd had to for years now. "You know I go by Olivia now."

"I like Sharlyn better. It's my favorite name. As a baby having a baby, it was the only thing I could give you."

How about loving her for who she was instead of what she was worth? "We've been through this," Olivia said. "I needed the change."

"You mean you wanted to get away from the paparazzi and the life."

The life being the craziness, and yeah. Especially since it'd been of her own making. Fact was, she'd been a Hollywood has-been before she'd even been legal. That she'd stayed in the public eye past that time had been due to—as her mom called it—living the life. Aka, being stupid. "How are you doing?"

"You know how I am," Tamilyn said. "So broke I can't even pay attention."

This was nothing new. Her mom had always been terrible with money, always looking for the next get-rich-quick scheme. She'd lucked out once and only once, and that had been the day that she'd heard about the open casting call in Lexington, Kentucky, where she'd been a housekeeper on a horse farm. A director had been looking for an "adorable young girl" for a commercial, and Jolyn had begged and begged to go audition.

Olivia had been dragged along. She could still remember being on the floor reading in a corner when the casting director had noticed her.

The next thing she knew, she'd filmed a commercial that had gone national.

Jolyn still hadn't forgiven her for that.

Or for all that came after. *Not Again, Hailey!* had catapulted them to Hollywood and changed their world, a world that then depended on Olivia.

"Doing this retro show won't change your life," Tamilyn said, "but it'll change mine. I need a girly surgery."

"Save it, Mom. Jolyn already told me you want another boob job."

"Well, damn it, they don't stay perky forever. You'll see."

"If you need money for living expenses, I can help you a little bit," Olivia said.

"Oh, no. I'm not a charity case. I just want what's mine. A fair cut as your manager, is all. Do the damn show. It's one day of filming. TV Land can start rerunning the series, and we'll be rolling in the royalties, and you can go back to hiding beneath a rock in Lucky Rock."

"Lucky Harbor." And she wasn't hiding. She was living. "It isn't just one day, Mom. If I do this, we both know the drill. TV Land's going to want a full-blown reunion show, and *TV Guide*'s gonna want to do a big deal on it, and..." And people here would realize who she was, and then she'd cease to be Olivia. She'd go back to being Sharlyn Peterson, a washed-up child star, complete with the humiliating public shenanigans.

Okay, maybe she was hiding just a little bit. "I'll think about it," she said.

"Well, think fast. Jolyn's talking of heading out there to see you."

Olivia's gut hit her toes. "Tell her no. I'll call."

"Soon?"

"Yes. But right now I've got to get to work." Olivia cut off the call and the usual wave of guilt rolled over her.

Damn it. She so didn't want to do the retrospective show. She liked her life just as it was right now.

Crossing the alley from the docks and beach, she came to the warehouse building she lived in. Once upon a time, it'd been a cannery, and then a saltwater taffy manufacturer, and then an arcade. Sometime in the past thirty years it'd been divided into three apartments.

Three poorly renovated, barely insulated, not-easily-heated apartments.

But there were bonuses. The ocean-facing wall was floor-to-ceiling windows that, yes, let in the cold wind, but also let in the glorious view and made her feel like... herself, just a woman who owned a vintage shop and lived as simply as she could here in sweet, quirky Lucky Harbor.

Olivia entered the building and stopped in the hallway at her front door. She occupied the middle unit. No one lived in the far right one. Her neighbor on the left was Becca Thorpe, soon to be Becca Brody, once sexy boat-builder Sam Brody got her down the aisle.

"Not the sharpest tool in the shed today," she said to herself. Because she hadn't hidden a key in case of idiocy—such as losing her keys rescuing a hot guy who didn't need rescuing. She sighed loudly.

A woman peeked out from the third and supposedly empty apartment. She was in yoga pants and a large sweatshirt, covered in dust from her strawberry-blond hair, which was piled on top of her head—although much of it had escaped its confines—to her battered tennis shoes. "Excuse me," she said to Olivia, "but are you talking to me?"

"No," Olivia said. "I'm talking to myself."

The woman smiled. "Gotcha. Carry on. Oh, and I'm Callie Sharpe. I'm moving in this weekend and just checking the place out. The walls are pretty thin."

"No insulation," Olivia said.

"Well then, I'll try to keep the wild parties to a minimum. You going to tell me your name, or should we just stick with Not the Sharpest Tool in the Shed?"

"Olivia." She didn't give a last name. She didn't like new people. Hell, she barely liked old people.

"Nice to meet you, Olivia," Callie said, and like a good neighbor, she vanished back inside without asking a bunch of questions.

Huh. Maybe Olivia would like her after all. She looked at her front door. Still locked. She eyeballed Becca's door, blew out a breath, and headed over there, knocking softly.

God, she really hated needing help.

Becca didn't answer at first and Olivia was debating her options—either go around to the back and break in through one of her windows or walk into town in Cole's big-ass shoes and break into her store—when Becca opened her front door.

She wore a man's T-shirt that said LUCKY HARBOR CHARTERS on one breast and, near as Olivia could tell, little else except a dreamy smile.

Dollars to doughnuts it was Sam's T-shirt. No doubt he'd been in Becca's bed directly before he'd arrived at the boat and was solely responsible for her dreamy smile, her mussed hair, and the whisker burns along her throat.

It wasn't envy that shot through Olivia, or so she told herself. But it was sure hard not to be at least a little wistful.

It'd been a damn long time since she'd had whisker burns.

"Hey," Becca said, and rubbed the heel of her hand over an eye as if trying to wake up. "You okay?"

Becca was a jingle writer, the local music teacher, and the only person Olivia knew who was newer to Lucky Harbor than herself. Becca was sweet and kind and unassuming, and at first Olivia had been suspicious of her because she didn't think anyone could really be so nice.

That was the city rat in her.

And the bitch.

But Becca had proven to be genuine, and they'd become friends as Becca had acclimated to Lucky Harbor. And yeah, acclimation was required. It was hard to believe a place with cozy, inviting Victorian architecture and a majestic mountain backdrop—a town that resembled a postcard picture—could actually exist.

But so far, it was living up to the promise. "I lost my key," Olivia admitted reluctantly. "Any ideas?"

"I'm a pretty good lock picker," Becca said. "Let me go get my tools."

Olivia was impressed. "You've got lock picking tools?"

"Bobby pins. Give me a sec, I also need something else."

"What?"

Becca blushed and tugged on the hem of the tee. "Panties," she whispered.

"Yeah, well, feel free to add a pair of pants to go with," Olivia called after her.

Two minutes later, Becca was back and they were standing at Olivia's door. Tongue between her teeth, Becca concentrated on breaking and entering.

"I appreciate this," Olivia said.

"You should, as I'm trying really hard to mind my own business. I know you're really private, and also that you can totally kick my ass, but…well, let's be honest, I'm dying of curiosity here. And also, I'm so not good at minding my own business."

No kidding. "I appreciate it, it's sweet of you," Olivia said. She was watching the hall and starting to sweat, getting nervous that this was taking so long. "Not to kick a gift horse in the mouth, or jeopardize the minding-your-own-business thing, but any chance we could speed this process up?"

Becca slid her gaze up, eyes sly. "Maybe."

"Did I say you were sweet?"

"Sweet's overrated. Spill. I want to know why your hair looks like you just went for a sea salt bath and you're wearing men's clothing."

Olivia slid another look down the hallway—and thank you sweet baby Jesus, it was still empty. "How about I give you a rain check on the explanation?"

"Pinkie swear."

"What?"

Becca thrust out her hand, pinkie first. "Pinkie swear you'll tell me later."

Olivia stared down at Becca's proffered pinkie. "Seriously?"

"Yes or no?"

Olivia sighed and wrapped her pinkie around Becca's. "Pinkie swear."

Thirty seconds later, Becca clicked the lock open on Olivia's apartment just as the door to the building opened at the end of the hall.

Olivia considered diving into her apartment and locking the door.

But Becca, definitely not-so-sweet, and most definitely ever-so-smart, subtly shifted, blocking Olivia's escape route as she waved at Cole. "Would you look at that," she said beneath her breath to Olivia. "He's got wet hair, too. And—he's injured?" She called out to him, "What happened? You okay?"

"Yep," Cole said, and locked eyes on Olivia for a beat before smiling at Becca. And for the record, it was a very different smile than anything he'd ever given Olivia. It was an easy, familiar, genuinely affectionate smile, the same he'd used when he'd spoken of his sisters.

"You've got a knot on your temple," Becca told him. "And you're wearing a sling. Last night we were singing at the piano at the Love Shack and all was well. What happened between then and now?"

Cole tugged on a strand of Becca's wild and crazy bedhead hair. "Nothing. I'm really fine."

"Uh-huh." Becca divided a look between Olivia and Cole, but Olivia had been born with secrets and knew how to hold 'em. Apparently Cole had the same skill.

"You pinkie swore," Becca said to Olivia. "Remember that."

"Hey," Cole said, head cocked. "Becca, is that your phone ringing?"

"Oh! Maybe, yes, thank you!" She vanished into her apartment.

"I didn't hear anything," Olivia said into the silence.

He smiled. "Me either." He nodded to Olivia's apartment, which was standing open. "You got in."

"Told you I could."

His warm blue eyes met hers. "Just wanted to make sure, since it was my fault you took an unplanned swim."

Nice of him to say so, but they both knew she'd reacted without thinking, and that if she'd only paused to observe for even a heartbeat, she'd have realized he was fine and not in danger.

"I can feel the cold draft coming out of your place," he said. "Is your heater broken?"

"No," she said ruefully. "Just my budget for the month."

He nodded like he understood. "So…you're okay? You warmed up enough?"

"I'm better off than you." She gestured to his shoulder. "Sling?"

"An old injury," he said casually.

He was good, but she was better. "You hurt yourself in the water," she accused, guilt slicing through her. "You said you didn't."

His eyes met hers. "And you said you were late."

"I am. I'm late getting to the shop. I've got a lot to do today." And yet she stood there, not moving, oddly reluctant to walk inside and shut the door.

"I keep hearing the faintest whisper of an accent," he said, eyes locked on her mouth. "Texas?"

"Kentucky," she admitted, a surprise to herself. Why had she told him that?

He smiled. "I like it. You grew up there?"

"Sort of. On a horse farm." It was what her bio said, that Sharlyn Peterson had grown up on a horse farm in Kentucky, and everyone knew that a bio was always true. And besides, her grandparents had worked on a horse farm, and so had Tamilyn. Six degrees and all that.

"You ride?" Cole asked.

"No, that was my grandpa mostly." Another sort of truth. He'd worked in the stables, but he'd been a rider at heart. He'd definitely had the touch with the fillies.

Both the two-legged *and* the four-legged variety.

"Well," she said, "thanks again for checking in on me. Good-bye." She moved to go inside, but Cole just stood there, studying her like she was fascinating. "You're supposed to be polite and say good-bye," she said.

"Good-bye," he said.

His smile was nothing but pure, unadulterated trouble, and at the sight of it, the devil on her left shoulder woke up and jumped up and down. *Oh please, can we have him, just once?*

But Olivia no longer gave in to frivolousness. Life wasn't about that. Life was a series of hard knocks that you had to be strong enough to survive.

She was still working on that.

Falling for a guy like sexy charter captain Cole Donovan was not only frivolous, it would be distracting in the extreme.

The falling for someone and having them walk—*that* she couldn't handle. Cole, with his tight-knit friends and family and perfect small-town life, was so far out of her league she couldn't even *see* the league.

With nothing else to say, Olivia stepped inside and, unable to break eye contact, stared at him as she reached out and gave the door a nudge.

Just before it shut, Cole flashed her a grin that said *game on*, a grin that she felt all the way to her toes and back. For a long moment she stared at the door, wondering if he was still standing there, wondering how to tell him that there was no way in hell she was going to play.

Chapter 7

Cole was lying in his hammock, his good arm up behind his head, a beer in his other hand as he idly swung in the afternoon breeze.

For the third day in a row.

He'd gone to the doctor in the hopes of getting him to say Cole was fine and that Sam and Tanner were being overly cautious not letting him work.

Dr. Josh Scott, an old friend, had agreed with the majority. No work for at least a week.

Cole was still pissed about it.

He had a radio on the grass beneath him so he could hear Tanner and Sam if either needed him. It absolutely wasn't because he was bored out of his mind.

The radio crackled to life. "Got some chop," Tanner said. "Move clients from swimming platform to below-decks. Over."

"No can do," came Sam's reply. "Head honcho says rough seas don't bother him. Over."

"Repeat: ten foot swells ahead," Tanner said. "Move him the hell off the swimming platform if you have to drag his ass with your own two hands. *Over*."

"Negative," Sam said. "He's trying to get a tan to impress the ladies and is wearing a Speedo and nothing else. You want him moved, you move him yourself. *Over*."

Okay, maybe he wasn't so sorry not to be there. Still, it was hard to be idle, and he hadn't had so many days off in a long time. None during his five years on the rigs. Not many more than that since starting up Lucky Harbor Charters. He'd spent all his time behind the controls of the boat, with Tanner at his back prepping whatever equipment they needed and Sam either helping or in their warehouse hand-building one of his many custom boats.

But now they were working without him. They'd be fine, he knew this. But he wasn't feeling fine. He was feeling left out. The three of them had been a team so long they operated by instinct, and their bond was strong.

And now they were operating without him.

It felt wrong. He'd always been the nucleus of the group, the one who kept them all together, and it hadn't been easy. The day after high school graduation, Tanner had gone off to the navy, and he'd eventually become a SEAL. Sam hadn't had money for college, so he'd gone straight to the gulf, to the rigs.

Cole had spent two years playing college baseball, a little bored, a lot unmotivated, snoozing his way through life. He'd watched two of his sisters get married and create their own families, until the holidays had become these huge, noisy, overwhelming affairs where no less than thirty people would bug him about his future.

He hadn't known then what his future would hold.

What he *had* known was that, while he loved his growing family and the insanity that came with it, he hadn't wanted that for himself. So when Sam had called him to the rigs, he'd gone without looking back. They'd met Gil there, and he'd fallen into the group like he'd been born to it.

And then Tanner had caught up with them after his navy stint and stayed. It'd worked. Everything had worked.

Until Gil had died—in Cole's arms, as a matter of fact.

His phone was vibrating like it was having a seizure, but as it was ten feet away in the wild grass where he'd chucked it an hour ago, he didn't give a shit. He sipped the beer and continued to swing idly, taking in the seagulls squawking, the waves hitting the rocky beach far below the bluffs where he lay, the sound of the wind whistling past him.

Inhale.

Exhale.

That's what he concentrated on.

"Hey," the nagging voice of his childhood said sometime later. "So you live."

His oldest sister, Clare.

"You know I'm okay," he said without opening his eyes. "You made me add you on that Find Your Friends app so you can stalk my dot."

"Yeah, well, your dot wasn't moving," she said. "I was voted to come check and make sure you were still breathing."

"Now you've seen firsthand that I am," he said. "Feel free to go back and report to the coven that I'm fine."

She made a sound that was half laugh, half pure annoyance at the old nickname he'd assigned to his sisters from the day they'd begun interfering in his life.

Which had been his birth.

Clare, Cindy, and Cara had been possessive of him from that day forward. His mom was the same. For most of Cole's life he and his dad had banded together to ward off the estrogen. Cole hoped the guy was sitting on a cloud in heaven eating a pizza as a big fuck-you to his cholesterol problem, amused at Cole's inability to fend off his sisters' nosiness on his own. "And just out of curiosity, why wouldn't I still be breathing?" Cole asked.

"Because you fell into the water two days ago, and apparently had to be rescued by some chick. I can't believe you about drowned and I had to hear about it on the street."

"What the hell?" Cole sat up, nearly upending himself off the hammock as he stared at Clare. "How did you hear that?"

"It's Lucky Harbor," she said in simple acceptance of the fact that while you could keep your car unlocked in the small coastal town and not worry about theft, you couldn't keep a damn secret to save your own life.

"That's not what happened," he said, pointing his beer at her.

Clare set the large brown bag she was carrying onto Cole's picnic table, her gaze going to his sling and then to the healing cut on his temple. "Then how did you get hurt?"

Well, shit. "Okay, I did fall into the water. But I did *not* need rescuing."

Clare absorbed this and sat at the table. This was a

problem because now he was stuck with her. "I'm fine," he said. "And it was days ago."

"Were you alone?"

"No."

Her eyes sharpened. "Is this where the chick comes in?"

"Her name is Olivia, and she doesn't come into anything."

Those sharp eyes studied him. "Olivia who?"

"Not telling," he said, well versed in this little game. "You'll have me married by next weekend."

"If you don't tell me, I'll just sic Cindy and Cara on you."

Her co–coven members, aka his other sisters—and they were all equally crazy. Well, actually, maybe Cara was the most crazy of them all, which was really saying something. "Don't even think about it," he said. "Cindy's busy with the baby, don't stress her out. And Cara doesn't need to bother herself."

Clare looked at him for a long beat. Probably using her powers to read his mind. "You ever going to tell me what she did to piss you off?" she eventually asked.

Yep, reading his mind.

"I'm not pissed," he said. "Do I look pissed?"

Clare snorted. "No, but then again, you never do. You put on this air that you let everything bead off your back. Nothing gets to you, isn't that your deal? You could be ready to jump off a cliff and no one would ever know it. You're just like Dad that way."

"And the problem?"

She met his gaze. Matching stubborn blue. "He dropped dead of a heart attack at fifty-five," she reminded him quietly.

Oh, yeah. That.

"Tell me about the Cara thing," she said. "Maybe I can help."

When their dad had died, Cara had pulled away from the family to grieve in her own way. Only Cole knew which way that was, and it was a huge bone of contention between the two of them. And it was literally just between them, as she'd sworn Cole to secrecy. "It's nothing," he told Clare.

"You're so full of shit your eyes just turned brown."

"You kiss Mitch with that mouth?" he asked.

Clare took a long breath. "Fine. Be stubborn. Change the subject. Works for me. I want to talk to you about something else anyway."

"I'm talked out."

Unconcerned, she rose, snatched the beer right out of his hands, and took a long pull from it as she looked around his yard.

He knew what she saw. A beach shack on the bluffs that had been built a hundred years ago and was in desperate need of renovation. He'd been working on the place slowly from the inside out, so most of his work didn't yet show.

He wasn't in a hurry. The most important thing was the mind-soothing view of his favorite place on earth.

The ocean.

"Do you want the truth?" Clare asked quietly.

"If I say no, will you go away?"

"Cole."

Of course she wasn't going to go away. She never did what he wanted.

"I'm worried about you," she said.

Ah, Christ. "Don't be."

"You've been in Lucky Harbor for two years, and near as I can tell, you haven't dated. You haven't dated at all since Susan—"

Shit. Cole snagged his beer back and finished it off, trying to remember whether he had more in his fridge. Doubtful, as he hadn't been to the store in recent memory. Rising, he peeked into the bag she'd brought. Homemade chili and cornbread. Nice. But beer would have been nicer. He reached in to pinch off a piece of the cornbread and Clare smacked his hand like he was her five-year-old son, Jonathan. "Save it for dinner," she said. "Now back to Susan—"

"Gee, this has been fun," he said. "But I have to go watch paint dry now."

"She dumped you two years ago—"

"Not going there, C," he said.

"*Two*. Years," she repeated.

Like he didn't know. It'd been Gil's funeral, a couple weeks short of two years ago now, and he remembered exactly.

Just as clearly as he remembered why. "Don't you have to get to work?" he asked. "Or, I don't know, stir your cauldron?"

She narrowed her eyes at him.

He stared back, holding the silence. It was his only weapon against her. Clare couldn't handle a silence. Not one of the coven could. Though in the old days, she'd used other techniques. Sitting on him had usually worked. Or ratting him out. His dad had never failed to fall for one flash of her baby blues, for any of his daughters' baby blues. He'd had a real soft spot for the girls.

For Cole, too, if he was being fair. He had no doubt of that, but he'd been taught that a female was to be loved, cherished, and pampered, and above all else, she was to get her way.

And he respected that. But he had different boundaries now, and he held his tongue.

"Fine," she finally said. "Subject closed. For now." Moving in, she hugged him hard, brushing a kiss to his jaw. "Love you, you big, stubborn ass." She pointed to the bag. "Heat the chili on the stovetop for dinner tonight. Save the bread to eat with it."

"Yes, ma'am."

"And Cole?" She flashed him a smile as she pulled her keys from her pocket. "Maybe you could ask this Olivia out sometime."

"For all you know, she's married with kids," he said. "Maybe she's a senior citizen and doesn't even have all of her own teeth. Maybe—"

"Maybe she's perfect for you, you ever think of that?" She smiled at his expression and wisely stepped back out of range. "Why don't you just try dropping *some* of those unrealistic expectations, baby brother, okay? Not every woman is going to be a hormonal wreck like your sisters or dump you like your ex."

That was the second time in three days he'd been told about his unrealistic expectations, and he rolled his eyes. His expectations, realistic or not, were just fine, thank you very much.

Clare shook her head at his lack of a response, blew him a kiss, and vanished.

Cole started to shove his hands into his pockets, but the left one couldn't bend that way thanks to the sling—and the bolt of pain. So only his right hand entered his pocket, and encountered soft silk.

Olivia's panties.

He'd forgotten they were there, and they must have gotten washed with his pants. Like a shockwave, arousal punched through his system, and he let himself get lost in that for a moment.

Olivia wasn't a mom—at least he didn't think so. She sure as hell wasn't a senior citizen. But beyond that, he didn't have a clue.

Well, that wasn't exactly true, either, was it. He knew she had amazing eyes, dark and full of secrets. He knew she could make him laugh. He knew she would literally risk her own life for a stranger's.

He'd told himself it didn't matter if he never talked to her again. He'd even bought it, at least in his waking moments. But in his sleeping moments he'd been dreaming about her. Fantasizing, really; hot, dark, erotic fantasies where they'd been back on the boat with none of the danger and all of the nakedness…

Okay, so yeah, seeing her again was a really bad idea. Clearly he was all sorts of fucked up.

And then there was Olivia. She was guarded, and not exactly eager. Cole fingered her panties again and let out a long exhale.

But she *had* attempted to save his life. That was a big deal. It'd be rude not to at least give her back her undies.

Chapter 8

♥

Three days after taking that unintentional swim, Olivia moved through her shop, reshelving and restocking, one ear cocked toward her tablet. She had it propped up on her desk, tuned to an *American Pickers* episode on Netflix.

Lord, she loved that guilty pleasure show. She loved all of them, *Pawn Stars*, *Storage Wars*, anything and everything about old stuff. It didn't take a shrink to tell her why, either. The art of digging through the neglected and discarded, giving those things a new lease, was a thinly veiled metaphor for her own life.

She'd been neglected and discarded.

She was working on that. She looked around. Unique Boutique was three rooms, two for her customers to wander through and one that was both a storeroom and an office. She'd done her best to re-create the same sense of warmth and mystic adventure that Mrs. Henderson had instilled within her all those years ago.

The location was great, near the end of Commercial Row downtown, in the bottom floor of a "quaint" old Victorian that her landlord claimed had been renovated before the turn of the century.

It was probably true. Olivia just wasn't sure which century.

The three rooms were tiny, but she'd made the most of them. They had the timeless look she'd always wanted, an old-fashioned parlor crammed full of wonderful old things that were strewn about, things that drew the eye and made you want to reach out and touch. She'd been careful with scents, too; today she'd used the vanilla oil and the whole place smelled like Grandma's kitchen.

If she'd had a grandma who'd baked.

She sold vintage clothing and assorted other things ranging from accessories to knickknacks to antique furniture. She'd accumulated everything herself, whether from estate auctions, garage sales, eBay, Craigslist, or her own closets.

Every piece had a story, a past, which was important to her. And though she loved it all, everything had a price—except the things she had stored in a special trunk that she kept for herself. Those things were pieces of her past, and her only luxury.

As she looked around the shop, it was with the usual surge of complicated emotions. Pride, which was easy to understand. And relief, which wasn't.

She'd left her old world, although, granted, not on her own terms. In fact, she'd been cut out of her old world, separated from everything and everyone she'd ever known.

In hindsight, it was easy to see that it hadn't been any-thing personal. Her show had come to an end, and that was Hollywood, baby.

But when she'd been in it, when the sets, her trailer, the food service, and the studio had been all the home she'd ever needed, losing it had been devastating. And yeah, she'd lost her way and gone a little wild. There was no disputing that it'd taken her a long time and a lot of screw-ups to figure her shit out, but she had figured it out.

So maybe the relief wasn't so hard to explain after all.

The shop bell rang, and three older women walked in. They were in polyester tracksuits in varying colors of the rainbow. Purple, pink, and green, all with bright white tennis shoes.

The leader, the one in purple, was Lucille. Hard to determine her exact age, but it was somewhere near the three-quarters-of-a-millennium mark.

"Heard you landed yourself in the drink and got saved by Captain Hottie," Lucille said in lieu of a greeting.

"Captain Hottie?" Olivia repeated.

Lucille grinned. "Sorry. I forget you're not a born-and-bred local. I'm talking about Cole Donovan. Did he give you mouth-to-mouth?"

"Uh, no," Olivia said. "And that's not exactly how it went, by the way."

Lucille's face fell. "Well, better luck next time, then."

Her cohorts nodded sagely.

Lucille leaned in close to Olivia. "You may not know this, either," she whispered like she was imparting a state secret, "but just about every woman in town would like to get with that."

Olivia just blinked.

"*Get with that*," Lucille repeated, enunciating each word as if she thought Olivia was half-deaf, or maybe just a little slow on the uptake. "It means—"

"I know what it means," Olivia said quickly, not wanting to hear Lucille spell it out. Good Lord. "I just...I don't know why you're telling me this."

"Because many have gone before you, but no one has succeeded," she said.

The others nodded like bobbleheads.

"Succeeded in what?" Olivia asked.

"Why, getting into his heart, of course," Lucille said. "Not since..." She hesitated. "Well," she said demurely, "far be it from me to spread rumors."

Riiiiight.

"It's just that he's such a good man," Lucille said. "And though women line up to try to catch him, he's been laying low, not nibbling at any lines."

"You are aware that he's not actually a fish," Olivia said.

"If he were, he'd be a really great fish," Lucille said. "You've seen him, you know what I'm talking about."

Olivia thought back to the Blanket Incident three days prior, when she'd taken a good, solid look at Cole in all his naked glory. And there'd been a lot of glory.

So she had to agree—she knew exactly what Lucille was talking about.

"And on top of looking so fine, he can fix anything," Lucille said. "You have any idea how rare that is in a man these days? And he coaches his five-year-old nephew's baseball team. He's worth a test drive, is all I'm saying."

"Now you're making him sound like a used car," Olivia joked, trying to think of a way to get out of this conversation without turning away customers. "How many miles does he have on him?"

Lucille didn't smile. "I'm serious, honey. He's... special. I want you to take very good care of him."

Olivia paused. "He's not mine to take care of."

A look of disappointment crossed Lucille's face, and Olivia sensed any purchase opportunities going down the drain. "Tea," she said. "How about tea?"

"You got the good stuff?" Lucille asked.

She was talking about the Keurig machine that Olivia had splurged on to serve her customers. Each cup she made cost a mint, but even though some people came in just for the tea—*cough*, Lucille, *cough*—it was worth it. "Always," Olivia said.

Lucille smiled. "Well, then, of course. We're here looking for some pearls." She gestured to the woman in the bright pink tracksuit next to her. "Mary needs a strand to wear to her sister's birthday party. Problem is, she already spent her social security check on bingo this week, so she's hoping you got something that looks real expensive but isn't, know what I'm saying?"

"Sure. What's the budget?" Olivia asked, trying to figure out if they wanted real pearls or imitation.

"Fifteen dollars."

Imitation it was, then. "I have just the thing," Olivia said. And she did. She'd been gifted with the ability to collect what others didn't even know they wanted to buy until they saw it. From a young age she could recognize a

Chanel at a garage sale as opposed to a Kohl's knockoff, and she could bargain like no other.

Stocking her shop was her one true joy.

She brought the women into the parlor, where she had several jewelry displays, and showed off a long strand of pearls that she'd gotten from a great estate sale of a set designer several years back.

The ladies oohed and aahed over the necklace.

"If you like it," Olivia said, "I've got the earrings to match, and a cashmere sweater set that they'd both look fantastic with."

The geriatrics got all aflutter at that, and Mary tried on the sweater. "Get a load of me," she breathed, staring at herself in the free-standing antique mirror, wearing the gorgeous pale-peach sweater and her neon pink track pants. "I'm…glamorous."

"Hollywood should be knocking," Olivia agreed, helping her arrange the necklace just right. "You belong on a set with your own name on a chair and everything."

Mary beamed. "I'll take it, all of it."

The other lady, Mrs. Betty Dettinger, was looking through a wooden bin of stuffed animals. "My granddaughter comes to your Drama Days," she said, referring to the weekly event Olivia hosted here at the shop for the local kids to play dress-up and act out small plays. "She was wondering if she could buy one of the costumes for Halloween."

"The costumes aren't for sale," Olivia responded. They lived in her favorite antique travel trunk, usually placed at the foot of her bed. The exception came once a week during Drama Day. The contents were her own personal collection from *Not Again, Hailey!*—the one-of-a-kind pieces of her childhood that she wouldn't sell.

The show had followed Hailey, the daughter of two professors, one who'd taught science and math, one who'd taught acting. Each week, Hailey had gotten herself into a mess, say forgetting to put a dessert in the fridge, so that her father could teach her a lesson, like what happened to food when it was left out. Hailey had played dress-up with her acting-professor mother's wardrobe—hence all the costumes—and had gotten herself in trouble for a variety of things, such as peeking into her siblings' private things. Every time she got in trouble, her parents or teachers or friends would say, "Not again, Hailey."

A simple premise, and shockingly popular.

"Are you sure they're not for sale?" Betty asked.

"Yes, I'm sorry."

"Such a shame," the woman said. "You'd make good money from them."

She didn't care about making good money. She'd done that. And then she'd lost it all. It was all the same to her.

When the ladies finally left, Olivia went into the back room and pulled out the box of cookies she'd picked up at the town bakery. Then she went back for the large antique trunk of costumes that she'd hauled into work earlier.

The costumes were just about all that was left of her earlier life. They represented the only good times from that period, times when she'd been loved and adored as Sharlyn Peterson, pre–public breakdown.

At age fourteen she'd been short and chunky and still playing age nine. One year later she'd started to grow up—and out—and from that moment on, she'd been under constant pressure to stay teeny-tiny.

Don't eat that, Olivia.

Or that...

But no matter what she'd done, she couldn't stop time. She'd grown like a weed, and they'd had to give the other actors in the show lifts in their shoes to make her look shorter.

Every year, Tamilyn had said a special prayer over Olivia's birthday cake. "Please God, don't let her go into puberty and ruin everything!"

Then it had happened. Olivia had turned sixteen, gotten boobs, and it'd been over. She could still remember being pulled into the producer's office and being told that they were going to have to recast someone younger, someone "fresher," or cancel the show.

The powers that be had chosen to cancel.

And just like that, her worth had dried up. In fact, she'd become of less than zero value to the studio. She'd become a liability.

The front door to the shop opened and kids piled in. Six of them, followed by their parents, with the exception of the two little girls holding hands with Becca, who occasionally helped out their father after school. The twins were identical, one in all pink, including her ponytail holder, the other in a variety of mismatched clothes indicating she'd been her own stylist that morning.

"Olivia, Olivia, Olivia!" Pink yelled—the only decibel level she seemed to know—jumping up and down at the sight of her. "What's today's play?"

It was silly, but Olivia got just as excited as they did.

When she'd first opened Unique Boutique, she'd known
she wanted to let her costumes be used by local kids.
She'd never been one to dream about marrying and having her own children to share her past with. Her life had
always been too chaotic for those kinds of settling-down
fantasies. And then when it had no longer been so chaotic,
she'd just figured that she wasn't exactly the maternal
type.

After all, she hadn't had a childhood. What did she
know about giving one?

But she could at least connect with kids in the one
way she was able to—through the world of make-believe.
"*Cinderella*," she said. She'd been Cinderella for one entire glorious week during her *Not Again, Hailey!* days,
and it had been her favorite episode.

Pink was jumping up and down again. "That's perfect!" She peered around Becca and looked wide-eyed
at her twin. "Kendra, you've always wanted to be
Cinderella!"

Kendra grinned from ear to ear. The two of them had
been raised in foster homes until only a few months ago,
when their father had relocated in order to take care of
them. There was precious little money in their household,
but Lucky Harbor did its best to take care of its own.
There'd been clothing and food donations. The rec center provided after-school care. Becca brought them in for
Drama Days.

It was reason number 1,000,003 that Olivia loved
Lucky Harbor. "We'll do something Halloweeny over the
next two weeks to celebrate the rest of October."

Pink clasped her hands together under her chin, her
face a mask of sheer delight. "We never got to have Hal-

loween before! Daddy says he's going to try to get us costumes this year!"

Kendra nodded her matching enthusiasm without saying a word. She very rarely spoke, which would make it interesting if she was going to be the lead in *Cinderella* today.

The moms had been looking through the store, and several had laid items on the checkout counter to purchase. Kids were wandering around, girls chattering excitedly, boys looking for trouble. Their energy ramped up even more when Olivia opened her trunk.

The kids gathered in close. The first time they'd done this, there'd been more than a few catfights over the costumes. Olivia had put a quick end to it by promising that the costumes were meant for sharing, that they'd seen a lot of wear over the years and they enjoyed being passed around. No one would be left out, ever. They'd reenact the short play over and over, until everyone got a turn at whatever part they wanted.

And she'd always kept that promise.

"So much stuff!" one of the girls said reverently.

It was true. Olivia had a lot of stuff. Tamilyn had always said she was one box of stuff away from a *Hoarders* Very Special Episode.

That might be true, too.

The next two hours flew by. They ran the "script" four times, enough to give everyone who wanted a shot at Cinderella a turn. Kendra went last, she insisted on it. Not with words. In fact, she never spoke at all, just gently pushed each of the girls ahead of her.

Finally she got her turn, and she glowed through the whole thing, even if she did make Pink speak her lines for her.

Afterward, as they filed through the door, Olivia hugged each kid as they left. They were all beaming, happy, and it meant so much to her that she'd given them that. She wondered if any of the people in her life—her agent, manager, director, acting coach, set dresser, tutor, any of them—had ever felt the same about what they'd given her.

But she knew they hadn't. Couldn't have. Not with the way they'd all vanished from her life the moment the show had been canceled.

Kendra was last to leave, and she wrapped her thin arms around Olivia's waist and pressed close, trustingly, sweetly, smelling like the chocolate chip cookies they'd consumed.

Unlike the others, the girl didn't say thank you—she didn't say anything. But as her gaze met Olivia's, she didn't have to. It was all there in her eyes: the gratitude, the joy, the relief that life was different for her these days, which was to say *much* better.

"You had fun?" Olivia asked, already knowing the answer.

Kendra nodded.

"You enjoyed the costume?"

Kendra's grip tightened and she nodded again, even more emphatically.

"Good." She squeezed the little girl, then concentrated on cleanup, dropping to her knees in the center of the Drama Days rug. When she picked up the Cinderella costume, she paused.

And then draped it over the front of her and looked down at herself. It would never fit her now but she could remember vividly when it had.

"I'd have guessed you were more the Xena, Warrior Princess, type than pink satin and lace."

Olivia whirled around and found Cole standing in the doorway to the shop, watching her hold the costume to herself.

Chapter 9

♥

Cole flashed that smile of his, the one that made Olivia's stomach feel like a butterfly sanctuary.

"What are you doing here?" she asked, rising to her feet.

"Just walking."

The same exact words she'd given him on the dock for the reason she'd been out so early.

A lie, of course. She'd been watching him work on the big, impressive boat that seemed as tough as he was, fascinated by the give and play of his muscles, the fluid, easy way he moved as if he was so sure in his own skin.

"You want to model that?" he asked.

She looked down at the Cinderella gown in her hands and snorted. "No."

"Too bad."

She gazed at him speculatively. He was toying with her. But two could play at that game, she thought. "You have a princess fetish?"

"No fetish, but I'm never opposed to roleplaying."

Her entire body hummed. Note to self: Not quite ready for prime time with Cole Donovan.

Laughing softly at whatever he saw on her face, Cole came all the way into the shop, letting the door close behind him.

"I'm closed," she said.

He helpfully flicked the lock, which resisted his efforts. He turned to eyeball it and then manhandled it the way she had to every single day.

"I could fix that," he said.

"That's okay," she said, looking at his sling. No way would she risk hurting him again. "I don't want you to spend your time. And besides, I have a handyman guy." She totally didn't have anything of the sort.

"It'd take me less than two minutes," he said. "And no charge."

"Cole—"

"You have any tools?"

She chewed on her lower lip.

He smiled. "You have all this stuff, and you don't have any tools?"

"I collect only pretty stuff," she said, and gave him a reluctant smile. "And I've never found a pretty tool, or I'd undoubtedly have some here for sale."

"It's okay," he said, unperturbed. "I'm packing."

This didn't surprise her. He was known as the local MacGyver, able to fix things in the blink of an eye with whatever he had on him…"Not necessary," she said, annoyingly breathless for no reason. It absolutely wasn't just the sight of him in one of his pairs of sexy cargo pants and a long-sleeved T-shirt that fit his rugged physique so well. She stood and dusted herself off. "Like I said, I was just closing, so…"

He flipped the OPEN sign to CLOSED.

"Yes," she said, "but you're on the wrong side of the door."

He just smiled. "You're good with kids, you know."

For some reason, that caught her completely off guard. Maybe it was because no one had said such a thing to her before, ever.

"Personal experience?" he asked.

"Are you feeling out if I *have* kids?"

"Or a husband," he said, unabashedly. "Kids I wouldn't mind at all. A husband…that's probably an obstacle I can't get around."

She laughed. "I have neither, not that it matters." She pointed to the sling. "Have you been to a doctor?"

"Yes, ma'am. It's just an old shoulder injury that I retweaked, that's all."

"Hauling me out of the water the other day."

"Hauling myself out of the water," he corrected.

She didn't buy that, not for a second, but looking into his stubborn expression, complete with squared jaw and that little bit of scruff she was determined not to find attractive in the slightest, she knew she'd get nowhere arguing the point. "Why are you here?"

"I don't tend to question the universe," he said blandly.

She had to laugh. "You know what I mean. Why are you here in my shop?"

"Maybe I'm here to buy something."

"You need a Halloween costume?" she asked.

"Maybe."

"I just got some new ones in," she said.

"Yeah?"

"Yeah, Dorothy from *The Wizard of Oz* and Miley Cyrus."

Not scared off, he grinned. "I could rock either."

That tore yet another laugh out of her, and his gaze slid to her mouth. "That's a really good look on you," he murmured. "More of that."

"You're pretty demanding for such a laid-back guy," she said. "Anyone ever tell you that?"

"I've had no complaints."

Of course not. Looking like he did, with that long, leanly muscled bod— Not going there...

Not even a little.

Too late! the devil on her shoulder cried gleefully, the slut. "I've really got to clean up," Olivia said.

"Need help?"

"No, thank you." She paused to wonder why it was that his voice, with its deep, low timbre, never failed to give her a shiver. The really good kind of shiver. "I've got it. I'm going out the back to lock up my car. Feel free to let yourself out."

For some reason this made him smile as he rocked back on his heels.

"What?" she asked.

"Nothing," he said, looking even more amused.

"You're a strange man," she said, and headed into the back. "You know the way out. Use it."

Assuming he'd do just that, she strode through her storage room to the back corner, which also served as her office. Her desk was as neat and organized as her storage room wasn't. She kept it so because the business side of

things didn't come easily to her. She had to work hard at
keeping herself on track with the bookkeeping.

The answering machine was blinking, reminding her
that she hadn't answered the phone during Drama Day
with the kids. Damn. She hit PLAY and sighed at the sound
of her mother's voice.

"What's it going to be on that happy reunion?" Tamilyn asked.

Delete.

The next message shouldn't have been too much of
a surprise. It was the producer from TV Land. He was
smart enough to get to the point. "Call me."

Delete.

Next to her desk was an antique armoire that had come
from the movie set of a remake of *A Christmas Carol*.
She'd played one of the orphans. It'd been one of her favorite jobs, and the piece meant a lot to her, which was why
it was back here in use and not out in the shop for sale.

She opened the armoire to pull out her coat.

The footsteps behind her shouldn't have been a surprise. Her back to Cole, she went utterly still for a beat
because he smelled...delicious, like he'd recently showered. She inhaled deeply, then pretended she wasn't trying to catch a bigger whiff of him as she turned, buttoning
up her coat. "Thought you left," she said.

"You thought wrong. Family reunion?"

"What?"

"Your first phone message."

Of course he'd heard the word "reunion" and assumed
it'd be a family reunion. This was because he was normal.
He could have no possible idea that this particular reunion had nothing to do with reality.

"I thought you didn't have any family."

"This is…extended family." As in *very* extended.

"Do you ever miss Kentucky?"

She nearly gave a choked laugh. Kentucky represented her first seven years of life, which had been spent in a single-wide on cement blocks that leaked in the rain, and it'd rained a lot. It had meant a lot of long, cold nights in the winter and longer hot, sticky nights in the summer. It had meant an unhappy, stressed-out mom, hungry bellies, and uncertainty.

But that had been a long time ago, a *lifetime* ago, in fact.

"No," she said as simply as she dared. "I don't miss Kentucky. Why are you here again?"

He pulled something from his pocket. Black lace.

Her panties.

"Oh, my God," she said.

"Thought you might want them back."

She gaped at him. "What if they'd fallen out of your pocket? What if you'd gotten in a wreck and been taken to the hospital with women's underwear on you? What if—"

Laughing, he put a finger over her lips. "You always worry about the worst-case scenario?"

Yes. Always.

She pushed his hand away from her mouth, snatched the panties, and then turned from him. She needed a moment without his sharp gaze to recover from the oddly electric touch of his finger on her mouth.

And what it had done to her.

"I was hoping to take you out to dinner as a thank-you for saving my life."

She hadn't been big on guys in a while. If she was being honest, she hadn't really even tried since the summer after college. The guy she'd been dating had discovered the *Not Again, Hailey!* DVDs. He'd had a showing with a hundred of his closest friends and charged admission, thinking it was funny as hell to promise people her autograph.

Instead, it'd been mortifying as hell.

"Long silence," Cole said. "Doesn't bode well. You're seeing someone, then."

She hesitated, considered lying, and then shook her head. She'd lied about enough already. "No."

"You sure? You need another minute to decide?"

He was laughing at her. She gave him a long look. "And what about you?"

"What about me?"

He was going to make her say it. She kept forgetting that his smile might be guileless and effortlessly easy, but he was no pushover. He was one of those sneak-up-on-you alphas; all charm and charisma, so that you barely noticed that you were doing exactly what he wanted, giving him whatever he was seeking…and all because of that sexy smile. "Are you seeing anyone?" she asked through her teeth.

"I'm hoping I'm seeing you. For dinner."

There was a pause, and their gazes locked. And then her pulse jumped the starting gate. "A thank-you dinner isn't necessary," she said. "You know exactly how the other morning went, which was *you* saving *me*."

He closed the distance between them.

Refusing to back up, she lifted her chin and met his gaze evenly.

"You put your life on the line for me, Supergirl," he

said quietly, no trace of his usual good humor in his low, husky voice. "I'm going to fix your lock. And then I'm going to buy you dinner."

Her heart skipped a beat. Dinner had implications. Dinner would be admitting there was an attraction, something she wasn't ready for, because once she went there, the countdown was on.

The countdown to him walking away.

Why let it get there at all? "No," she said.

"Why not?"

"I don't think you're supposed to ask why after you've been turned down for a date," she said. "It's in the Man Handbook under the instructions on how to deal with women."

He flashed a grin. "I never read instructions."

"And I suppose you don't ask for directions, either," she said.

"Don't need 'em. I always know where I'm going."

Oh boy. She just bet he did. But she couldn't do this, no matter how tempting his mischievous, sexy smile was. She had no track record, at least no good track record. She never managed to keep anyone in her life, and yes, she knew that was all on her. She'd never quite been lovable enough.

Some things couldn't be changed.

"Okay," she said, "this has been fun, but I've got to get home now, so—"

He turned and headed out to the front room. To leave, she thought. Perfect.

So why she felt like grabbing him was beyond her.

She followed to lock up behind him, but though he went to the door, he didn't go. He pulled something from one of his cargo pockets and went to work on the lock.

And then two minutes later, slid the tool back into his pocket and locked the door.

With ease.

He turned to her with a smile. "You've also got a few bulbs out in the back office. You got lightbulbs?"

"I'll do it myself when I borrow a ladder—"

"You don't need a ladder."

"Yes, I do."

"Okay, maybe *you* need a ladder. I don't," he said. "Bulbs?"

"It's not just the bulbs," she said. "I've already tried replacing them."

"So something's wrong with the electrical. I'll take a look."

She thought about what had happened on the boat when he'd been working on the electrical wiring. He'd been shocked and had fallen into the water. "Don't worry about it."

"I can fix it."

"But I don't need you to," she said.

He cocked his head and looked at her. "Is there some sort of problem here?"

She bit her lower lip. "Fine. It's just that the last time you tried to fix something electrical, you…" She grimaced. "You know."

He paused. "No," he said, "I don't know."

Well, crap. God save her from a man's fragile ego. "You had an…issue."

He looked at her like she'd just questioned his manhood. "First you think I can't swim," he said, "and now you think I can't fix an electrical problem. Jesus, woman, why don't you just castrate me while you're at it?"

"Listen, this isn't necessary. I—" She broke off when he held out his hand, palm up.

"Lightbulb," he said shortly.

She blew out a sigh and gave up, opening the bottom drawer of an oak filing cabinet, then pulling out the box of free bulbs she'd gotten at the Green Fair on the pier the week before.

Cole took a bulb and nudged her out of the way. Then he carefully scooped aside a stack of receipts on her desk. Planting a hand there, he vaulted onto the surface with the ease of a track and field Olympian.

A really hot Olympian.

She stared at his running shoes. Battered. Her gaze moved north up his long legs. He had a lot of pockets in those cargoes, and she wondered what else was in them.

She didn't have to wonder what was *beneath* them; she'd seen it all.

And just remembering had her swallowing hard.

Stretching up with his good arm, he unscrewed the dark bulb. As he did, his T-shirt rose, revealing the low-riding waistband of the cargoes and the equally low-riding waistband of his BVDs—navy blue, if one was taking notes—and...

A strip of tanned male skin with just the hint of two dimples—

"Olivia."

She blinked at the laughter in his voice and tilted her head back to find him staring down at her with great amusement.

"Hit the lights," he said, thankfully not commenting on the fact she'd just gotten caught staring at his ass. "I'd hate to electrocute myself and prove you right that I'm indeed an idiot. Sam and Tanner would love that."

"They'd love it if you electrocuted yourself?"

"No, but they'd enjoy the shit out of me making a fool of myself in front of you."

"I don't get men," she said, baffled.

He laughed low in his throat with what might have been agreement as she turned off the lights. Since the sun was just setting but hadn't yet vanished, they still had ambient lighting slanting in the two windows that faced the street, but it wasn't much. As a result, the room had been plunged into a sort of black-and-white landscape.

Cole easily replaced the bulb with a new one. "Hit 'em again," he said.

She turned on the lights.

The new bulb sparked, made a loud pop, and went out.

Olivia jumped about a mile.

Cole didn't. He didn't move a single inch. In fact, it was like he was frozen in place.

"You okay?" she asked.

Not even a flicker.

"Cole?"

At his name, he blinked, took a very careful breath, and said, "Off."

Again, she hit the switch. "Are you—"

"It's all good," he said lightly. Casually.

But she wasn't fooled. She could actually feel the tension in his every muscle—of which he had plenty—coming off him in waves.

Just as she could feel him shoving back that tension, clearly trying to let it go. She got that, she understood that. Hell, she'd lived life like that. "Did you shock yourself?"

He didn't answer. Didn't, in fact, move.

"Maybe you should get down," she said quietly.

That got his attention. He inhaled deeply, then slanted her a long look and unscrewed the bulb.

"Seriously," she said softly. "I'll hire an electrician."

Another long look, and she shut it.

He muttered something she didn't quite catch and crouched low to set the bulb at his feet on the desk. As he did, his pants slid a little lower, into nearly indecent territory.

Like a moth to the flame, Olivia's gaze went right back to his butt. It was a really great butt.

Pulling a screwdriver from a pocket, he rose again, fiddling with whatever was up there, and then held out a hand to her without looking.

She narrowed her eyes at the unspoken demand but set another bulb into his palm.

"Lights," he said.

She hit the switch, and this time both lights flicked on. She stared at him. "What did you do?"

He shrugged.

"Nice," she said. "Thank you."

"You're welcome."

She bit her lip but she couldn't keep it in. "So what was that before? Just now, and also on the boat?"

"If I answer that, then you have to answer a hard one, too. You ready to go there?"

She paused. "Define hard."

"I want to know why you lied to me."

She sucked in a breath. Had he guessed? Oh, God, what did he know? "*Lied* is a strong word."

"Misled. You misled me into thinking you had a handyman."

Oh. That. She nearly sagged with relief.

"No?" he murmured. "Not going there, huh?" He slipped his screwdriver into the pocket running along one thigh.

"Who carries a screwdriver and a…lock-fix-it-thingie in their pocket?" she asked, a little desperate for a subject change.

"Me," he said.

"What else do you have in there?"

He smiled. "Come to dinner and I'll show you."

She arched a brow. "You'd bribe me into going out with you?"

"I'm a man without shame," he said easily. He hopped down from her desk and waited with what she was beginning to realize was characteristic patience for her response.

It was just dinner, she told herself. A simple invitation.

But they both knew nothing about it would be simple.

There would be…hard stuff.

She wasn't particularly good at that. She'd spent her entire childhood weighed down by the obligations and heavy expectations that had been placed on her. And when she'd failed to meet those expectations, people she'd cared about and counted on had abandoned her.

Repeatedly.

As an adult, she'd come to realize that she was much happier going without the weight of those things.

Giving up relationships had been a by-product.

She was okay with that. Very okay.

"This isn't brain surgery, you know," he said. "Just dinner. Hell, we don't even have to commit to needing utensils. We can grab a burger. How does that sound?"

Sounded right up her alley. Nothing serious.

Problem was, Cole, with his sexy MacGyver ways and those cargoes with the screwdriver sticking out of his pocket, had a little bit of serious in his eyes. "I can't," she finally said. "I'm busy tonight. But thanks for fixing the lock and light. Good-bye, Cole."

He met her gaze, his own lit with amusement and the knowledge that she wasn't the only one who thought she was a chicken.

And then he was gone.

Leaving her wondering why, if she'd done the right thing, her heart was burning with disappointment.

Chapter 10

♥

It was late afternoon two days later when Cole walked into the Love Shack and nodded to Jax Cullen, who co-owned the bar and grill.

"Sight for sore eyes," Jax said. "I've got a broken dishwasher—again—and no plumber for two days. Tell me you can jury-rig it to work that long, and I'll feed you all week on the house."

This was a good deal for Cole, who could cook but would rather have a hot poker shoved beneath his toenail. He went into the back and fixed the dishwasher with a roll of duct tape and his screwdriver. "A bacon blue with fries," he told Jax.

"Done," Jax said. "Your boys are already here. I'll bring the burger to you."

Cole headed to his usual table. Indeed, Tanner and Sam were already there, with burgers in front of them, along with a pitcher of beer, half gone. Tanner kicked out a chair for Cole.

Cole poured himself a glass and the three of them made their usual toast.

"To Gil," they said in unison.

"You're late," Tanner said.

Cole scrubbed a hand over his face. He'd been at his mom's all afternoon, building her a set of shelves for the hundreds of books she kept buying even though he'd given her a Kindle.

It had been the last thing on his to-do list.

He was bored out of his mind, not a good place to be. Plus, he was still overthinking Olivia's flat-out rejection. And she hadn't been playing coy, either. She hadn't been playing anything. She honestly hadn't wanted or expected a thing from him.

He didn't know what to make of that, or understand why he even cared. "I'm coming back to work," he said, half expecting them to fuss like old women.

They didn't. Sam thumbed his way through the calendar on his phone. "Talked to Josh today. The doc said another week, right?"

Cole blew out a breath. "Yeah. But not one day more."

"Great," Sam said. "Because I've already got you on the schedule for next week."

Cole looked at him. "Great?"

"Yep. Looks like your first client is already scheduled for six a.m. one week from today. It's all yours."

Cole looked at Tanner, who was studying the ceiling like it held the secret to life. "Alright," Cole said. "Why did that feel too easy?"

Tanner smiled. "'Cause it's for Lucille and her cronies. They want fishing lessons."

Well, hell.

"She said all this talk of you dating Olivia gave her the idea," Tanner said.

"And both of you told her the truth," Cole said, "that I'm not dating Olivia. Right?"

Neither responded to this. "Shit," he said. "Seriously?"

"Hey, if she's focused on you," Tanner said, "then she's not focused on us."

"Nice. Thanks." But Cole didn't bother to sigh, as the reasoning was pretty rock solid. "Either of you know anything about this woman I'm supposedly seeing?"

Sam and Tanner exchanged a look.

"What?" Cole asked.

"Nothing," both Tanner and Sam said, and sipped their beers.

"It's something," Cole said.

"Okay," Tanner said. "It's the first time you've asked about a woman since Susan— Ouch! Shit, man," he said to Sam, and rubbed his kicked shin. "What's your problem?"

Sam ignored him and said to Cole, "I know she's a loyal, fierce friend to Becca."

"And I know she's got a sweet ass," Tanner added.

Sam must have kicked him again, because Tanner spilled his beer and swore. "Whatever," he said. "It's true. And you know the rules. If he'd claim her, I'd stop noticing her assets."

"I'm not claiming anyone," Cole said.

"So her ass is fair game," Tanner said. "That's all I'm saying."

"You know what?" Cole pointed at him. "I *am* claiming her, just so you can't."

"You can't do that," Tanner said. "That's against the rules."

"What the hell rules are you talking about?"

"I don't know. The rules," Tanner said.

"Let me put this another way," Cole said. "Look at her ass again and—"

And he didn't know what, exactly, but it didn't matter because Tanner was grinning.

"All you had to do was say you're into her, man."

Cole ground his teeth and leaned toward him but Sam put a hand on his chest. "Yeah, he's an asshole," Sam said, "but maybe you could stop making yourself such an easy target for him."

Cole thought about it and realized Sam was right. They had another beer and Tanner nodded at Cole's shoulder. He'd removed the sling on the walk over. "You really better, or just bored out of your ever-loving mind?"

Cole leaned back and sighed in disgust. "Do you know how exhausting it is to do jackshit for days on end?"

"You didn't do jackshit for days on end," Sam said. "You tried to pick a fight with Clare, who didn't bite because she's smarter than you, and then you went sniffing around Unique Boutique. And then you spent the day building shelves instead of resting your shoulder."

Cole froze for a beat before drinking more of his beer. "You don't have enough to do with me out, you've got to hunt up gossip?"

"He sleeps with your new girlfriend's BFF," Tanner reminded him. "And Becca and Olivia live in the same building. Becca shares her updates with Sam, who shared with me. We all know that you asked Olivia out and got shut down."

Sam shook his head at Tanner. "You're a real dick tonight."

Tanner didn't look bothered by this assessment of his character.

"Olivia's not my girlfriend," Cole said. "I just met her a week ago."

"Uh-huh. And had her naked two minutes later," Tanner reminded him. "For two years the women in town have been falling all over themselves trying to get your attention, and you've ignored them all. Until now. Let's just say I find this…interesting."

Cole might've jumped down his throat again, or simply told him to shut his pie hole and mind his own business, except the fact was that they *were* each other's business.

And there was another reason. Tanner's eyes were dark, his body tense.

He was having a rough go of it. Cole knew it, Sam knew it, and Tanner himself surely knew it. Not that he'd complain. That was the problem with Tanner. He kept his shit to himself and deeply protected.

Hell. They all did. "Next time," Cole said, "you can rescue the pretty girl."

That got a rare smile out of the ex–Navy SEAL. "I don't need to rescue them, man."

This was true. Women had been attracted to him since the day he'd hit puberty, and he'd made the most of it— until karma had caught up with him and bitten him in the ass in the form of a teenage son with as much wild and crazy as Tanner had shown. Maybe even more.

Sam pulled out his tablet, and Cole groaned.

"Whatever," Sam muttered. "It's financial planning night and you both know it. We've got shit to do."

Tanner poured himself another beer. "Hit me, Grandma."

Sam narrowed his eyes at the age-old nickname for the one of the three of them who always worried about everything. "Don't tempt me," he said, and turned the tablet so that they could see the screen.

Cole settled himself in for the numbers crunch. Sam started talking and he tuned out, confident that the financial wizard with the Midas touch had taken good care of them as always.

Instead, he let other worries sink in. His mom, for one, who kept saying she was fine, but they were coming into another holiday season soon, her second without his dad, and that was going to be rough.

His sisters, specifically Cara, who still refused to let him help her.

Tanner, who seemed to be getting more and more bitchy as time went on instead of…well, better—

"He's gone, baby, gone." This from Tanner himself, and Cole blinked, realizing that they were both staring at him.

"What?" he asked.

Sam swore. "You haven't heard a damn word, have you?"

"Nope," Tanner said, answering for him. "He's running through all his shit in his head again."

"I am not," Cole said.

"Right," Sam said. "Then what did I say?"

"That we're done?" he asked hopefully.

Sam shoved the tablet beneath Cole's nose and started again. They went over receivables, payables, the bottom line. They went over their expectations for the next quarter and whether or not they wanted to get a second boat by next summer season.

Which brought a whole new level to the word *expectations*.

Half an hour later they were done, and in spite of themselves, the three guys who'd started out with literally nothing had come out okay.

More than okay. They had a big, fat bank account and more business than they knew what to do with.

They left the bar together and took in the gray dusk, their breath crystallizing in front of their faces. Daylight Saving Time hadn't ended yet, so it was still staying light late, but the chill didn't wait for dark.

Fall in the Pacific Northwest was predictable in its unpredictability.

"Getting cold," Sam noted, hands shoved into his pockets.

"Yeah," Tanner said. "Cole might want to stay out of the water in the mornings."

Sam just shook his head and walked off, no doubt heading straight to Becca's place.

Tanner stood there a moment, silent. Tense.

Cole blew out a breath. "You all right?"

Tanner made a sound of affirmation that didn't fool Cole for a second, but then he walked off in the opposite direction as Sam.

Alone, Cole crossed the street and hit the pier. The arcade and Ferris wheel were open until Halloween, and Cole headed straight for the ice cream stand. He bought a chocolate shake from Lance, who ran the stand.

"Heard you're dating that hot Unique Boutique chick," Lance said.

Lance and Cole went way back. Cole had been a sickly kid, though not like Lance, who had suffered his entire life with cystic fibrosis. The guy meant a whole hell of a lot to Cole, and he was a walking time bomb, which sucked so hard that Cole tried not to think about it much. "I'm not dating anyone," he said.

"Tumblr says otherwise," Lance said.

Cole groaned, and Lance laughed. "So it's true? You're finally seeing someone again?"

"Not you too," Cole grumbled.

"Hey," Lance said, losing the teasing tone. "Life's too fucking short, man. You know that better than anyone else I know."

True statement. He and Lance bumped fists and then Cole kept moving down the pier, sucking down his shake.

Ahead was the Ferris wheel, backlit against the deepening purple sky. It was operated by Tiny, the six-foot-nine badass biker who owned both the Ferris wheel and the arcade.

Tiny wasn't alone. There was one other person standing there with him, a dark brunette who Cole had no trouble recognizing, even from the back.

Olivia.

Olivia stared up at the Ferris wheel, which was lit with strings of lights that twinkled like stars far above. The thing was huge against the quickly darkening sky. Huge, and both a little terrifying and exciting, she thought as she just watched, slurping her chocolate shake.

She hadn't had a shake since she was a kid.

And she'd never been on a real Ferris wheel. She'd been on a pretend one on a set once. She'd also been pretend horseback riding. And on a pretend helicopter.

Hell, she'd been to the White House.

Also a set.

Maybe it was time to start doing stuff for real.

"You want to buy a ticket?" This was asked by a giant linebacker of a guy in head-to-toe leather and studs. He smiled at her with straight white teeth. "Half off," he said, "just for you."

"Why?" she asked.

He shrugged his broad-as-a-mountain shoulders. "You've been standing here for five minutes looking up at the Ferris wheel like it's your Kryptonite. You're either chicken or broke. I figured I'd find out. So…which is it? You want a ticket?"

No way was she going up alone. "Yeah, I don't think—"

"Two tickets."

Olivia whirled around and came face-to-face with, of all people, Cole. "What are you doing?" she asked.

He touched his shake cup to hers. "Same thing as you, apparently." He turned to Biker Dude. "Hey, Tiny."

Tiny?

The two of them did some complicated male bonding handshake thing, and then Cole pulled a five out of his pocket and handed it over.

And then she was being ushered onto the Ferris wheel.

"Wait," she said, stopping. "Wait a damn minute. I didn't say yes."

"She's chicken," Tiny said helpfully. "I thought maybe she was broke, but you just offered to pay for her and she's still dragging her feet."

Cole cocked his head at her. "You're afraid?"

Try petrified. "Of course not."

He smiled as if delighted by her big, fat, obvious lie.

Tiny did the same.

With a low laugh, Cole took her hand.

"I'm not afraid," she told him, as if repeating this statement would make it more true, as they—deep breath—took a seat on the ride.

Tiny locked them in and winked at Olivia.

"It's okay," he said. "I hardly ever kill people on this thing anymore."

Oh, God.

Cole grinned at Tiny.

Tiny pointed at him. "You get a kiss because of me, you owe me."

Cole saluted him and turned to Olivia.

"You're not getting a kiss," she said.

Ignoring that, he put a big, warm hand over the cold-fingered clench she had on the bar in front of her. "Wait till you get a glimpse of the view from the top," he said. "You can see everything, the whole world in a glance."

"I don't need to see— Oh, crap," she whispered as the Ferris wheel jerked and began to move.

Cole laughed softly but tightened his grip on her hand.

"This isn't funny," she said.

"It's okay, I'm right here."

She'd been staring down at her shoes to avoid the dizzying view, but she turned to eyeball him. "What are you going to do if we get stuck up here?"

"Get us unstuck."

He said this so calmly, so reasonably, that she had to laugh too, but it was a breathless laugh.

He sipped at his shake, looking steady as a rock.

"We're both drinking shakes," she said inanely.

He nodded.

"And walking the pier," she said.

Another nod.

"Do you do this a lot?" she asked.

"Always have," he said. "Started when I was young. I told you I was the runt of the house, right? I'd escape and come here."

The idea that he'd had anything to escape from caught at her, even more than the night air in her face, ocean-scented and chilly. "What was wrong at your house?"

"Estrogen overload in the form of three bossy older sisters," he said. "Ever been held down and had your hair curled, makeup put on, and your toenails painted?"

Actually, yes. It was called the makeup trailer. She took in his long, leanly muscled build. He was strong as hell, and she knew it. "You were the runt?" she asked in disbelief.

"Yep," he said. "Small and puny. I weighed about eighty-five pounds soaking wet until high school."

"What happened in high school?" she asked, unable to help herself.

"I caught up." He met her gaze, his smile fading. "So we both came looking for comfort tonight."

"I hardly call being a million feet in the air comfort," she said. And though she hadn't looked out, she could feel her stomach drop, signaling that they were getting higher. And higher. She closed her eyes.

"What were you seeking comfort from?" he asked.

"Oh, no," she said, shaking her head. "Not going there. Not in space." Or ever.

"All right," he said. "I'll go first." She felt him shift slightly and risked a quick peek. He was leaning back now, long legs stretched out in front of him as if he didn't have a care. He was staring out into the admittedly glorious night, and still they were rising, rising, rising, and she slammed her eyes closed again.

"I just left a meeting with Sam and Tanner," he said casually. "It was a good meeting. Our business is solid, we're solid. But it's a lot of pressure to keep up with our expectations. Open your eyes, Olivia."

She squeezed them tighter. "Hell no."

She felt him shift again, felt his arm settle along the back of the bench, brushing her shoulders comfortingly, his fingers lightly stroking the nape of her neck.

She shivered. "Still no."

Something brushed her jaw. His mouth? Her entire body tightened at the thought and her eyes flew involuntarily open.

And met his.

It wasn't his mouth touching her, it was his thumb, though he was close enough that they could—and did—share their next breath. He stroked her jaw again. "We're at the top."

Chapter 11

♥

We're at the top...

That's what Olivia used to hear every week when the ratings would come in. And then the network would shower her with love and appreciation, and life would go on.

Until it'd come to a crashing halt.

She opened her eyes, going stock still. Behind Cole, the sky was purple, with only a hint of the stars that would light it up when full darkness hit. The ocean swells stretched out as far as the eye could see, meeting the horizon. Far below them were the twinkling lights of Lucky Harbor.

He was right. She could see everything, the whole world in a glance.

"Breathe," he said quietly, entwining their hands and bringing them up to his torso, letting her feel his chest rise and fall steadily. "Just breathe."

She sucked in some air, suitably distracted by the feel of the hard pecs beneath her hand. He looked so deceptively normal in his clothes that she forgot that beneath he was anything but. She'd seen that for herself, every single perfectly sculpted inch.

And a certain number of those inches? Mouthwatering.

She'd been wondering about him over the past few days. The town had gotten it in its collective head that they were seeing each other, and she'd been fending off the "So you and Cole?" question at least once a day.

At night she had only her own questions to fend off…

"Better?" he asked, still holding her hand to his chest.

She thought of his reaction to her peeking beneath the blankets at him and smiled in spite of herself.

"Yeah," he said, watching her face carefully. "Better."

Good thing he didn't know why.

His gaze never left hers, and his mouth twitched. "Care to share?" he asked.

"Expectations." She breathed some more and stared out as they—finally!—began their slow descent back to earth, the cool, salty ocean air blowing in her face. "You said it was hard to live up to the expectations you had of your business." Her entire life had been nothing but one long expectation. "I know how that feels."

"You don't say much about yourself," he said after a moment. "When did you leave home?"

"You never really leave, do you?" she said.

"You mean you can take the girl out of Kentucky, but you can't take Kentucky out of the girl?"

She laughed. "Something like that."

"You said you didn't miss it, but I'm getting the feeling you do. At least on some level."

She stared out at the black sea. Did she miss Hollywood? That was the place she really considered home. Not Kentucky.

Never Kentucky.

"I miss the people," she finally said. God's honest truth. She missed her director, and the producer. She missed the caterer, the wardrobe people…her agent. He'd been like a father to her. In fact, she'd often pretended he was her father, which was better than the truth—that she'd been conceived during a one-night stand at a party and Tamilyn had never named the guy.

Olivia had found her real family on set. The wardrobe lady had been the grandma she'd never had, since her mother had been estranged from her own family for decades. The set director had been like an uncle. The other kids on the set were her siblings. It'd been a dysfunctional family, but still a family, and she missed the close camaraderie. "I miss the people a lot."

"You were close."

They'd been lucky. Their cast had been a large, young, boisterous, happy one. After spending the first seven years of her life poorer than dirt, life on that set had been a dream come true. Food tables, constantly filled. Games, toys, books, whatever she'd wanted. "Extremely," she said, knowing damn well that he thought they were talking about her real family. But these people had been her family, for all intents and purposes.

Until, of course, she'd hit puberty and the show had been canceled. Her identity had, *poof*, vanished, and the people she'd cared about had all moved on, leaving her alone, confused, and more than a little frightened at the easy abandonment.

As an adult, she'd come to realize it hadn't been anything personal. It'd simply been the way of the industry. The way of the world, in fact.

Didn't make it hurt any less.

"How about you?" she asked. "You're close to your family."

He laughed and rubbed his jaw. He had at least a day's worth of growth there, and the scraping sound it made against his palm activated the butterfly colony living in her belly.

"My dad's gone now," he said, "but both he and my mom grew up here, and they never left. Raised all four of us here, and yeah, we're close. Though I think *nosy*'s a better word. We're all up in each other's business a lot."

"And you all stuck in Lucky Harbor?" she marveled, unable to fathom that. He'd said his sisters were crazy, but she could tell by the softness in his gaze that he was just joking, that he had the real deal in his family.

"All of us," he said. "I left for a while after graduation. Worked on the oil rigs in the Gulf of Mexico for five years before coming back here."

"Wow," she breathed. "Five years. What did you do?"

"I was the chief positioning operator and navigator for the ship and in charge of the equipment and safety for all the guys. Eighty-five, to be exact."

"I'm trying to imagine living with eighty-five guys on a rig for that long."

"Three were women, actually."

"Not the best of odds," she said, fascinated by him, by his family, by everything.

He shrugged, but something in his gaze caught her interest. "You beat the odds," she said, guessing. She laughed when he grimaced. "You did," she said. "Eighty-two to three, and you caught one of them."

He grimaced again and scrubbed a hand over his face. "Only because as a supervisor, I stuck out from the general population," he said. "Authority tends to look good to some women."

She studied him. Heart-stopping blue eyes. Silky brown hair that tended to fall over his forehead when he was wet from head to toe, and also when he was riding Ferris wheels.

He looked pretty damn good to her, and she wasn't into authority figures. "You don't think you're hot?" she asked.

He actually squirmed, and she laughed again.

He met her gaze, his own rueful. "You know I love your laugh, but this is starting to remind me of when you were pointing and laughing at my naked ass on the boat last week."

"I never pointed and laughed at your naked ass. I never saw your naked ass. I saw…other parts." Oh boy, had she. "And I wasn't laughing at…it."

He arched a brow. "*It*?"

Now she squirmed. "You've got a better term?"

"Absolutely," he said. "It's called a co—"

She put her hand over his mouth. "We were talking about the rigs," she said firmly, doing her damnedest not to blush—as if she had any control over that. "You had a girlfriend out there."

He nodded, a little reluctantly she thought. She had no business wondering, being so curious about him, but she couldn't seem to stop herself. She dropped her hand from his mouth. "You and One-of-Three go out for a long time?" she asked.

"Three years."

"Three years…in the past tense?" she asked.

"You fishing?"

Hell yes. She just didn't know why.

"Past tense," he said, letting her off the hook. "I don't still see Susan."

There was something in his expression. No, scratch that. There was absolutely nothing in his expression at all. He was carefully…blank. "Real life wasn't as romantic on the mainland as it had been on the rig?" she asked, trying to joke.

He laughed at that, drily. "You think things were romantic on the rig?"

"They must have been at least a little romantic," she said, "if you and Susan did the deed there for three years."

"The deed? We really need to work on your sexual vocabulary, Supergirl. 'The deed' could refer to any number of things—"

"I don't need to know specifics!" she said quickly. *Yes, you do*, said the devil on her left shoulder. Olivia ignored her. "But three years together, that's a long time. You must have really been in love."

"Thought so at the time," he said. "But it didn't work out. It's been over for a while."

He looked a little sad, which was hard to take for some reason, but it suitably distracted her from panicking that they were still moving. "Over over?" she asked.

He looked at her for a long beat, and then a ghost of

a smile crossed his lips. "You asking for any particular reason?"

She huffed out a forced laugh. "No. Of course not."

"You're interested in me."

"That's absurd. That's…ridiculous. I don't even know you. I—"

He leaned into her so that she felt cradled between the arm along the back of the ride and the hand he'd set on the armrest at her far hip. "It's over over," he said, and held her gaze. "You know what this means, right?"

She shook her head.

"It means it's your turn to share with the class."

She stared at him, those butterflies in her belly fluttering to life again. Her longest relationship had been with her handheld shower massager.

"You ever love anyone, Olivia?"

Well, she loved her shower massager, but somehow she didn't see herself admitting that. "Love?"

"Yeah. Love."

She'd been with guys. She'd had crushes. She'd even really liked a few here and there…but she'd never been particularly successful at getting to the next stage and staying there.

Maybe because your first kiss happened on camera.

Or maybe because your first boyfriend was a fellow actor, who'd been…acting.

But the real answer was even more revealing—she'd never figured out how to let anyone know the real her. Instead of answering, she risked another look around. They were on the upswing again. "Oh, good God. We're going around another time."

"Breathe," he murmured. "Just keep breathing."

Right. She gulped in air. "I've heard it's a pretty rough existence out there on the rigs," she said, desperate for a subject change.

"Yeah," he said. "Rough. You could definitely say that."

She met his gaze.

"We lost someone out there," he told her. "My best friend, Gil. And nearly Tanner, too."

"My God, how awful," she breathed. "What happened?"

"We had a gas explosion, and a fire."

She couldn't even imagine. Here she'd been thinking about how hard she'd had it. Poor little Hollywood kid, abandoned by her people, boo hoo. "Were you hurt?"

"Minimally," he said. "I don't remember much of it, not the last few moments leading up to it, or right after. Opened my eyes in the water, and that was it."

He looked angry at himself that he couldn't remember. "Sometimes," she said quietly, "remembering isn't all it's cracked up to be. Sometimes we're better off not remembering."

He nodded and looked off into the night. "Sam, Tanner, and I left the gulf after that. We'd saved every penny we could during those five years to start a charter company together. We did it in Gil's memory."

"Pretty great way to honor him," she said.

He gave her a small smile. "Gil would've been real pissed off if we hadn't followed through with the plan because of him."

So he'd come home with Sam and Tanner and started the charter company, she thought. And then his dad had died, leaving him as the man of the house for his mom and sisters.

Which she knew he most likely had taken on without complaint, because he had a backbone of steel.

She'd never met anyone like him. "You've had a rough few years," she said.

"And also a pretty great few years."

She stared at him, warmed by just looking at him and also by the realization that she liked him. The man he was. She liked him, and trusted him. And she was tempted by him in a way she'd not been tempted in…well, ever. She hadn't let herself become attached to anyone because this way she was always prepared when they left.

But with Cole, she had the feeling it was already too late.

"What about you?" he asked. "What did you do before coming to Lucky Harbor?"

"I went to college." Several times, in fact.

He smiled. "You're going to make me work for this. That's okay, I'm a patient sort. Where did you go?"

"NYU." The first time.

"Impressive," he said.

"And then San Francisco University." She paused. "And New Mexico."

"Ah," he said. "You had the wanderlust bug."

"More like the ADHD bug," she admitted. She'd happily gone along collecting degrees like some women collect earrings, soaking up being in school for the first time in her life, loving the freedom.

She'd finally stopped when she'd had no choice, when the money had run out and both her mother and her sister were hounding her to go back to acting.

She'd refused. Still aimless, she'd gathered all the stuff she'd collected and had in storage and had done what no one would have ever expected of her, the one thing she'd been yearning to do since Mrs. Henderson had told her of the idyllic Lucky Harbor.

She'd moved here and opened up a shop and, for the first time, was living like a real person. Not off a script or her forged bio.

That had been a year ago, and though she was literally living paycheck to paycheck, she'd been happy—until the past month, when her mom had started making noises about needing money again.

But the night pushed that worry away for now. So did sitting so close to Cole, close enough that she could feel the warmth of his thigh pressed to hers, the easy strength of him, not to mention the fact that he smelled more delicious than chocolate fudge brownies—which was really saying something.

"I'd love to hear about your family sometime," he said quietly, as if he didn't want to spook her.

She'd been telling tales about her past for so long that they always slipped easily off her tongue. Naturally. And since she'd never really cared what anyone had thought of her, she'd never felt particularly guilty.

But she did now, because already Cole was different. She found she cared that she'd let him believe her family was gone, that she was alone, and she wished she could take it back and start again. But she couldn't.

You could try the truth…

She opened her mouth to say…what? What could she possibly say? *I lied because I'm a coward*? Or *I lied because you don't know this yet but you're going to leave me like everyone else always does, and it's my little way of protecting myself from pain*?

Lame, and she was afraid it was also a little pathetic.

Tell him, said the usually silent angel on her right shoulder.

Don't tell him, the devil on her other shoulder said. *We haven't gotten to sleep with him yet! You'll blow it!*

Olivia shook her head. Cole wouldn't understand. He was strong of mind and body. He was honest to the very core. He didn't shy away from the difficult or the hard-to-take. He didn't shy away from anything. If she told him the truth now, he'd stop looking at her like…like she was interesting.

Like he wanted to eat her up with a spoon.

The Ferris wheel clicked to a stop before she could decide what to do. They were back on the ground. She stared at Cole in amazement, and he grinned.

"Yeah," he said. "You lived."

Tiny let them off the ride. Full dark had fallen now. Long fingers of fog were riding in, sliding along the water's surface, dancing around their heads. They walked back to the beginning of the pier, where Olivia expected Cole to break off and go his own merry way. Instead, he kept stride alongside her toward her shop. "Where are you going?" she asked.

"Walking you back to your car."

"No need," she said. "It's not like this was a date or anything. There's no getting lucky at the end of the night, you know."

Apparently uninsulted and not at all bothered, he laughed. She wasn't sure what was so funny.

"You are," he said, reading her mind.

At her block, she headed around to the back door of her shop, where it was pitch-black, as usual.

Cole stared up at the light that wasn't lit. "You need to put that on a timer so you're never out here in the dark like this."

"I have a timer," she said, fumbling through her purse for her keys. "I just can't get it to work."

"I can—"

"Not necessary."

He waited until she opened the shop door, and then he stepped in behind her.

"Hey," she said. "I said you're not going to get lucky…" She trailed off because he wasn't even looking at her. He was flicking the light by the door on and off.

Nothing was happening.

"New bulb?" he asked.

She sighed. "It doesn't work, never has."

He shook his head in reproach. "You have a new bulb?"

"You've already fixed my front door and office lights, Cole. I can't let you—"

"Could've been done by now, Supergirl." Then he leapt onto the landing railing, balancing there with absolute ease as he reached up with his good arm and unscrewed the bulb.

She stared up at him. "You're injured. You can't—"

"Here." He handed her the old bulb. "Grab me a new one, yeah?"

She blinked. How the hell could such a laid-back, easygoing guy also be so alpha? "Please?"

"No worries, babe. I won't go until I've fixed this."

"No." She had to laugh. "I meant 'go grab me a new bulb, *please*.'"

He looked down at her, eyes glittering. "I like the way you say please."

She narrowed her eyes.

"Fine," he said. "Would you get me a new bulb, *please*?"

So of course she did.

When she got back with the bulb, he had a penlight in his teeth, shining it at his hands, which were working a piece of duct tape around and around a wire. He looked like he knew exactly what he was doing, and her pulse kicked.

Which was absolutely juvenile. She'd seen good-looking guys handling tools before.

Actors, she reminded herself.

Fakers.

And there wasn't a single fake bone in Cole's body.

He reached down for the bulb without looking at her, and she handed it over.

"Where did you get the duct tape?" she asked.

"Had some in my pocket."

Of course he did. She watched as he shoved the roll of duct tape back in said pocket and pulled a screwdriver from another.

He twisted one end off, and in the blink of an eye, the thing had turned into a hammer. He hit something a few times, turned it into yet another tool, played with the wiring, and then screwed in the new bulb.

"Hit the switch," he said. He paused. "Please."

Damn, he was good. She hit the switch, and then blinked as a circle of light flooded over them.

He hopped down with his usual easy agility. "Turn it off again."

She turned it off without question.

Then he stepped into her, bumping her body with his.

"Why did I turn it off?" she whispered.

"For this. Which, by the way, I'm going to owe Tiny for after all."

And then...

Oh, God, and then.

He kissed her.

Chapter 12

The moment Cole's mouth touched Olivia's, he caught some serious voltage. Not electrical this time, but two hundred volts of pure sexual energy.

Her lips were soft, and sweet.

So damn sweet.

And yet somehow *not* sweet at the same time. Wanting to savor her, he moved slowly, sliding his hands up her arms, over her throat to her jaw, his thumbs caressing her as he tilted her head to suit him.

And man, did she suit him.

She let out a soft, wordless murmur, and then her hands were on his chest. He liked that. Her fingers dug in a little bit, signaling that she was about to either push him away or pull him in.

What's it going to be, babe?

After the longest heartbeat of his life, those fingers of hers curled, gripping his shirt.

He was going to take that as a good sign.

Her mouth parted, and then she was kissing him back. He let her take control for a moment, a rough groan escaping him when her hands slid from his chest into his hair.

Things went hot then, detonation hot, and only when they were both breathless did she pull away.

"Don't take that the wrong way," she gasped.

"There's no wrong way to take that." His voice was more than a little rough. He couldn't help it; all the blood had drained out of his head.

Staring at him, she put her fingers to her own lips. "That was…"

Spectacular, he thought. Heart-pounding. Perfect—

"Interesting," she finally said.

He stared at her and then had to laugh. "You're not easy on the ego."

She made it worse by smiling. "I'm sorry."

"Yeah, I can see that." But he couldn't help smiling, too, as he turned to go. "'Night, Olivia."

She didn't say anything, so he turned back to look at her. She was standing there in the doorway, lit only by the moonlight. But he didn't need to see her face to know she was still looking a little dazed.

Which was only fair. He was dazed all the way into next week.

"Bye," came her soft whisper.

"I said good night," he said, "not bye."

"What's the difference?"

"A whole hell of a lot," he said.

"Not to me." And then she slipped inside, the click of the lock sounding in the night.

A challenge.

* * *

Cole was halfway home when his cell rang. His mom. "Everything okay?" he asked. The question was habit, one born of fear. When his father'd had his heart attack, Amelia had called Cole first. It'd fallen to him to handle his mom, his sisters, all the arrangements, everything, and he'd done it without fail.

But his heart still skipped a beat whenever she called him late at night.

"I'm fine," she said, her voice light and happy, signaling that everything truly was okay. And given the party atmosphere he could now hear in the background, things were more than okay.

"I'm just wondering about you," she said in the way people did when they were trying to get you to spill your guts.

There was no possible way the gossip mill could've gotten ahold of the mind-boggling, heart-stopping, pulse-racing kiss he'd just laid on Olivia.

Right?

He stopped right there in the middle of the sidewalk and looked around. Nope. All alone. "I'm fine," he said.

"No," she said. "Fine would be you married with kids so I could be a busybody grandma to them—"

"Mom. Focus."

"I am. You'd make a great husband and father, Cole."

He'd never been one to see himself with a wife and a family. He had all that craziness already on his plate with his mom and sisters. "Mom, what did you need?"

"To know why you aren't here."

He tried to visualize the calendar he rarely bothered to keep updated, tried to remember whatever it was that he'd forgotten. Not that anyone could blame him, because there was some sort of family gathering every week. He did his best to skip as many of them as possible, but he was rarely successful in this endeavor.

Blood was much thicker than water.

"Need a hint?" his mom asked.

Apparently so, since his brain was currently replaying that kiss with Olivia on repeat, leaving little room for anything else. "No, I remember."

"Uh-huh," his mom said, sounding amused. "So we'll see you in a few then, yes?"

"Absolutely." Cole disconnected. "*Shit*," he said, and called Tanner.

Tanner's phone connected, but he didn't speak. Through the phone Cole could hear the same party sounds he'd just heard from his mom's phone. "*Shit*," he said again.

Tanner laughed. "Need a hint?"

"No!" Cole disconnected. He stared off into the distance, racking his brain, but nothing came to him. On the off chance Sam was in bed with Becca—which was where any red-blooded man would be if he were engaged to the gorgeous brunette—Cole texted him instead of calling, and went with casual. He had to, because if Sam sniffed out that Cole had forgotten tonight's gig, he'd laugh his ass off and not respond.

So what's up?

Cole was pretty confident that Sam would know, as they'd had Sam as a foster kid on and off through his teen years and he was part of the family. And sure enough, Sam responded almost immediately:

You forgot, huh?

Hell. Cole stared down at the phone, pride warring with good sense. Good sense won, and he texted:

Just %#!#$@# tell me.

Again, Sam responded within seconds.

Your great-aunt's second husband's retirement party.

Cole's eye twitched. He pressed a thumb into his eye socket and got into his truck to drive over to his mom's house.

She lived on the bluffs overlooking the bowl shape of the town and the harbor, and the house was lit up bright as day. He no sooner entered the place than he was pounced on by everyone.

"Darling," his mom said, and pulled him in for a hug. She was petite and fit, making her look a decade younger than her fifty-one. "So sweet of you to finally show up."

He sighed. "Who ratted me out?"

"Tanner."

Cole lifted his head, searched the crowd, and found Tanner leaning against the mantel nursing a drink, which he lifted in a mock toast to Cole. "Ratfink bastard," Cole muttered. "He could have told me at the Love Shack earlier."

"Don't blame him," his mom said. "I withheld my meringue pie until he squealed. Not even a Navy SEAL can hold back from my pie."

This was true.

Amelia ran a hand over Cole's shoulder. "You're going to get this looked at again before you go back to work, yes?"

"It's fine." Judging from the sounds of laughter and talking and music coming from the living room, the party was still raging. He ignored it. "How are you doing, Mom?"

She smiled with no little amount of irony as she repeated his earlier words back to him: "I'm fine."

He rolled his eyes, and she laughed as they entered the fray together. His sisters Clare and Cindy were there, with their rug rats and husbands, and it took him twenty minutes to wade through them.

"Where's Cara?" he asked.

Clare's smile faded, and she jerked her chin toward the back of the house.

"She alone?" he asked.

"Yes. She said she broke up with that guy she was seeing. Ward."

If only it were that simple, Cole thought. He took in Clare's worried expression and tugged on a strand of her hair. "It's going to be fine," he said.

His mantra tonight, apparently.

He went through the house, stopped along the way by what felt like a billion people, including Sam and Tanner, but he didn't find Cara anywhere. The house was a sprawling one-story ranch-style, shaped like a big U. The party had spilled out into the courtyard that the house surrounded on three sides. Beyond the courtyard was a small grove of trees, one of which held their childhood tree house. His dad had built it for him.

For most of his childhood, that tree house had been his

escape from pesky sisters who couldn't, or wouldn't, be bothered to climb it and get at him.

He walked through the courtyard, past the pool, and to the grove, stopping at the base of the biggest tree. He drew a big breath, preparing for battle. Because it was always a battle with Cara. "Hey," he said upward to the flicker of light he could see between the wood slats.

No answer.

"Aw, come on," he said. "Don't make me climb up there."

More nothing.

"Shit, Cara. Really?"

The tree house door creaked open and a head peeked out. "Go away!"

There she was. "I'd love to, but my sister's miserable and sharing that misery with everyone in the family, and they're all clueless as to why. Only I know that she's a big, fancy liar and her guilt's eating her up. If she'd stop being an idiot, then yeah, maybe—"

"Must be nice to be perfect!" she yelled down at him.

He pinched the bridge of his nose. "There's something seriously wrong with you if you think my life's perfect." No answer, and he sighed. "Look, I think you—"

"Stop thinking for me! You think you know everything, but you don't!" With that, she slammed the door shut.

"What the hell," he muttered. He looked around, but not a single tree or breeze or jackshit offered to help him out here.

Then he heard it.

The sound of Cara's quiet sobs.

He tipped his head back and stared at the stars for a beat, but nothing came to him, no miracle cure. Grinding his teeth, he began to climb. Which, thanks to his shoulder, hurt like a son of a bitch. It wasn't an easy climb, either; that had been the beauty of the design, and his dad had done it on purpose. No ladder, no easy steps. If you couldn't climb a tree, you didn't get into the tree house. That simple.

And that difficult.

"Haven't done this in over a decade," he muttered halfway up. He was pretty sure he heard Cara's derisive snort, and the sound spurred him on. Two minutes later he flopped into the tree house and lay flat on his back, breathing heavily.

"You're out of shape," came Cara's disembodied voice in the dark.

"My shoulder's killing me."

There was a rustling, and then a bright light in his eyes.

Her Kindle.

He slammed his eyes shut and covered them with his arm. "Jesus—"

"I thought your shoulder might be better by now. How did you climb the tree if it's not better?"

"I could climb this tree in my sleep," he said. "Why are you out here in the dark?"

"Why do you care?"

He resisted the urge to strangle her. "You know I care."

"I know you're angry with me."

"So?" he asked. "What's new about that?"

She set the Kindle—still on—between them. "I want to be alone. I'm reading."

"Yeah?" he asked. "The party boring you?"

Her gaze met his in the pale light from the e-reader. "The constant, nonstop questions are," she said.

"Questions?"

"The usual," she said. "How's school, what am I majoring in again, how many units am I taking, when am I going to be finished, am I the oldest one there, what am I going to do with my life…pick one."

"You sound like a sixteen-year-old," he said.

"Yes, well, as it turns out, being thirty-two is no picnic either."

"Because you're lying to everyone," he said.

"Hi, Kettle. Black much?"

"Telling people my shoulder doesn't hurt so they won't worry about me is different from letting everyone think you've gone back to law school when you haven't," he said. "Or hiding the fact that you ran off and eloped with the guy you'd known for a week."

She went still, then backed up just enough that he could no longer see her face from the glow of the e-reader. "I thought I loved him."

"After a week."

"You and your unrealistic expectations," she said. "What do you know about love?"

Well, she had him there. "You told me you were going to have the marriage annulled. That didn't happen. Then you said you were going to divorce him."

"It's not that easy," she said.

"Why?"

"Because, damn it, I still love him. Sort of."

Sort of. Jesus. "He cheated on you," Cole reminded her.

"He thought I'd left him."

Cole wasn't going to win this fight. "And lying to Mom?"

"I'm going to tell her."

"About which?" he asked. "That you're not really in school, or that you got married without telling her?"

"It's so easy for you," she said. "You went to college for a couple of years, found your thing, hit the rigs, made bank, and now get to sit around on your boat all day. You've got it easy."

"Is that really what you think?" he asked incredulously. "You think I have it easy?"

She just looked at him.

He struggled to find something to say that wouldn't have her chucking her e-reader at his head. At least she'd turned it off so they were in the dark.

Easy. Christ. The rigs had been anything but easy. It'd been hard work, the hardest fucking work of his life, day in and day out. And yeah, he'd been lucky enough to be with the guys, and for a while, Susan.

Until Gil had died. Until the day of his funeral, when Cole had turned to Susan for comfort and realized that she was grieving for Gil even more than he was. She'd been grieving for Gil like a woman who'd lost the love of her life.

Kind of a game changer in a relationship, realizing that you were the only one in love…

He thunked his head back on the wall a few times to clear it, shoving the memory deep as he waited for his sister to say something more.

He'd given up on that when she finally spoke, her

voice once again disembodied in the dark. "I get that I've disappointed you, Cole. But it's my life."

"You didn't disappoint me," he said. "This isn't about me."

"Could've fooled me," she muttered.

"You let Dad think you were going back to law school, to be an attorney, like he was. For the entire last year of his life he thought that," Cole said.

"And I was in school."

"For what, three weeks?"

She blew out a sigh and there was some more rustling, and then he felt her lie flat on her back next to him, so that only their arms were touching. It was something she'd done when they'd been young, when he'd been so sick. She'd lay with him, and it made him ache.

"I miss you," he said.

"I'm still right here," she said, but they both knew that wasn't true.

"I hate it that you have to keep my secrets," she whispered in the dark.

"Then stop the madness. Either tell everyone you married Ward, or dump him. Stop taking Mom's money for tuition and books. Come clean with everyone."

"It's not that simple, Cole."

"Yeah, it is. No one's going to judge you for your life choices, Cara. But they will for the lies."

"I'm not spending Mom's money, you know. I have it all in my account. I haven't spent a penny of it."

"Whatever, Cara; lying is lying."

Another long silence. "What am I supposed to tell them?" she asked softly.

"The truth. That you followed your heart, for better

or worse. That you quit school two semesters ago. That you're working at some store."

"I'm a personal shopper for Macy's, which thankfully is a forty-five-minute drive so the nosy-bodies from Lucky Harbor haven't discovered me. And you know what? I happen to be really good at it. In fact, I love it," she said. "In case you wanted to know."

He sat up and moved to the door.

"Where are you going?"

"Home," he said. "I'm tired from sitting around on my boat all day long."

She turned on the e-reader again, and her face was bathed in soft ambient light. She had the good grace to grimace. "I shouldn't have said that, I'm sorry. I know you work your ass off. But I'm doing the same now, I promise. And I'll figure out the Ward thing. Soon."

He crouched at her side. "If you love this job, then just tell Mom and the rest of the coven the truth. Make up with Ward or don't. But tell them. That's all I'm asking."

She bit her lower lip and gave a barely there nod.

Good enough, he thought, and hoped she meant it. He moved to climb down.

"Cole?"

"Yeah?"

"Thanks for not telling on me."

"It's not my place to tell," he said.

"I appreciate that—"

"Because it's yours."

She blew out a sigh. "You suck."

"I care."

"Damn it. And now the guilt…"

"No guilt," he said. "We're family. Family doesn't lie to each other. You hear me?"

She sighed again.

"Cara."

"Yeah," she said. "I hear you."

Their gazes met and held, and then he left her alone, hoping she'd do the right thing.

Chapter 13

A few days after Holy-Cow-Didn't-See-That-Kiss-Coming Night, Olivia woke early. A storm had blown in at some point and she could hear the wind pounding the warehouse, whistling through the rafters high above her.

The heat hadn't kicked on, so she huddled beneath her blankets, not wanting to get up. From bed she checked on a few of her pending eBay bids and Craigslist items she had her eye on for the shop. Next up was email, which she tackled with one eye closed because everyone knew that made it easier to ignore the bad ones.

Yep. Her sister had emailed.

And so had her mother, which was new. Tamilyn had finally stepped into the twenty-first century, God help them all.

She also had an email from the TV Land producer, in which he quickly and efficiently outlined the retro special he'd planned.

A nightmare in the making.

She was in a good place, damn it, a really good place. She didn't want to go back. Not even for a day.

Braving the icy morning, she got up, showered until she ran out of hot water—which took only about five minutes—and then dressed and headed out. Down the hall, she knocked on Becca's door.

It took knocking a second time before Becca opened up, her hair wild, cheeks rosy, wearing a grin that wouldn't quit.

Olivia shook her head. "We're going to have to switch our weekly breakfasts to dinners."

"No, I promise I can get ready in two minutes."

"It's not because you're late," Olivia said, stepping inside while Becca searched for clothes.

"Why then?" Becca asked, throwing on a sweater that was clearly Sam's, since the chunky cream cable-knit hit her at midthigh.

"Because I'm jealous," Olivia said. "And anyway, it's been a bunch of months already. Aren't you tired of having sex all the time yet?"

Becca laughed. "Are you kidding? You've seen who I'm sleeping with, right?"

It was true, Sam was pretty damn fine. As was Tanner. But Olivia's brain had a perma-pic of Cole on her frontal lobe, wearing the same heavy-lidded, sensual look in his eyes that he'd had after kissing her. No doubt even if she spent every night in Cole's bed for months, she wouldn't be tired of him yet, either.

Becca hopped into a pair of jeans and fought with the top button. "Damn it, I'm going to have to order oatmeal this morning instead of my usual bacon-and-eggs special. I'm getting to be a chunk."

"Yeah right," Olivia said, looking at Becca's warm, soft curves.

"It's true," Becca said. "Oh, and I invited the new girl to join us. Callie."

"But you know I don't like new people."

"Oh good," came a female voice from the doorway. "And here I was nervous that this would be all awkward, like high school."

Olivia sighed and turned to the door.

Callie stood there, not looking awkward in the slightest. In fact, she was smirking slightly at Olivia. She was in another pair of yoga pants, sans dust this time, and a long, soft sweater the same blue as her eyes. Her smile was a mix of dry wit and bravado, and Olivia felt like a jerk.

"I'm sorry," she said genuinely. "I didn't actually do high school."

The words slipped out of her, and before the questions could start, she gave the truth. Of sorts. "I was home-schooled."

Tutored on set. Same thing.

"Man, I wished for that," Callie said. "I did the opposite of homeschooling. I went to a small-town high school."

"Really?" Becca asked. "Where?"

"Right here in Lucky Harbor."

When both Olivia and Becca just stared at Callie, she smiled. "Left after graduation and vowed to never again live in a town small enough that you could run into your gyno at the grocery store. Or your parole officer at the post office." She shrugged. "And yet ten years later, here I am."

Silence.

"Hey," Callie said. "I was kidding about the parole officer."

"So…you missed Lucky Harbor?" Olivia asked, drawn to the idea. She'd been in town just long enough to know she loved it here and hoped to never leave.

But Callie laughed. "No, I didn't miss much about Lucky Harbor, actually."

"So why are you back?" Becca asked.

"My grandma," Callie said. "She's acting a little…" She swirled her finger on the outside of her ear. "Cuckoo. Like maybe her box of crayons is missing a few colors. My family took a vote on who had to come back to check on her. I drew the short straw."

"Your grandma's living here with you?" Becca asked.

"No, Grandma owns the local art gallery," Callie said. "There's room there for me, or at her house, but I need my own space."

"Art gallery." Becca smiled. "Your grandma's Lucille? The oracle of Lucky Harbor?"

"Oh, God. You know her?" Callie asked. "It's true then, she's been making trouble?"

Becca laughed. "Well, that depends on who you ask."

"Great." Callie shook her head and looked around the interior of Becca's apartment. "Looks like yours is as big a piece of crap as mine."

"Yeah, but not Olivia's," Becca said. "She owns Unique Boutique, that really great vintage shop downtown. She did up her apartment as pretty as her store."

Pride filled Olivia at the unexpected praise. "It's all older stuff," she said, "nothing new."

"Some of the very best stuff is old," Callie said, and she came up in stature in Olivia's eyes.

They left the warehouse and stood outside a moment, taking in the vicious dark clouds coming in off the water, churning up the sky like black cotton candy.

"Gonna be a hell of a storm tonight," Becca noted.

"I remember Lucky Harbor's fall storms," Callie said, wrapping her arms around herself. "Does the power still go out all the time?"

Becca and Olivia, both relatively new to Lucky Harbor, looked at each other.

"Never been here during fall," Becca said, not sounding quite as excited about the storm now.

"Stock up on candles," Callie warned. "Just a tip. Although that's not going to keep me online and working, so hopefully I'm wrong."

"What do you do?" Olivia asked.

Callie paused for the briefest second. "I run an online one-stop wedding website."

"Wow," Becca said, sounding impressed. "You can make a living off that?"

"People are pretty serious about their weddings," Callie said.

They walked past the docks toward the pier. While Becca and Callie chatted, Olivia took in the empty slip where Lucky Harbor Charters' boat was usually moored.

"The guys took out a big group of fishermen," Becca said, noticing the direction of Olivia's gaze. "It was supposed to be Lucille and her cronies, but they decided on bingo instead."

"You mean Sam and Tanner took out the fishermen?" Olivia asked.

"Not Sam. He's building a boat in their warehouse today."

"But Cole's shoulder," Olivia said. "He shouldn't be out yet."

"He's not. He's working the hut," Becca said.

Lucky Harbor Charters operated out of a large warehouse on the harbor. A smaller building functioned as their client reception area. They called it the hut. Olivia knew this thanks to Becca. The two of them had often sat and watched—and also drooled—over the three guys either out on their boat, surfing, or having pull-up contests in the alley between their warehouses...and Becca had just as often suggested Olivia go for one of them.

Olivia had declined.

"I should probably tell you," Becca said. "Cole asked Sam about you."

Olivia stopped breathing. "Why?"

"Maybe for the same reason you're pretending not to notice that he exists," Becca said slowly, watching Olivia.

"I know he exists. A girl can't see a guy naked and not know he exists."

Oh, shit. Had she really said that?

Both Becca and Callie choked. "Okay," Becca said. "You owe me a story. Now."

"We were wet," Olivia said. "Cold. Possibly hypothermic. We had to...lose our clothes."

Callie grinned. "Nice."

Becca blinked. "How did I not see this one coming? Damn, I'm losing my touch."

"You saw everything?" Callie asked. "Is he still hot?"

Becca turned to Callie. "You know Cole?"

"And Sam and Tanner too," their new neighbor said. "Went to high school with them all eons ago, though I was behind them a few years, and I was the biggest computer geek to ever live, so they didn't know I existed." She winced. "I had this really pathetic crush on Tanner. Haven't seen any of them in forever. Is Cole still the sexy nerd, the MacGyver guy who can fix anything with a roll of duct tape and a screwdriver and those big ol' hands of his?"

"Yes," Olivia heard herself say, and then she bit her own tongue when Becca refocused her attention on her as if to say *Really?* "Fine, I saw him naked and he was amazing, okay? Can we drop it now? It's not like we're dating or anything. I don't even know him." Look at her fib. Because actually, she knew a lot about him. She knew that although he was easygoing and laid-back and didn't appear to let things get to him, he'd been deeply hurt by his last relationship. She knew he loved his family, crazy or otherwise, and that he'd do anything for them and expected the same in return. It was those expectations of those he cared about that terrified her.

She'd never done so well with expectations. In fact, it was safe to say she failed at them, spectacularly.

Becca whipped out her phone. "You know what I want to know? Why my soon-to-be-husband didn't tell me there was nakedness." She was texting as she spoke. She paused as an answer came back and blew out a sigh. Then she showed Olivia and Callie the screen.

Stay out of it.

Callie laughed. "Still Sam, then. Grumpy as ever."

"And dead," Becca muttered, shoving her phone away. She pointed at Olivia. "And you. You pinkie promised me a story. Don't you think I've forgotten."

"I can't wait to see everyone again," Callie said. "It's gonna be fun."

"Well, since I'm going to have to kill Sam, I'm sorry ahead of time for your loss," Becca said.

They came to the pier and the local diner. Eat Me was open for business, and Becca pushed Olivia in ahead of her.

"Food first," she said. "And then you start spilling some serious deets."

Cole stopped outside Olivia's shop at the end of the day. It was pouring buckets and had been for hours. He'd called their chartered fishing group in early, which had turned out to be a good idea, since ten minutes after Tanner had moored, the swells were being clocked at twelve feet.

Hood up, hands shoved in his pockets, he took a peek inside Unique Boutique. The place was the picture of a warm, old-fashioned gift shop where you could find just about anything. The lights were on and so was the music, but he couldn't see a single soul.

Above him, lightning cracked. And then a beat later, thunder rolled.

And rolled.

Cole let himself inside, tossed back his wet hood, and moved through the place. He had the pleasure of finding Olivia bent over a hip-high shelving unit in her office. It was a most excellent view, the best view he'd had all damn day, in fact.

Her feet were barely touching the floor as she reached for something on the floor, out of range.

But that wasn't the best part. No, that honor went to what she was wearing—some sort of Valkyrie woman warrior costume, complete with a leather bustier dress and matching arm bands with high-heeled gladiator sandals that might as well have been the on switch to his libido.

Topping off the vision, she was swearing up a storm.

"Damn sonofabitch, piece-of-shit—"

"Problem?" he asked.

She squeaked, jerked, and then the entire shelving unit collapsed, taking her down with it.

Chapter 14

♥

Cole rushed forward and scooped Olivia up, setting her on her feet. "You okay?"

"Yeah." She blew a strand of hair from her eyes. "Well, except for my pride."

He found himself grinning. "Nice costume."

"Got it from eBay. It came from the set of *Game of Thrones*."

He didn't care if it'd come from the moon. He loved the leather skirt, the straps wrapped up her calves, and especially the corset barely containing her breasts. He wanted to pull on the tie of the corset and unravel her. "You going to be a warrior princess for Halloween?" he asked.

"No, but I'm hoping someone in Lucky Harbor will want to be—"

Lightning burst.

Olivia jerked. "One, two, three," she whispered, and cringed as thunder rolled through the shop. "That's awfully close," she said shakily. "Too close."

"Hey." He pulled her into him. "It's okay. We've had worse."

"But what if the power goes out?"

"It probably will," he said.

She chewed on her lower lip, looking worried.

"You afraid of the dark?"

At this, her spine snapped straight. "No."

He smiled, and she sagged. "Okay, maybe just a little," she said. "I blame the *Sleepy Hollow* marathon I just watched."

"I could get your mind off of being scared."

She met his gaze. "That'd be like jumping from the frying pan into the fire."

True enough. He looked at the collapsed shelving unit at their feet. Cheap laminated plywood, and poorly constructed at that. "New?"

"Yes." Olivia gave the pile a little kick. "And it's a piece of crap."

"Yeah," he agreed. "But it's more how it was put together that was the problem."

"Hey," she said, then sighed. "And true."

He picked up a small plastic bag with three screws in it. "Here's problem number one. You're supposed to use all the screws, Supergirl."

"Well, *now* you tell me."

He laughed, which he realized he did a lot around her, and crouched low to gather the pieces together.

"I didn't see that baggie of screws. Do you need my tool kit?" she asked.

He looked up at her. Up those long, bare legs to the leather kick-ass costume that made his mouth water. "You don't have a tool kit."

"I do now," she said proudly. "Brand new, too. Got it yesterday at the hardware store." She went to a closet and pulled out a small toolbox with a variety of dollar-store tools in it. She lifted the cheap battery-operated screw gun. "Look at this baby. It's what I used to put the shelves together."

"Cute," he said, enjoying thinking about her sitting right here on the floor, piecing the shelving unit together. "But let's use all the screws this time."

"Good idea." She revved the screw gun. Annie Oakley meets Xena, Warrior Princess.

"You can direct," she said, "but I get to do all the screwing."

He grinned. "A guy's greatest fantasy."

But he did indeed direct, and she screwed, her brow furrowed in concentration, lower lip being tortured between her teeth as she worked.

It was sexy as hell.

"You like doing things for yourself," he said when they'd gotten the shelving unit back together and she stood there, hands on hips, staring proudly at her finished product.

"Always have," she said. "It's the city rat in me."

"I thought you were a country kid."

She stilled briefly, then turned away. "I'm a hybrid."

He came around the shelving unit to look at her. She was studying the shelves, her expression faraway, lost in memories. "How did you lose them?" he asked softly.

Her head jerked to his. "Who?"

"Your family."

Her face closed up. Just closed up entirely. "I...don't like to talk about it."

He nodded. That was something he could understand all too well. "When my dad died," he said, "I couldn't talk about it, either. He was such an important part of my life for so long. It was always him and me against the wave of estrogen in my house growing up. We were a team."

"But you love them," she said. "Your sisters."

"Yeah, of course." He gave her a small smile. "They're family, you know?"

She just kept staring at him, and the oddest feeling came over him, the feeling that she really didn't know. "You've been on your own for a long time, haven't you?" he asked.

Still staring at him, she hesitated and then nodded. She opened her mouth to say something, and he leaned in to hear her over the driving rain slanting against the windows because he didn't want to miss a word.

But in the next blink, lightning again lit up the shop, and again she jerked.

"One," she said shakily. "Two—"

The crack of thunder had her taking a quick step closer to him, and then...

The lights flickered and went out.

Her hand slipped into his. He immediately pulled her closer. "It's okay," he said. "I've got you."

"I'm not scared," she said, and then pressed her face into his chest. "I just don't want you to be."

He smiled into her hair. "Sweet."

Her arms slipped around his waist as she pressed even closer. "That's me. Sweet Olivia."

She was trembling, and he stroked a hand down her back. "Come on, Supergirl. Let's lock up and get you home." He grabbed her coat and held it out for her.

"I need to change."

He eyed her in that mouthwatering costume and shook his head. "Leave it on," he said. "You might have to protect me on the way home."

"Don't be silly."

"Okay, then leave it on because it's the sexiest thing I've ever seen."

She buttoned her coat over the costume without another word. "My truck," he said. "I'll drive." They braved the stormy night together and ran hand in hand to his truck.

Inside her warehouse, her place was dark and the usual frigid temperature. "You have candles?" he asked as they stepped inside. "Or a lantern?"

"Candles." She moved forward, bumped into something, swore, and was ripped from his hands.

He flicked on a penlight from his pocket and once again found her sprawled on the floor.

"Not a word," she said as she hopped up and dusted herself off. "I don't want to hear it."

"What did you trip over?" He aimed the light at the floor, but there was nothing.

"My own feet, if you must know," she said. "And I said I don't want to talk about it."

He smiled. "Remind me to keep you in the center of the boat when you're out on the water. I don't want to lose you overboard." He continued to direct the light around the place, curious about her. It looked just like her store. "It's nice in here."

"So on top of a screwdriver and some duct tape, you also carry a flashlight. What else do you keep in your pants?"

He grinned, and she blushed. "You know what I mean!" she said, clapping a hand to her cheeks. "Oh, never mind. Candles. I'm getting candles."

She moved to an antique hutch and opened some drawers, pulling out two armfuls of candles, which she spread around the place. "Here," she said, handing him some more. "I'll start lighting them." She struck a match along the matchbox, and it sizzled, went *whoomp*, and burst into flame.

He startled. It pissed him off, but he did. There was no getting around it, and there was no missing it either. He'd just jumped like a goddamn baby because a goddamn match had been lit.

Over the small, flickering flame, Olivia met his gaze. She didn't say a word, just slowly touched the tip of the match to a candle and then repeated the process on the other candles until the match's flame got too low and she had to blow it out.

She didn't light another.

The five candles she'd lit brought a little glow to the place, and some desperately needed warmth.

Or maybe that was the look in her eyes.

She set the matchbox down and came to him. "I'm scared," she said.

Bullshit. She wasn't scared. But then she slid her arms around him again, and he couldn't think beyond the fact that she was clearly cold. Letting out a low sound, he pulled her into him. "You're shaking."

"That's you," she said softly.

Well, hell.

She slid her fingers into his hair and met his gaze. "What's going on, Cole?"

"Nothing."

"Nothing is why you're jumpy around flames?"

"I'm never jumpy."

She ticked the moments off on her fingers. "You fell off your boat at a spark. You froze at my shop at another spark, and then just now with a flame."

"Maybe I'm just a fucking pussy," he said.

"Or maybe things are bothering you."

His gaze locked on hers. "And you think badgering me about it will help?"

A bolt of lightning lit the room like day for one single heartbeat. Thunder immediately boomed, shaking the ground and rattling the windows. She shivered and shifted closer. "I think I know something that will help."

Chapter 15

♥

Olivia pressed closer to Cole, tilting her head up to see his face. But it was dark, and he'd closed his eyes.

It was a technique she knew well. She'd just never had it used against her before.

"Not talking about it," he said. "Not right now."

She got that. She could understand that. "You're wet," she said softly.

"So are you." He opened his eyes then, and with some of his usual good humor, met her gaze. "And déjà vu."

Had it been only a week since that morning they'd dragged themselves to his boat, frozen, shivering, needing to get warm, stripping down to the skin beneath a blanket?

Why did it seem like a million years ago?

The reason was both obvious and uncomfortable. There was the amount of time you'd known someone, and then there was the way you'd spent that time.

They hadn't had much, she and Cole, and though the time they'd spent together had been intensely intimate, bonding them, she still didn't know his favorite color or whether he was a lid up or down sort of guy.

But she knew something was wrong. Something was haunting him from deep inside. And she was driven to help.

Odd, because he was just about the least helpless male she'd ever met. But she wanted to bring him comfort. She wanted to be his comfort. "You know what comes next, right?" she asked, keeping her voice light, teasing.

He shook his head.

"I get you warmed up." So she took him by the hand and led him over to her bed, where she pushed him down to sit. Then she wasn't sure what to do with herself.

He arched a brow.

His facade. That amused, laid-back expression, like *Everything's cool, no worries*. He was damned good at that, so good that she imagined most people never saw past it.

But because she had that same look mastered, she could see beneath it. She didn't know exactly what was wrong, only that something was. And if he was half as good at hiding his emotions as she was, then he wasn't going to let go easily.

"Strip," she said.

He smiled. "Love it when you get rough," he said, but didn't move.

Fine. She got that too. Holding back, building barriers. Hard to keep up any barriers without clothes, however, and on a mission, she pulled off her coat, tossing it on a chair by her bed.

His smile widened at the costume beneath. "You going to let me peek this time?" he asked.

"You peeked last time," she reminded him, willing to let him think he was running the show. She unlaced the costume and it fell from her. This left her in leather arm bands and...neon pink panties. She bent to the sandals and he groaned.

"Leave them," he said.

She yanked the covers down and sat on the bed, eyeing him expectantly.

Eyes on her, he stood up and toed off his shoes, then did that sexy guy thing where he one-handed his shirt off over his head. Then his hands went to the zipper on his cargoes. "You going to warm me up, Supergirl?"

"That's Warrior Princess to you," she said, sucking in a breath when he shucked his pants. He was commando. Cole wore clothes extremely well, but he wore nothing even better. She loved his build, all those rangy, lean muscles. There wasn't an ounce of extra fat on him.

Still holding her gaze prisoner, he came to the edge of the bed. "In the name of honesty," he said, his voice low and a little rough, "you should know I'm not all that cold."

"Good. I'm not all that scared."

This time Cole pushed her down on the bed and climbed over the top of her. He was solid and warm, so deliciously warm. She'd been colder than she'd thought, but it wasn't his heat that had her burrowing into him. There was something about him, as if just Cole being Cole somehow reached her deep inside and...lit up her dark places.

He cupped her face and looked into her eyes, silently demanding one hundred percent of her attention before his callused fingers skimmed her breasts, her belly, and then hooked into the pink lace at her hips.

"Lift up," he said.

She did, and then the panties were gone, sailing into the air somewhere behind them.

"There," he said, sounding deeply satisfied as he hauled her in against him, and not particularly gently either. "Better."

Her senses were on complete overdrive. Back on his boat, huddled with him beneath that pile of blankets, shivering with fear and adrenaline, she hadn't been able to appreciate the situation.

She was appreciating it now.

And he was right. He wasn't cold. He was a furnace, and she pressed close, her soft body plastered up against his hard one. He was something else, too. He was hard.

Everywhere.

Another burst of lightning, and she cringed, waiting for the thunder. When it hit, her windows rattled.

Cole breathed her name, the whisper of it incredibly erotic. She pressed even closer, feeling his hands stroke down her body.

Tender.

Cautious.

No, wait, not cautious.

Careful.

"What are you doing?" she asked.

He lifted his head, his hair all sexy bedhead, his eyes hot by flickering candlelight. "If you don't know, then I've forgotten how to do this."

"You're being careful," she accused.

He blinked once, slow as an owl. "Careful," he repeated. "And here I thought I was being the sexiest guy you've ever had."

If he only knew. He was the sexiest guy she'd ever had and he'd barely touched her yet. "I told you I'm not that scared. I don't want you to be careful."

"So you'd like me to what," he said, sounding a bit like she was amusing him, "just jump you?"

Yes, actually.

He took in her expression, laughed in disbelief, and rolled to his back on the mattress, covering his eyes with a forearm.

She turned her head and stared at him. Was it wrong that the first thing she noticed was how the muscles in his shoulder and biceps were flexed? Probably.

In any case, he didn't move.

She came up on an elbow and poked him in the chest. "Hey."

"Yeah."

"What are you doing?"

"Trying to figure you out," he said.

"Is that going to take a while?"

"I'm quite certain yes."

Biting her lip, she chose her words as carefully as she could. "I don't need anyone to take care of me," she said. "Never have, never will."

Lowering his arm, he met her gaze, his eyes glittering in the dark, his skin looking golden by the candle's glow. "I get that about you," he said. "I admire that about you. But sometimes a guy wants to take care of the woman he's about to make scream his name. It doesn't make you weak, Olivia. It makes you mine to take care of, at least until one of us walks away."

She had a hard time catching enough air in her lungs. "Yours?" she repeated, trying to decide if she was pissed at the possessive display, or—damn it—even more turned on.

"Until one of us walks away," he said again, not apologizing, not looking away, just meeting her gaze and waiting for her to decide.

She went with humor; she had nothing else. "We going steady, Cole?"

He didn't play. Instead, he raised his head and nipped her jaw. *Not* gently.

She sucked in a breath and felt herself go wet. Damn.

Lifting his head, he looked at her. "I haven't slept with a woman in two years," he said, "so *steady* has little to do with what I'm feeling right now."

Two years…Since Susan then. "Good to know," she finally said.

"Something else you should know. Once I get inside you, I won't share you. No one else for either of us, not until—"

"One of us walks away?" she asked softly.

His blue, blue eyes hadn't wavered from hers. "Yeah."

So they were going to do this, and if they kept doing it, there would be no one else until they were done.

"Olivia."

He was waiting for an answer. "I can live with that," she said.

Heat and something else flared in his eyes, and he kissed her until everything left her brain but this, the feel of him, here and now. She didn't breathe as his hands familiarized themselves with her body. Nothing slid past his intense exploration; he touched and kissed everything—her shoulders, her breasts, her stomach, her hips, her thighs, and then he pushed them apart and held them there, bracing his weight up on an elbow, his gaze never shifting from hers. "You're beautiful," he said.

"You're not even looking."

He shook his head very slowly from side to side, his expression starting a slow burn deep in her belly. "I'm looking right at you," he said, and then before she knew what he was about, he slid back up her body, wrapped his fingers around her wrists and tugged her arms up so they slid around his neck.

"Better," he said, and rolled so that she was on top of him, pressing all his sinewy, hard perfection into the mattress.

The truth was that *he* was the beautiful one, all long, lean planes and hard muscle. She had no idea how long this thing between them could possibly last, but she didn't fool herself. It wasn't forever. It wasn't even long term. She'd ensured that already by not being honest. Because she knew that it was only a matter of time now before that came back and bit her on the ass.

But when this was over, she'd miss him. She'd miss his laugh, his wit, his inner strength…She'd miss everything, including just looking at him. She wanted to memorize him, every single inch: his square jaw and the perpetual scruff, his sexy chest, the cut of the muscles at his hips, his thighs, and what he had between them—which, for the record, was just about the most gorgeous thing she'd ever seen. And that was saying a lot, because in general, guy parts weren't all that gorgeous.

It was then, halfway through her inspection of his body, that his warm breath tickled her ear as his teeth sank gently into her earlobe. His tongue flickered over the spot before his lips slid down her neck to the hollow at the base of her throat, and that slow burn in her belly spread south.

His scent was already familiar to her and still so erotic, making her dizzy with longing. "Cole…"

"Kiss me," he said, as if he was feeling all the same things. And then, without waiting for her, he yanked her down and kissed her, a soft, openmouthed connection that made her gasp as the tip of his tongue outlined her lips. She opened for him, but he pulled back.

Watching her, eyes hot, he smiled. She stared at his mouth, wanting it back on hers so badly she could taste him.

He gave in with a soft, fleeting kiss. And then another. One more…

He was teasing her.

"Cole."

"Come here, Warrior Woman," he murmured, and gathering her in, he finally gave her what she wanted. It was a really great kiss too, hot and sexy, with just the right amount of tongue to make her breathing quicken and her entire body quiver for more.

He knew what he was doing.

And she didn't. Not when it came to him. Oh, she knew the mechanics, but he'd taken it so far beyond simple mechanics that she felt a little lost, and more than a little panicky.

"You feel good," he said, tucking her beneath him. "You feel right."

His words infused her with confidence, and not done with being on top, she rolled them back.

And right off the bed.

She gasped and he laughed as he planted his fists on either side of her shoulders to lift his weigh off her. But she liked it, and wrapped her legs around his hips to show him how much—

A knock sounded on the wall right above them. The wall that she shared with the next apartment over. Callie's.

Both Cole and Olivia went still.

"Hello?" came Callie's voice through the wall. "Olivia? Is that you? Are you okay?"

Olivia stared wide-eyed at Cole. "Yes," she said, but had to clear her throat of the sexual rasp and try again. "Yes, it's me. I'm—"

Cole slid down her body and put his mouth to a breast, sucking her into his mouth hard, and her entire body quivered. "Oh, my God."

"What?" Callie asked. "You got a spider? Did you fall? It sounded like you fell."

"Thin walls," Olivia whispered to Cole.

Lifting his head, he flashed a grin and switched to her other breast, which he licked and nuzzled, and then gently closed his teeth over her nipple.

"Oh, my God," she gasped again.

"What?" Callie asked. "You keep saying that! Listen, I'm coming over—"

"No!" Olivia sucked in a desperately needed gulp of air as Cole shifted down her body. "No," she said. "I'm—" God, his tongue was shockingly talented. For a guy who professed to not having done this for two years, he hadn't forgotten a damn thing about a woman's body. "I'm fine," she managed, squirming as Cole kissed her hip and worked his way inward from there. All she could see of him now was the top of his head and the broad width of his shoulders, gleaming by candlelight between her legs.

"You sure?" Callie asked. "I've got a lantern. We could—"

"No!" Sweet baby Jesus. She tried to soften her voice, but Cole had her about to sing the Hallelujah Chorus. "Don't come!"

"Well, jeez. Okay," Callie said.

Again Olivia lifted her head and stared down her torso at Cole. He had a big hand on each of her inner thighs. Holding her gaze for a beat, he then dropped his head and locked in on her goods.

"Beautiful," he mouthed, and let his thumbs brush her core.

And then again, and this time his thumbs were slick from her arousal.

Eyes on hers, he brought one of those thumbs to his mouth and sucked her wetness like it—she—was a delicacy. Her mouth fell open, and she must have made some sort of sound because Callie knocked again. "Olivia? You sure you're okay?"

Not appearing to be concerned that he was driving her to the very brink of sanity, or that she was trying to shoo Callie off, Cole bent his head back to his task, using his tongue now, up and down, and back up…

Olivia arched into him, managing to rasp out "I'm sure!" to Callie. She looked at Cole. "She's not coming," she whispered.

"Good," Cole said. "'Cause you are."

Oh, goodie! cried the devil on Olivia's shoulder, jumping up and down with excitement.

"No," she gasped. "We can't, the insulation—there's no insulation— She can hear everything—"

"Then you'll have to be quiet." He accompanied this with another devastating stroke of his fingers.

And another.

More whimpers escaped her, unintelligible.

"Shh," he murmured. "Not a sound or we'll have to stop."

"If you stop," she gritted out, "I'll kill you."

With a badass smile, he brought her hand up to cover her own mouth, squeezing gently, silently telling her to keep a lid on it.

She tried, she really did, but she moaned when he slid back down her body. She lifted her hand enough to whisper, "Maybe we should just get to the main event."

"No."

No? "I've got a condom in my bathroom," she whispered, "but I'm on the pill and haven't done this in a long time, either, so it's probably okay—"

His mouth closed over her and she whimpered again, tightening her hand over her lips as his talented fingers joined the fray and...drove her right over the edge. Her hips bucked and she shuddered wildly as she came.

In less than five minutes.

In another time and place, say when her head was actually sitting on her shoulders, she'd have to think about how he'd managed to do what even she couldn't do for herself. Oh, she could give herself an orgasm, and so could a guy. It just usually took a lot of effort and some general fantasizing about Channing Tatum.

This time it took nothing but Cole.

By the time she came back to herself, he was pulling

a condom from one of the myriad pockets of his cargoes. "Someday you're going to show me what else you keep in your pants," she said.

With a snort, he brought her hand to his impressive erection.

"This," he said. "This is the most important item—" The laughter seemed to back up in his throat with a sharp inhale when she stroked him slow and long.

"Jesus, Olivia," he groaned.

"Shh," she said, mocking him. "Not a sound or we'll have to stop." And then she guided him home.

He pushed inside her, a delicious, warm, wet slide, and she had one last thought before a tidal wave of sensuality took her away.

She needed to enjoy the hell out of every single second of this, because just as surely as the sun would rise tomorrow and then set tomorrow night, Cole *would* eventually walk away.

Chapter 16

♥

Holy mother of God. That was Cole's only rational thought. He was balls deep inside Olivia's tight body and reeling from sensory overload. It took everything he had to bite back the groan that wanted to escape.

She was having trouble keeping quiet, too. Her hand was still over her mouth, fingers white from pressing so hard. Leaning over her, he kissed those fingers as he pulled out of her and…pushed back in.

She caught his hips, wrapping her legs around him, digging her nails into his ass as he began to move, keeping him close and deep.

Right where he wanted to be. He couldn't get enough of her. He loved her body, loved being all over it, and especially loved the reactions he got from it. But then she rocked up into him, tightening her long legs around him, and his entire world narrowed to senses, to how wet she was, to the way she clutched at him, the sound of her panting, the heat of her skin.

Planting an elbow near her head, he lowered himself enough to kiss her fingers, nudging them away from her lips so he could cover her mouth with his.

Beneath him, she shook as she came again, and watching her took him right along with her.

It might have been five minutes, an hour, or a lifetime later when he opened his eyes. He was warm. Actually he was toasty as hell, thanks to the woman curled into his side.

She was all over him. She had a leg thrown over his, an arm across his chest, her face pressed into his throat.

Either she was in a sexual coma or he'd killed her. "Olivia."

She mumbled something and cuddled closer, rubbing the cold tip of her nose against his throat. Nope, not dead. "Supergirl."

She tightened her leg and arm on him and then shifted her hips closer.

Yeah. He was on board with that and considered round two. The thought was tempting, so fucking tempting. How long had it been since he'd lost himself in a woman?

Since Susan.

Two years…

He hadn't missed having someone in his life. He'd been busy holding on to his hurt, his fury. Holding on to it, nursing it, enjoying it even. But now, for the life of him, he couldn't remember why.

Moving on was a much better strategy, and he was mad at himself for not thinking of it sooner. Brushing the hair from Olivia's face, he watched as her dark eyes opened.

"Hi," she said softly.

"Hi."

"I was sleeping a little bit."

"And drooling," he said.

"I was not!" But she wiped her mouth and then narrowed her eyes when he laughed. "I don't drool."

"Okay, maybe you were just snoring," he said.

She blinked. "I snore?"

"Loud enough to rattle the windows."

She started to slip out from beneath him, but laughing, he tightened his grip and held her still. "My mistake, it was just the thunder."

She fell to her back, and he leaned over her and kissed her, a long, lazy, hey-how-ya-doin' sort of kiss that was perfect for stormy nights with no electricity and nowhere else to be in any hurry.

"What?" she asked, pulling back. "You're smiling at me."

"You're purring," he said, and laughed when her dark eyes narrowed to slits. "You are. It's cute."

"Well, you're smug as hell. And it's *not* cute."

"Liar."

Once again she started to escape, but another burst of lightning lit the place, and she went still.

Flat on his back, he reached over and ran a hand up the back of her thigh to cup her ass. "Where you going?"

A shockingly close roar of thunder sounded, rattling the windows, the ceiling, hell, even the floors, and Olivia turned and leapt on top of him. "Nowhere."

Laughing softly, he tugged her into him, made a Herculean effort to get them both on the bed, and pulled the covers over them until they were cocooned. "Nowhere sounds good to me."

Olivia snuggled into Cole's body. Snuggled. She was still trembling and feeling a little bit like she'd revealed her tender underbelly. She felt…exposed and vulnerable, and as a rule, she didn't do either very well.

And neither did Cole, she was guessing, given how he'd shut down after what had happened with the match. She'd managed to distract him from that, but he'd distracted her right back.

Still, she hadn't forgotten that look of utter hollowness and despair. "Does it have to do with the rig explosion?" she asked quietly.

He'd been stroking a hand up and down her back, and his hand froze low on her spine.

"A little bit," she guessed.

"The anniversary of Gil's death is this week." He said this into her hair, voice low, so low as to be almost inaudible, but she felt the vibration of the words rumble through his chest into hers as the words sank in.

She had one hand on his biceps, the other on his jaw. She stroked down his arm, around to his back, where beneath smooth, heated skin and muscle, she could feel the coiled tension in him. "You miss him."

He let out a low breath and brushed his jaw to hers, saying nothing.

"I'm sorry," she said softly.

"It's not just the loss," he said. "It's that I thought…" He shook his head. "It's turning out that maybe he wasn't exactly the guy I thought."

Her fingers trailed up and down his spine, the way he'd done to her only a little while before, and she realized his grief was mixed with something more. Anger.

She was definitely missing a piece of this puzzle. "What do you mean?" she asked.

He shook his head.

"It's okay," she murmured, "if you still don't want to talk about it." After all, she had plenty of her own secrets to protect.

"Something came out after," he said. "After Gil died. And it changed…things. For me."

She squeezed her eyes shut. Oh, boy. Okay, so they were going to go there. And she couldn't be surprised. He was not a man to hold back for long, if at all. "And whatever it is," she said softly, "it affected your feelings for him?"

"Yeah. Though I'm trying to get past it." He slid out of her arms and rose from the bed. "I'm getting water. Need anything?"

A moment to herself to regroup would be nice, to back away from the emotions that were entirely too close to the surface when it came to him. "No, thanks."

Cole turned toward the kitchen and promptly tripped over the old trunk at the foot of her bed. When he righted it, the lid popped open. Inside were the costumes of her own personal collection, the ones she shared at Drama Days but couldn't bear to part with. On top was the Cinderella costume, which he reached for.

The trunk lid slammed closed, just missing Cole's fingers. He glanced at Olivia.

"Sorry," she said, kneeling at the foot of the bed, holding the trunk closed while all gloriously rumpled. And gloriously nude. "You okay?"

"Private collection?" he asked.

She wrapped herself in the sheet they'd kicked to the foot of the bed. "Maybe I'll take a glass of water after all," she said.

In other words, *Yes, asshole, private collection.* Message received. Cole crossed the open space and hit the kitchen, filling up a glass of water, downing it in a few gulps before filling it again and bringing it to Olivia.

While she drank, he slid back into the bed with her. "Not exactly an open book," he said.

She didn't pretend to not know what he was talking about. She simply shrugged. "Old habits."

He studied her face by the ambient candlelight flickering around the room. "You can tell me anything. You know that, right?"

"Nothing much to tell."

Right.

One of their phones was going off; he could hear it vibrating across her nightstand. He lifted his head and found it was hers.

It said: DICKWAD CALLING—DON'T ANSWER!

He glanced at Olivia. She did not meet his gaze. "Ignore it," she said.

A minute later, another call came in. This time the screen read: EVIL QUEEN CALLING—DON'T ANSWER!

He was starting to see a pattern.

Olivia's hand came into view, and she scooped the phone from under his nose and brought it to her nose. "Damn," she said.

And then she tossed the phone across the room, where it landed in her laundry basket.

"Nice shot," he said.

"Yeah, I make that shot a lot. The trick is remembering to rescue the phone before I do laundry."

"Expensive mistake," he noted.

"Tell me about it. I'm on phone number three this year

already." She rolled away from him and started to climb out of the bed. "Listen, I need to get up early, so you should probably go."

He pinned her on her belly, letting the erotic feel of her beneath him take over from everything else.

She blew hair from her face, craned her neck, and narrowed her eyes at him. "What's with the caveman hold? I think we've both had our jollies here tonight, so we can consider ourselves over the whole 'I'm yours' thing, right?"

"Wrong." He rocked his hips against her sweet ass.

A soft moan escaped her, and her eyes softened momentarily, until her phone began vibrating again.

"How much you want to bet it's another 'Don't Answer'?" he asked.

She turned her head so he couldn't see her expression.

Ah. The brick wall. He was getting good at bashing his head up against it. "So who's Dickwad?" Lowering his head, he brushed his scruffy jaw against the nape of her neck.

She shivered. She liked. So he did it again. "Olivia?"

"No one important."

Uh-huh. Whoever he was, he was important enough to label. "And the Evil Queen?"

"Wrong number."

He laughed softly. "Such a beautiful liar." Scooping her hair aside, he pressed his lips to the spot. "I bet I could get you to tell me all your secrets, Supergirl."

"They're not very interesting," she said, and then hissed in a breath when he nibbled his way down her spine, the sound muffled against the pillow, like she was pressing her face hard into it so he couldn't hear her.

But he *wanted* to hear her. "I think everything about you is interesting," he said, and when she growled at his hold, he merely spread her legs with one of his thighs. And then made room for the other.

"I said I have to go to sleep," she muttered, but she pushed her ass into his crotch.

And then it was his turn to groan.

One hand braced at her shoulder, holding the bulk of his weight off her, he slid his other beneath her and cupped a soft, warm breast.

Her nipple immediately tightened and pressed into his palm.

"Okay," she said panting. "Fine. You've got ten minutes."

"I can do a lot with ten minutes," he said. And then he proved it.

Chapter 17

♥

It was a sneaky, cowardly thing to do, but Olivia got up before dawn and…left.

Yeah. She left her own place, with Cole in her bed and her phone still in her laundry basket.

She stopped at the Eat Me diner for coffee, hit up the bakery for a croissant, and then wasted more time by walking the pier, telling herself she needed the exercise.

She didn't. She'd burned a bazillion calories riding Cole like a bronco all night…Just remembering burned a bunch more.

The sun came up behind the mountains, highlighting the choppy water. She watched awhile longer while finishing her coffee and croissant and then went back home.

Cole was gone.

She'd thought she'd be relieved, but she was something else entirely.

Disappointed. In herself, not him. She'd long ago decided that as Olivia she was going to be a better version of herself, and she had been.

Until this morning.

By the time she showered, dressed, grabbed her phone, and got out the door—for the second time—she was having a hard time maintaining her distance about the night she'd just had.

What had Cole thought when he'd woken alone? And why did she care? He wanted to know more about her, and she got that. She wanted to know about him, too. But she didn't want to share her past with him, not now.

Not ever, if she could help it.

Not because she didn't trust him. As ridiculous as it sounded, she already trusted him. There was just something about him that instilled a boatload of trust.

But with that came a healthy dose of reality. She'd learned the hard way not to give too much of herself. Nothing good came from it. She needed to remember that.

Just a little bit longer with him, the devil on her left shoulder begged. *Oh, please.*

You shouldn't, the angel on her right shoulder said, clearly worried. *Guard your past, walk away.*

Olivia's heart clutched. She knew she couldn't keep her distance, couldn't resist him.

But tick-tock, the clock was counting down. She knew it. Behind that easygoing, laid-back nature of Cole's, he was sharp as a fox. And intense. He had questions, and he wanted answers.

He was going to complicate the world she'd built for herself. He was going to huff and puff, and if she wasn't careful, he was going to blow her carefully constructed house down.

Right around her ears.

Even as she thought it, her evil, *evil* phone buzzed in her pocket, and she took a look. Not a DON'T ANSWER this time, but Becca. "Hey," Olivia said, cradling the phone in the crook of her neck as she unlocked the door to her shop.

"You missed mine and Callie's impromptu breakfast. Did you get my text?"

"I did," Olivia said, walking inside, flipping on lights and the heater. "Sorry. I was…busy."

"Doing?"

"Uh…" Shit. She kept forgetting that friends, the real ones, liked the details. "Going through stock, getting the shop ready for Halloween, stuff like that."

"Oh," Becca said. "Because Callie and I thought maybe you were busy doing something else." She paused meaningfully. "Like, say…someone else."

Olivia went still. "Um." Her brain started racing. "Why would you think such a thing?"

"Because we both saw Cole leave your place earlier. He was whistling, by the way."

"He was fixing my…" What? "Stuff," she said, then grimaced. Lame.

"Yeah?" Becca asked, sounding amused. "Is that what put that smile on his face? Fixing your stuff?"

Olivia closed her eyes and thunked her head to the front countertop. It did not knock any sense into her.

"Because in my humble opinion," Becca went on, not sounding all that humble actually, "a smile like the one Cole was wearing screams 'just got lucky.'"

In Olivia's ear came the welcome beep telling her she had another call. "I gotta go."

"I bet."

"No, really. I've got another call."

"Uh-huh," Becca said drily. "Later."

Olivia disconnected and eyed the screen to see who was calling her.

BEST LOVER YOU'VE EVER HAD—ANSWER.

She stared at it for a moment and then burst out laughing. She had no idea when Cole had managed to get ahold of her phone and program himself in, but she had to give him creativity points. She connected. "Someone a little full of themselves this morning?"

"And yet you don't deny the Best Lover Ever claim," he noted, voice low and playful.

Damn, she was cheesing from ear to ear. She tried to curtail the stupid grin but couldn't. "Why are you calling?" she asked, walking around and adjusting some of the Halloween decorations that she'd put up earlier in the week. She was thinking she could use some more. One could never have enough Halloween decorations. "Didn't I just see you?"

"Ouch. And yes. I need a favor. I've got this thing I've got to attend Friday night. Was hoping you'd come with."

Friday was three nights away, and Halloween. "Define thing," she said warily. A date? Yes, they'd slept together, but that hadn't exactly been a planned thing. A date would take them to yet another level, and she wasn't sure she was ready for that.

"Suspicious much?" he asked, sounding amused. "I can see the wheels turning from here. Just say yes, Olivia."

"I don't think—"

"It's a Halloween gig. Costume required."

Excitement trumped reluctance. She loved to wear costumes. Loved. And he knew it. She eyed the rack of costumes she had displayed, already imagining at least three she wanted for herself. "You know," she said casually, "that whole bossy thing you've got going was fun in bed, but it's not as much fun in real life."

"Okay," he said. "Say yes, *please*."

She let out a short laugh. He was a quick learner.

"I promise you a good time," he said in that low, sexy voice, the one that had coaxed her right out of her shell last night and had her doing whatever he'd wanted.

And loving it.

Shaking her head, she walked through the shop to her office and flipped on a few more lights. The one over her desk actually went on and stayed on as it had all week now and she had to smile. "Fine," she said. "Yes."

"Was it me, or the fact that you get to wear a costume?"

"Do you really want to know?"

He laughed softly, so damn sure of himself. "I know it was me."

She told herself she didn't have time for this, or him. Her voice mail was filled with calls from the TV Land producer, her mom, her sister…All wanting their piece of her. A little bit of her after-sex glow eroded. She needed to stand firm. Because if she didn't, if she caved and did this for them, they'd take what they needed and they'd leave her.

Again.

Which, actually, was a good reminder. This happiness

in Lucky Harbor was tenuous, and it all depended on the facade that she'd built remaining in place.

Here she wasn't the child star.

She was just herself. A sole proprietor. A simple woman with simple needs.

The minute she became Sharlyn again, everything would change. This happy life would vanish. Everything good would go away. Her friends. Maybe her business. Cole.

And if that wasn't a sobering thought, there was the re-alization that this too, this life she'd made for herself in Lucky Harbor, was temporary.

God. God, she hated that. But the truth was, this life was nothing more than another show, another illusion.

Or delusion, as it were…

"Olivia? You still with me?" Cole asked.

Yeah. She was. The question was, how long would he be with her? "Yes."

He paused, and this time the good humor was gone from his voice when he spoke. "Gotta say, it was unex-pected waking up alone."

She cleared her throat. "The whole night was unex-pected. I didn't plan on sleeping with you, Cole."

"And I didn't plan on you being gone in the morning."

So honest. So up front. Again, no games, no hidden agendas, just…Cole.

She had no idea what to do with that. Or him, for that matter. She'd never met anyone like him. He'd probably never hidden from the truth about anything, and she knew damn well he expected the same from those he cared about. And that openness of his, not to mention those un-spoken expectations, were a mystery to her.

"Women who are brave and pull perfect strangers out of the ocean shouldn't make a run for the door," he said.

She wasn't sure what to say, but she did get a warm glow from him calling her brave.

"We need a do-over, Olivia."

Her body quivered at the thought of a do-over and what it might entail. After last night, she no longer had to wonder how he'd be in bed. She could close her eyes and feel him moving over her, hear the rough timbre of his voice in her ear. He'd been…amazing. Intuitive, giving… deliciously commanding.

Which, of course, meant one thing. They couldn't do this again. Because the closer they became, the more intimate things got between them, the sooner the end would come. "I've got to go," she said.

"Me too. I'm late for a swim with Tanner."

She pictured that for a moment, two of the hottest guys she'd ever known powering through the water. "That sounds…" Hot. "Crazy. It's freezing."

"We have special wetsuits."

"Still crazy."

"Nah," he said. "It's fun. We have extra gear, if you wanna join. Except no trying to save me. Copping a feel? Hell, yeah, go for it all you want. But no rescuing."

She smiled and realized she felt…light as a feather.

Happy.

Terrified. "Can I ask you something?" she asked quietly.

"Anything."

And wasn't that just the thing. He was an open book. And she…she didn't even have a book.

"When you walk away, just do it, okay?" she asked. "Don't try to sugarcoat it or drag it out. Just walk."

There was a beat of silence. "Just walk," he repeated, an odd note in his voice.

"Yeah," she said. "And I'll do the same. No hard feelings, I promise."

Another beat of silence. "Is that how things are done in Kentucky, Olivia?" he asked softly.

Oh, God, that voice, that low, gentle but slightly pissed-off voice. She flinched at what he believed to be her past, the reminder harsh and unwelcome. Panic licked at her.

Trapped by her own lies.

"It's how things are done in my world," she said.

In her *real* world.

"Well, not in mine," he said. "I don't just walk away."

Chapter 18

The day before Halloween, Olivia found herself having difficulty concentrating on anything. She blamed another sleepless night where she'd tossed and turned, reliving the time she'd spent with Cole in this very bed. And on her floor. And back in her bed…

He was hard to forget.

I don't just walk away.

His words, and the meaning behind them, kept replaying in her head. They meant that she was sleeping with, and quite possibly falling in serious *like* with, a guy who had a moral compass that never wavered.

She liked that. She loved that. But it would only make it worse in the end. She was already counting down to the day he would leave her—and no matter what he said, he'd eventually leave her—and she was both needing it and dreading it at the same time.

Instead of dwelling on that, she buried herself in work. When the kids arrived for Drama Day, Pink and Kendra came in holding hands with Becca. As talk turned to Halloween, it came out that the twins were the only two kids who wouldn't be trick-or-treating, because they didn't have costumes.

"That's okay," Pink bravely told Olivia. "We get to dress up today, right?"

Olivia met Becca's subdued gaze and understood the problem—their dad was still facing serious financial woes. She swallowed the lump at the back of her throat. "Absolutely," she said. "Everyone dresses up for Drama Day."

The girls squealed and bounced up and down like pogo sticks. Then they raced for the dress-up circle and sat with mock patience, restless as if it were the last day of school.

Olivia went into the back and dragged out her trunk, which she'd brought in as she did every week.

Pink pulled out the Cinderella costume and handed it to Kendra. "Here, Sissy."

Kendra reverently clutched the frothy pink thing to her torso, her expression rapturous as she stroked the material.

Drama Day went on as usual, with each kid playing the part of their choice from a script Olivia had saved for today because it revolved around Halloween. She'd brought candy for them as well, and afterward, when everyone had changed back into their own clothes, they were allowed to dig in.

Olivia found Kendra in the back alone, still Cinderella. "Kendra?"

The little girl didn't look up at her. Instead she let out a telltale sniff and kept her head lowered.

And Olivia's heart cracked right in two. Becca came up behind Olivia and took in the situation. "I'm stopping at the drugstore with them on the way home," she whispered softly to Olivia. "I'm going to buy them costumes."

No. Not going to happen. Not on Olivia's watch. Dropping to her knees before Kendra, Olivia gently lifted the girl's chin and looked into huge, swimming green eyes. "I want you to take the Cinderella costume for tomorrow night," she said.

Kendra's impossibly huge eyes widened even farther, and her mouth fell open.

Pink had come in behind Becca. "We don't have any money," she said.

"I'm not selling it," Olivia told her. "I'm giving it to her."

Pink let out a joyous whoop, jumped up and down, and then grabbed Kendra and spun her around. "You hear that?" she asked her twin. "You get to be Cinderella for Halloween, just like you've always wished for! That means wishes come true. And that means that maybe we'll get our other wish!"

Kendra grinned.

"What's your other wish?" Olivia asked.

"That Santa comes for Daddy this year and brings him what we hear him asking for on the phone sometimes."

"And what's that, honey?" Becca asked.

"Something called credit so he can buy us a house."

The lump in Olivia's throat was back. "Well," she finally said softly, "I'm betting Santa will do his absolute best."

Pink nodded and reached for Kendra's hand. "Come on, Sissy, we gotta go. The others are waiting."

"You're forgetting something," Olivia said to Pink. "Your costume."

Pink's eyes got as big as Kendra's. "Wow, I get one too?"

"Of course you do," Olivia said, choked up anew at the thought that Pink had actually believed that she and Kendra couldn't possibly be lucky enough to each get a costume. "Your pick."

Pink threw herself at Olivia and hugged her around the waist tight. "I hope Santa comes for you too," she whispered fiercely.

And then they ran out of the back room into the front, right past Cole standing in the doorway, holding two to-go coffee cups. He smiled at each of the twins, exchanged a quiet, familiar greeting with Becca, and then, when they were all gone, he handed Olivia one of the cups.

"I like watching you with the kids," he said. He stepped closer and put his mouth to her ear. "Admit it, you're just a big softie."

She pulled back and met his gaze. "Am not."

Leaning in again, he kissed her jaw, working his way back to her ear. "*Softie.*"

Her knees were wobbly and she was breathing erratically, but she tried to keep her cool. "Bite your tongue," she said.

Instead, he nipped her ear, making her quiver all the more. "You gave them costumes from your trunk, the one you so carefully keep separate from your usual stock because the things in there mean something to you."

She sucked in a breath. "How do you know?"

"Because you almost took my finger off when I touched it the other night."

Well, he had her there. "I'm not a softie," she repeated.

He just smiled.

"Am I that transparent?"

"No," he said. "You're actually hard as hell to read.

You don't give away much." He paused, waiting until she met his gaze. "I just happen to know you now. I'm guessing I know you more than you usually allow."

She sucked in a breath, getting a good lungful of his scent while she was at it, which had her body doing a repeat on the quiver. "You think you know me?"

He grinned a confident, alpha grin that said why yes, he thought he knew her well. "Just because we've done… it," she said, "doesn't mean—"

"We discussed your sexual vocabulary. 'It' is not on the list of acceptable descriptions for what we did."

"Fine," she said. "We had wild monkey sex that ruined me for all other men. Happy?"

"Getting there." He moved in close. Real close. "Tell me more," he said.

She rolled her eyes, pushed him away, and sipped her coffee. "Thanks for this, by the way," she said, studying him over the steaming rim. He wasn't dressed in his usual cargoes today, but in basketball shorts and a T-shirt. "What brings you by?"

He shrugged. "On my way home from a run."

"How's your shoulder? Your doctor okay with you running?"

He rolled his shoulder. "It's great."

"Is that what your doctor says?"

He flashed a small smile. "Okay, so the great part's my own personal opinion."

"And the professional opinion?"

"A few more days before I'm one hundred percent," he said. Paused. "Maybe a week or two."

Her breath shuddered out and she set down the coffee. "Oh, Cole. I'm so sorry."

"It's no big deal," he said. "I've got plenty to do while Sam and Tanner take over. I could watch paint dry, for instance. Or—"

"Bring me coffee," she said with a smile.

"Yeah. And I'm looking at that hanging dress display," he said, his gaze on the contraption she'd created the day before to show off some vintage designer dresses. "No offense, but it looks like you jury-rigged it with…yarn and silk ties?" He shook his head. "It's about two minutes from falling on someone's head."

"I know," she said. "I've got to take it down before I kill someone."

"I can fix it."

"No one can fix it," she said. "It was a whim, and it's a disaster."

"Bet me."

She looked at him, startled. "What?"

He smiled that smile she imagined the spider gave to the fly. "Bet me. If I fix it, I win."

Her heart tripped. "You win what?"

"Winner's choice," he said, and casually sipped his coffee.

Casual, her ass. "So if you can't fix it?" she asked.

"Your choice," he said simply. Except nothing with him was simple for her. Not a single thing.

"Now?" she asked, stalling for time, but she was talking to his back because he'd passed by her and was studying her haphazard display. "You're in workout clothes," she said. "You're not packing any goodies in your shorts."

He chuckled low in his throat, as if he knew damn well he was packing plenty of goodies, just no tools.

"Is sex all you think about?" she asked.

"Around you, yeah. You have anything stronger than the ties? Rope, maybe?"

"I've got two sets of handcuffs to go with the police costumes I ordered."

He craned his neck and looked at her, his expression showing first surprise and then a wicked, sexy mischievousness. "You feeling playful?" he asked softly.

She bit her lower lip and made him laugh.

"Good to know," he said. "But one thing at a time."

Half an hour later, he'd fixed the display. When he was done, he rose to his full height, the silk ties she'd used in hand.

He smiled, a badass smile, and then headed toward her.

"Wait," she said with a laugh, backing up right into her desk, lifting a hand to ward him off. "I never said—"

He kept coming at her until her hand bumped into his chest and then got sandwiched between them, his eyes shining with both amusement and heat. "I win," he said.

Her heart skipped a beat. And there were all sorts of other reactions as well. "And you pick…?"

"You," he whispered, and slid his hands to her wrists and pulled them behind her back.

Oh, boy…

Cole smiled against her jaw, she could feel it, and then she felt the soft silk of the tie as he began to wrap it around her wrists, and then…she felt something else.

His phone vibrating.

And vibrating.

"You going to get that?" she asked.

With a rough exhale, he let her go, pulled his phone from his pocket, and stared at the screen. "Shit."

"Problem?"

"It's Tanner, and we have a rule. We can't ignore each other's calls unless we're in a life-or-death situation."

Olivia had to smile at the look on his face. "This is hardly life or death, Cole."

He looked down at himself and she followed suit. His arousal was making a tent of the front of his basketball shorts.

"Speak for yourself," he muttered, and answered the phone without a greeting. He listened for thirty seconds, swore viciously, and shoved the phone back in his pocket.

"Well?" she asked, already knowing.

"I've got to go." He set himself away from her with grim regret. "Remember where we're at," he said, shoving the ties in his pocket.

Her thighs quivered and she took another look at the way he was straining the front of his shorts.

He followed her gaze and a sound like a growl escaped his throat, along with a rough laugh. "Not helping," he said gruffly, and adjusted himself.

And then he was gone.

Remember where we were at? she thought, having to lean against the desk for support.

She wasn't likely to forget.

Chapter 19

♥

Cole headed straight for the hut after Tanner's call.

Tanner wasn't there, but Sam's dad was. Mark worked for them part time, along with Becca when she wasn't teaching. He answered phones and handled client needs.

Mark looked up from the gear he was cataloguing and nodded at Cole. "How's the shoulder?"

"Totally fine," Cole said.

Mark grinned at the lie. "You're as bad as the two idiots you're saddled with."

"Speaking of the two idiots, what's up?"

"Sam's in the warehouse. Tanner's here somewhere, checking diving equipment, seeing what we need to order for next year."

Their diving season was just about over. Not many people out there wanted to brave the fall and winter waters. Sam would spend the winter holed up in the warehouse making boats to spec for clients who had disposable cash. Tanner tended to head south. Way south,

across a few borders into South America, where he
hired himself out as a diving expert for big bucks.

Cole didn't get much of a break, but that was by
choice. There were plenty of clients who wanted to go
winter deep-sea fishing, or out cruising, so he more than
anyone tended to keep busy all year long.

Heading down the dock, he boarded the boat. There
was a line of equipment portside, in three piles. As Cole
stopped in front of the gear, Tanner emerged from the water onto the swimming platform, pulling the diving gear
from his face.

"What's up?" Cole asked.

Tanner shoved his wet hair back and tossed the mask
into the far right pile. "Separating the shit gear from the
good gear. I'm going to need to spend some money. The
rental gear didn't hold up."

They had done a much bigger rental business this year
than they'd anticipated, which was good. None of them
had realized how hard they'd be working, which wasn't
quite as good. On the rigs, they'd worked their asses off
for years. The goal had been to come here and enjoy life.

Tanner went belowdecks. By the time Cole followed,
he'd stripped out of his wetsuit and was standing in the
middle of the galley buck naked, dripping wet.

"Christ," Cole said, and tossed him a towel. "Cover
that shit up."

Tanner swiped the towel over his head to dry his hair
and then made a halfhearted attempt to dry his face,
shoulders, and arms before wrapping the towel low and
loose on his hips. "I've got a problem."

"So you said on the phone," Cole said. "You have
some craptastic timing, by the way."

Tanner's brows went up. "I interrupt anything good?"

"Let's just say you owe me. Big."

Tanner looked at him for a long moment. "You were with Olivia."

"I didn't say that."

"Didn't have to," Tanner said. "Face it, you can't keep shit to yourself."

"I can when I want to."

Tanner was quiet for a beat. "Two weeks ago you fell into the water and needed a rescue—"

"Jesus, I misstepped. I fell. No rescue. And you've never made a stupid mistake?"

"I've made plenty, as you damn well know. Now shut your pie hole a second and listen." Tanner pointed at Cole's mouth when he opened it. "You've been going twenty-four/seven since we got here, for two straight years."

"We all have," Cole said, unable to keep it zipped.

"Yeah," Tanner said. "But it's different. Sam gets off on the boats he makes, so that's not work to him. Diving is the same for me. But you, you work around the clock, not because it's your passion but because you want the charter company to succeed, and—"

"Like you don't want that?"

"—And because you don't want to deal."

Cole stared at him, getting pissed off. "Deal with what?"

"You know what. Gil's death. Your dad's death. Both unexpected and huge blows—"

Cole made a no-shit-Sherlock sound and shoved his hands into his pockets rather than punch something. Like Tanner's face.

"And then there's Susan and the way she left you—"

"Okay," Cole said tightly. "We're not going there."

"—On the day of Gil's funeral."

Right, like Cole had forgotten not only being dumped on the worst day of his life, but finding out that his best friend and his almost-fiancée had fallen in love.

Behind his back.

"I know you think you've moved on," Tanner said, "but you haven't, at least not until now. That's why we're happy about Olivia. She's the first woman to catch your attention since—"

Cole spun on his heel and started off the boat.

Tanner grabbed his arm.

Cole shoved him hard.

"Fine." Tanner lifted his hands and backed off. "It's best that we don't tangle right now, anyway."

"I don't tangle with naked-ass motherfuckers."

Tanner's smile was much more real this time. "Aw, now you're just trying to hurt my tender feelings."

"You called me here," Cole said. "I'm giving you five seconds to get to your point."

"Christ, take a Midol already." Tanner dropped the towel and snatched up a pair of Levi's. "I needed to ask you something."

"The answer is yes, you're definitely suffering cold water shrinkage."

Tanner snorted as he pulled up his jeans. "You wish." His smile faded. "I'm going to owe you for this one."

"What's up?"

"Elisa and Troy are back."

Tanner's ex and his son.

Tanner had married Elisa at age seventeen to give her

and the baby his name, and he'd done his absolute best to make them a family. But kids having kids was never easy. Especially wild-ass kids like Tanner and Elisa.

When he had gone into the navy—the only way he'd been able to figure out how to support them—Elisa had packed baby Troy up and moved to Florida to be with her grandparents. The divorce papers had reached Tanner the day he'd become a SEAL.

Tanner had supported Elisa and Troy all these years, gone to see Troy as often as he was allowed, but it hadn't been an easy relationship.

Troy had turned fifteen last week and celebrated by lighting a bag of dog shit on fire and leaving it on the front porch of the girl who'd dumped him. Problem was, she happened to be the principal's daughter.

"Elisa wants Troy to live with me for a while," Tanner said.

Cole nodded. "Good."

Tanner choked. "Good?"

"You've wanted him closer to you for years," Cole said.

"Yeah, but now he's fifteen and out of control," Tanner said. "And hates all authority, including his parents."

"Yeah?" Cole asked. "Is it like looking in a mirror?"

Tanner didn't smile.

"You're not alone," Cole said. "We'll help."

"Good," Tanner said. "You start tonight. I'm taking a group out that I can't cancel on." Tanner tossed him his keys. "Be at my place by six. He's going to show up by six thirty. Don't close your eyes, turn your back, or relax. Tie him up if you have to."

Cole was pretty sure he was kidding about the last part, but damn. He stared down at Tanner's keys and blew out a breath. He'd been hoping to tie up someone else tonight…

"This isn't a date," Olivia said. It was the next night. Halloween. And she was crowded in her small bathroom with Becca and Callie.

"Okay," Callie said. "But then why are you wearing lip gloss?"

"I always wear lip gloss," Olivia said.

"Not your Tom Ford lip gloss," Becca said. "That thing costs an arm and a leg, which I know because I looked it up. Out of my budget. And your budget can't be that much bigger than mine. Which means that stuff is sacred. And yet you're wearing it."

"Damn, you're smarter than you look," Olivia murmured. She was staring at herself in the mirror over the bathroom sink in disbelief. Long, flowing wig, red. Silk corset, brilliant green. Matching skirt so snug she'd practically had to spray paint it on.

She was Ariel, the Little Mermaid.

She'd gotten the brilliant idea because Cole was a sea captain. It'd made perfect sense in her mind. But now she felt…silly. "I should cancel."

Her peanut gallery stared at her reflection in the mirror. "You can't cancel," Callie said.

Becca shook her head. "Absolutely not."

"Why?" Olivia asked.

"Because I haven't been out on a date in a long time," Callie said. "I'm living vicariously through you. I need this date, Olivia. Ariel."

Olivia sighed and stared at herself some more. "It's not going to work. The costume is…too much."

"It's perfect," Becca said. "It's gorgeous. *You're* gorgeous. I mean, who knew you had that rockin' of a body? Good Lord, woman, you're going to knock Cole's socks right off."

"It's not a date," Olivia repeated. "It's a…favor." Or so she'd thought, but now she wasn't so sure. Sleeping with him had changed things in a big way, and she was trying to ignore that, but some things couldn't be easily ignored.

Callie shook her head. "Honey, trust me, you looking like that makes it a date. His tongue's going to fall right out of his head."

"Where in the world do you get all these fantastic costumes?" Becca asked. "This thing looks like the real deal."

That's because it was. She'd got it off eBay from a *Stars on Ice* production assistant. "eBay—"

Someone knocked at her door and she froze.

Becca jumped up and down and clapped her hands, looking for all the world like Pink or Kendra in her excitement. "I can't wait to see what he's wearing."

"Don't you have anything else to do?" Olivia asked in desperation.

"Nope!" Becca said cheerfully.

Olivia walked out of the bathroom. Although in the skintight "fin," *walked* was a bit of a misnomer.

"Your ass looks really great," Callie said helpfully from behind her. "But you might not want to sit down. I don't see you getting up again without splitting that thing. You're wearing undies, right?"

"Yes!" If a teeny-tiny thong that was really more like a G-string counted…Olivia stopped at the front door, drew a deep breath that threatened to pop open her corset, and then answered the door to…

Captain Jack Sparrow.

She'd always had sort of a secret thing for Johnny Depp in the Pirates movies, but Johnny had nothing on Cole Donovan. In his pirate's hat, bandana, and long dreads, not to mention sexy scruff, he was smokin' hot.

And that was before she followed the lines of his leanly muscled body down the white shirt and leather vest to the various weaponry, such as the sword strapped at one lean hip, and boots.

"Wow," she whispered.

Chapter 20

Cole's eyes just about popped out of his head at the sight of Olivia, and when the irony of her costume hit him, he laughed. "Ariel, fair maiden of the sea," he said, and bowed.

When he rose again she was...blushing? Fascinating that his confident, hot Supergirl would be, but she most definitely was.

Becca and Callie were right behind her, staring at him with their jaws dropped open.

"Wow is right," Becca said with serious ego-stroking awe in her voice.

"You're engaged to be married," Callie reminded her.

"Yes, but it's Captain Jack Sparrow," Becca said. "He's a fictional character. You're allowed to lust after fictional characters when you're engaged. It's in the Engaged Handbook somewhere."

Cole smiled at her.

Becca smiled back dreamily.

Olivia rolled her eyes and pointed at Callie and Becca. "Do *not* eat my brownies." And then she shoved Cole over the threshold, followed, and shut the door behind them.

"Brownies?" he asked, leading her to his truck.

"Yeah, I—" She stopped at the passenger side and stared up into the cab, and then down at her tight skirt.

"No worries, I've got ya." He scooped her up and set her on the seat, taking his time putting her seat belt on for her and retrieving his hands from her delicious curves.

"I could have done that," she said, a little breathless.

"What fun would that have been?"

"I…" She closed her mouth, blushed wildly, and sighed. "I forgot what I was going to say."

He grinned.

"Not helping," she said. "I made the brownies last night. They were to be my reward if I survive this *favor*. I could use them right now."

"I've got something better than chocolate."

"No kidding," she muttered.

He laughed and pulled the truck out onto the road. A few minutes later, they were driving up the bluffs. He parked and Olivia glanced around at the house at the top of the driveway and then the tumbling sea far below.

"What are we doing?" she asked. "Where are we?"

"My place," he said. "I didn't have time to stop at home before picking you up. I've just got to get the wine and beer I promised to bring tonight. Do you want to come in, or wait here?"

Their gazes met and held a moment. "I'll come in," she said. "But you should know it's because I'm curious about your house, not because I want to do…" She almost said "it," he could tell. "The wild monkey sex," she said instead.

He grinned at her. "Look at you with the big-girl vocabulary." He unlocked the front door and held it open for her to walk in ahead of him. "Fair warning," he said. "I wasn't expecting company."

He'd had the house for a year now, and loved the small beach shack that he was slowly renovating. Slowly being the key word.

Olivia took in the sights. Cole looked around, trying to see his place as she might. The living room and kitchen were all one room, a wall of windows allowing a stunning view of the water.

That was his favorite part of the place.

There were some dishes on the counter, books on the kitchen table, and a tumble of shoes and boots in a huge wooden box, above which a ton of weather gear hung on pegs. Yeah, he probably could've done a better job on the cleanup efforts.

The furniture was big and comfy, and well used. The TV was a massive flat-screen, new. "Home sweet home," he said.

"It's nice," she said.

"Working on it." He stepped into the kitchen and grabbed the beer and wine. Striding toward Olivia, his little mermaid for the evening, he set the boxes down on the bench by the front door and stepped into her. "Hi."

"Hi," she said a little breathlessly. He wasn't sure, it could've been how tight her costume was, but he wanted to think it was because of him. He ran his hands down her body. "I like this costume. A *lot*."

"Yours isn't bad either." Her gaze lingered on his open shirt.

Her eyes dilated.

"Say the word," he said, done teasing, "and we skip the party."

"I'm wearing mermaid hair."

"I know." He wasn't sure what that had to do with wild monkey sex. He let his fingers run through the hip-length red wig she was sporting, and because he was a multitasker, he could picture what she'd look like riding him in that wig, the locks flowing over her breasts, brushing his chest. It was a real good image. "I like the hair. And that skirt."

"It took three of us to get me into this skirt," she said. "Callie broke a nail and Becca fell on her ass helping me tug it into place. That should've been a clue."

Cole had started to pull away but he stilled. "Your friends had to help you dress?"

She slid him a look. "Is that all you heard?"

"Pretty much," he admitted.

"Oh, for God's sake—"

"Shh a minute," he said. "I'm not done picturing it."

She shook her head and gave him a shove. Grinning, he pulled free, led her back to his truck, made sure she was buckled up, and shut the door.

"You mentioned surviving the night," he said when they were on the road again. "What do I get if I survive the night?" he asked.

She glanced over at him, clearly startled. "Where are we going, exactly?"

He stopped at a light. "My sister's annual Halloween surprise party for her husband."

She stared at him like there were so many problems with that statement that she didn't know where to start. "How can an annual party be a surprise?"

"My sister's husband loves her, God knows why. She gets a kick out of giving him a surprise party, so he pretends to be surprised."

More staring from gorgeous mermaid. "You're bringing me to a family party," she said.

"Yeah."

She opened her mouth. And then closed it. "Is your family that bad that you need a prize to survive them?"

"There are days, yes," he said.

She just stared at him.

"Don't worry, they're going to love you. And that costume? Hot. I'm going to have to fight off the cousins and brothers-in-law," he said half jokingly as he pulled up to his sister's house. There were already a bunch of cars, and judging from the loud music and laughter coming from the house, the party was already well under way. "Perfect. Looks like we're late enough that everyone's already going to be a few red Solo cups into the evening's festivities."

"We're late?"

"Perfectly late," he said.

She blinked at him. "So we're at a family party, and we're late. On purpose."

She was mad, he realized. "I was saving you from having to be with them longer than necessary."

"You were saving me," she said, and then nodded. But then she shook her head. "And you think I'm going to make a good impression here. In a ridiculously revealing costume that screams 'ho on a stick,' and also, we're late."

He couldn't help it, he laughed.

Wrong move.

He got that immediately, but as she fumbled for the door handle it was all he could do to hit the locks before she escaped. "Wait," he said, knowing that if she got out, she would take off like a bat out of hell. "Wait a minute. Let me catch up."

She whirled back to him, brow knitted, lips—those perfect red lips—ready to blast him. "I'm waiting."

"You're mad that we're at a family party."

"Give the man a point," she said.

"And you're mad that we're late."

"Another point," she said. "Want to go for a three-pointer and win the game?"

"No one's going to care that we're late," he said to soothe her. "I'm the only son; they're going to be grateful I showed up at all. And having you with me, you're like my get-out-of-jail-free card."

"Don't you think it's a little early for this?"

"No," he said. "We missed the 'Surprise' already. I hate that part."

"Your family," she said. "Don't you think it's a little early to have me meet your family? We're not even…" She trailed off, clearly at a complete loss.

"It's going to be okay," he said.

She gave him a look that he imagined could shrivel a guy's balls right off. But the truth was, he liked her show of temper. Her eyes were sparking, her skin was flushed, and she looked like she wanted to kick his ass from here to next week. He had a good fifty pounds on her, but he wanted to tangle.

With her in that costume.

And out of it.

She made him feel so damn...alive. He looked down at the erection he was sporting—not smart in the stupid pirate pants that didn't hide a damn thing—and snorted.

She followed his gaze and narrowed her eyes. "Are you kidding me? My pissiness is turning you on?"

"I'm pretty sure it's just you," he said. "No worries. I'll do multiplication. That usually works. Twelve times twelve—" He caught movement at the front windows. "The coven's watching."

"The coven?"

"My sisters."

She just stared at him. "You call your sisters 'the coven'?"

"Just sometimes."

"And they're watching us."

"Little bit. They like to stick their noses in my business. It's like they can't help themselves."

"And you're still hard?" she asked, heavy on the irony.

"Good point," he said. He looked over and saw Cindy peeking out the window and pointing at him, probably to Clare or Cara. "Problem solved," he muttered.

"I should have eaten the brownies first," she said.

Cole was beginning to understand that family meant something entirely different to her than it did to him. "Hey, it's going to be fun." He wished he knew what had put that look on her face, that distrust, that...vulnerability. He hadn't wanted to push because she'd been so reluctant to talk about her family, but he was undeniably curious.

And more than that. He was concerned that maybe her past wasn't anything that she *wanted* to remember. And he hated thinking about why that might be.

He really wanted to know more about her, but now wasn't the time. Now was the time to try to get her to relax and enjoy. Reaching across the console, he squeezed her hand. "Listen," he said, dipping down a little to look into her eyes. "I know you're skittish about this, but it's going to be okay."

She didn't respond, but he could read her now, or he was starting to be able to. She had a wealth of old soul in those dark depths. And pain.

It killed him.

He cupped her jaw. "I promise not to hurt you, Olivia."

She shook her head, her eyes never leaving his. "People can't promise things like that."

"Try me."

She stared at him some more, got out of the truck, and then started walking toward the front door.

They didn't even hit the first step before the door flew open and the music and laughter spilled out.

So did a sister or two.

"Clare, Cindy," he said, pointing to the two people dressed up as Dr. Seuss's Thing One and Thing Two.

If it hadn't been for the five-year-old minion gripping Thing One's thigh—Clare's son, Jonathan—he couldn't have said who was who. "This is Olivia."

"Gorgeous costume," Clare said. "You look fantastic."

"Thanks," Olivia said.

"Is that hair real?" Thing Two asked, reaching out to touch it.

"No," Olivia said. "It's just a wig."

"Good," Cindy said. "Or I'd have to hate you. It's amazing. You didn't get this at any old costume shop."

"No," Olivia said, "I didn't."

"She owns the Unique Boutique," Cole told them. "She's got some pretty amazing stuff in there." He felt Olivia's glance and turned his head to meet it.

He'd surprised her. Getting that his family could be completely overwhelming to him, and he'd known them all his life, he could only imagine how bad it might be for a perfect stranger. Reaching out, he grabbed her hand in his and pulled her in a little closer, smiling at her.

She smiled back—for his sisters' sake, he was pretty sure, and he was proven right when she went up on tiptoe to murmur in his ear.

"I don't care how hot you look, Captain Sparrow, if I survive this night, *I* win. And my spoils are going to be more than brownies."

Chapter 21

♥

"You can't call a woman's things 'stuff,'" Clare said to Cole. She looked at Olivia. "Sorry. We raised him better than that."

Olivia did her best to smile. No way was she going to admit that walking into this all-Donovan party had shaken her to her core. No way. She shook her head, like *It's all good*. "It's okay. It *is* mostly…stuff."

Iron Man came up behind Cole and began to strangle him. Cole reached behind him and junk-punched the superhero, dropping the giant guy to the floor. As Iron Man went down, he hooked a foot around Cole's legs and brought him down with him, hard.

The floor shook like thunder.

The two of them wrestled and rolled around, crashing into a coffee table. They were evenly matched, which was a good thing for Jack Sparrow, given that Iron Man had a hundred pounds and six inches on him.

"Squash him like a bug, honey," Thing Two yelled.

Okay, that was sweet in a way, Olivia thought, Cindy calling her brother "honey."

"Nail his sorry ass," Cindy yelled. "Come on, Garrett, you can totally take that pipsqueak!"

Whoops, Olivia's mistake. Thing Two wasn't encouraging Cole. She was yelling for Iron Man to squash Cole like a bug.

And indeed, Iron Man rolled onto Cole and bent him like a pretzel.

"Excuse me," Olivia said to Thing Two, "but you know he's injured, right?"

"Eh, he's tough," Cindy said. "Honey," she yelled, "sit on him if you have to!"

The entire party of about thirty people had gathered around and were cheering and egging on the wrestling match. They seemed pretty evenly divided between Jack Sparrow and Iron Man.

Iron Man was winning. He had Jack Sparrow in what looked like an impossible hold, eating hardwood floor.

"He's injured," Olivia tried again, this time to Miley Cyrus and Robin Thicke, who'd come up beside her. "His shoulder—"

The guy dressed as Robin Thicke grinned. "He's scrappy as hell, darlin', no worries."

Olivia glared at them, and then at his sisters, but clearly no help was going to come for Cole from either source. Whatever. She'd help him herself then, and she strode directly into the melee and—

Cole managed to turn his face and smile up at her. He actually smiled, like *I got this, babe*.

She stopped and shook her head, and Cole made his move. He rolled Iron Man onto his belly, climbed on top of him, and wrapped his forearm around Iron Man's beefy neck, yanking his head up off the floor.

"Oh, come on!" Cindy yelled at Iron Man. "It's like you're not even trying!"

Cole leaned low over Iron Man, his mouth near the guy's ear. "Say it."

Iron Man shook his head.

"I'm going to offer this one last time," Cole said, calm as you please, sitting on Iron Man's back. "Say it or eat dust."

Iron Man huffed out a huge sigh. "Fine. I bow to your greatness."

"Sorry," Cole said, cupping a hand around his ear. "Didn't hear you."

"I bow to your greatness! Jesus! You're going to wrinkle the suit, man! And you might want to lay off the pizza and beer, you're getting fat."

Cole grinned—clearly he knew damn well he didn't have a spare ounce of fat on him—and sprang up to his feet.

Iron Man flopped to his back. "Shit. You suck."

Cole strode over to Olivia and slung an arm around her neck. Pulling her in, he kissed her temple. "Ariel, this is Garrett, my brother-in-law."

Olivia just stared up at Cole. "Are you okay?"

"I won, didn't I?" He glanced back at Iron Man, still lying on the floor sucking in wind.

"Yes," she said, "but—"

"Princess of the sea," he said, and let out another laugh in her ear, "you can inspect me for injuries later."

She stared at him. "Men are so weird."

"Good weird, right?"

That was when Elvira walked up to them. She was lean and regal, and she gave Cole a long look.

"What?" he said, lifting his hands. "He started it."

Elvira shook her head and looked at Olivia. "You'll have to excuse my son," she said.

Oh, God. Her son? This gorgeous creature was Cole's mom?

"Seriously," Cole said. "He started it."

"Your father taught you how to walk away from a fight." Elvira took Olivia's hands in hers. "He also taught you manners, which you've clearly forgotten. I'm Amelia," she said. "And you are?"

"Olivia Bentley."

"You own that lovely boutique. It's wonderful to meet you. I love your costume."

"Thank you."

"You're certainly giving Jack Sparrow some class tonight."

Cole laughed. "I think it's fair to say she can outclass me on any night, Mom." Again he slipped an arm around Olivia.

Did she look like she needed the support? Olivia wondered. She'd thought she was managing the terror pretty well. To be on the safe side, she flashed him the small, bullshit I'm-fine smile that had worked on every single person she'd ever let into her life.

But Cole wasn't buying what she was selling, which she realized when he gently squeezed her waist like he was offering her comfort on top of support. She turned to Mrs. Donovan. "This house is beautiful. Is it yours?"

"Yes, and call me Amelia. It was built in 1905, and you wouldn't believe how cranky it can get." She patted Cole on the shoulder, which she had to reach up to do. "Cole helps me keep it fixed up. I don't know what I'd do without him, especially since his dad died last year. He's my rock."

Thing Two was back, holding a two-year-old dressed up as the Lorax. "I want Ariel to tell us about when she knocked Cole into the ocean."

Cole swore beneath his breath, and got smacked upside the head for it. "Watch your mouth," Elvira said.

Cole straightened his dreads and bandana and slid his mom a look.

The toddler started fussing as a stunningly beautiful woman came up to them. She wore a long white column dress and dazzling bling. "Wait for me, I want to hear about the chick who got the best of Cole, too!"

"Cara," Cole said to Olivia before turning back to his sister. "And who are you supposed to be?"

"One of the Real Housewives of Lucky Harbor."

"But you're not married," Thing Two said.

Cara shrugged. "Details." She smiled at Olivia. "Normally Cole counts on us to take him down a peg or two, so we appreciate the assist."

"Maybe you should've dressed as the family comedienne," Cole said.

There was something here, Olivia thought, a different dynamic between these two than the others. Tension, for one.

And a lingering anger and resentment that surprised Olivia.

Thing Two shoved her fussy, drooling two-year-old into Cole's arms. "Mom's kitchen sink isn't draining again. Can you fix it?"

Cole bounced the Lorax up and down in his arms, making the toddler give a full belly giggle and drool some more. Olivia was having a similar reaction watching him easily handle and charm the baby.

"Grannie's sink isn't draining 'cause she keeps putting food into it," Cole told the little guy, lifting him high in the air, "even though she's still on a septic tank and not the sewer system."

The boy gave another belly laugh that was utterly contagious, and Cole brought him in for a smacking kiss that had the toddler's legs kicking in sheer joy.

Something deep within Olivia quivered.

"Why does he always stop crying for you?" Cindy demanded, and took the Lorax back.

The baby lifted his hands back out to Cole. "Mine! Mine Cole!"

Cole grinned at him. "You and me later, dude. We've got 'nap' written all over us."

The baby cooed.

Cindy was staring at Olivia, head cocked. "You know," she said. "You look really familiar. I feel like I've seen you before, somewhere."

"Her shop," Cole said while Olivia's pulse kicked, knowing where that somewhere had been.

"No, not her shop," Cindy said. "Somewhere else."

"Cara, offer our guest something to drink," Elvira said.

"What's your poison?" Cara asked Olivia.

Olivia looked around and saw that everyone was drinking wine or beer. "I'll have a beer, thank you."

Clare pointed at Cole. "Keep her," she said.

Cindy was still staring at Olivia. "You look familiar," she said.

"I have that kind of a face," Olivia said.

Cindy let the subject drop, though her gaze never left Olivia. She was close to figuring it out. On borrowed time, Olivia thought…

The party engulfed them then. There was a pool table, and some fierce games were going on there, and also on the two dartboards. Turned out the Donovans took their competition extremely seriously. That was okay, because so did she.

In college, she'd kept to herself, but had been drawn to both pool and darts. They'd appealed to her competitive nature, and also were games she could play without being on a team. She was good.

But Cole was better. He killed her at pool.

And then he had his ass handed to him at the dartboards. By Olivia.

The crowd went nuts, and she was toasted by everyone in the family for keeping Cole humble.

Cole ignored them all and good-naturedly high-fived her, and then shocked her by dipping her low over his arm and kissing the hell out of her.

They were separated for a while after that. Cindy's husband grabbed Cole for another game, and Olivia found herself at the bar with someone dressed up as an orc, helping restock. Afterward, she grabbed two more beers and went in search of Cole.

She didn't find him in the living room or the courtyard, where people were milling and dancing. He wasn't in the den, either, or in the large kitchen that was filled with every sort of kitchen appliance known to man, along with the personal signs of a big family. Family pictures decorated the fridge, and then there was stuff scattered over the counters, including a stack of mail, empty food containers, a cat sniffing around in the sink, and…

Cole and Cara's voices, coming from…

The pantry?

"I said I would," Cara was saying, sounding irritated. "Happy? You've finally worn me down. I'm telling Mom everything."

"When?" came Cole's voice. "*When* are you going to come clean with everyone?"

"Jesus, Cole, you're like a dog with a bone."

"Or a pissed-off, tired-of-keeping-your-fucking-secret brother?" he asked.

"Oh, get off your high horse," Cara snapped. "You're one to talk."

"We've had this conversation. *I'm* not lying to everyone I care about."

"No, of course not. You're better than that, right? Your world is black and white, right and wrong. There's a clear line drawn, and if someone crosses it, you're done with them."

"Jesus, dramatic much?" he asked. "Your costume's fitting tonight."

"Whatever."

"Cara, look at me."

"Aye, aye, Captain."

"Shut up, smart-ass," he said. "I'm here bitching you out. Does that seem like I'm done with you?"

Olivia shook herself, realized she was eavesdropping, and crossed the room to tell them she was standing right there, but by the time she poked her head into the pantry, they were hugging. She jerked back out of sight, leaving the kitchen to stand in the hallway, both uncomfortable at interfering and incredibly moved by their relationship, which seemed…real. More real than anything she'd ever had with her own sister.

Too late she realized Cara had stepped out of the pantry and was now right in front of her. Damn. Way too late to make it look like she was doing anything other than listening in on a private conversation. "I'm sorry. I didn't mean to eavesdrop."

"The more the merrier in this house of crazy," Cara said. "You like him, right?"

Olivia shot a startled glance toward the pantry. "Oh. Well…I—"

Cara smiled. "Yeah. You do." She started to pass by Olivia, but then stopped and met her gaze. "Thanks for coming with him," she said. "It's nice to see him smiling."

And then she was gone.

Olivia sucked in a breath and thought about how close the siblings were. About how the concept was both alien and yet something she yearned for with all her heart and soul.

She wasn't used to this sort of group dynamic, hadn't been for a long time. But suddenly she missed the feeling of being on a set, the family sense of the crew.

Because that's what this felt like to her, one big, happy set.

Only this couldn't be canceled when ratings tanked. This was Cole's real life.

Which reminded her how different they were. She couldn't even imagine what it would be like to be a part of a family like this, one that stuck, that stayed no matter what, whose members loved each other and all their individual faults.

Unconditionally.

They weren't dependent on each other financially. They each had their own jobs and took care of themselves.

But they also took care of each other.

Willingly.

They loved each other.

A hand slipped into hers. Cole. He smiled and drew her back into the kitchen, where he pressed something in her hand.

A napkin.

Which was when she realized she had tears on her cheeks.

"Hey," he said softly. "We overwhelming you with our obnoxiousness?"

She blew her nose. "No. I've got something in my eye is all."

He smiled with such understanding that she nearly cried some more. "We're harmless," he promised. "Well, mostly."

He was about as harmless as a python. "You've got a pretty great family," she said. She was trying to wrap her head around that while reminding herself that this wasn't her future, much as she might secretly love it to be.

Because she'd lied to him.

"Great?" Cole asked. "Or terrifying?"

"Great."

He looked at her for a beat and then backed her into the pantry, pressed in close, and shut the door at his back. "You look like you need a moment." He leaned against a shelving unit filled to the gills with cans and bins and spices. His pose was relaxed, his smile easy, his eyes appreciative.

"We can't be in here," she said. "Your mother—"

"Knows her son is an adult."

She stared at him. "But…"

"I'm the youngest," he said. "Do you really think there's anything I can do to shock her that one of my sisters hasn't already done? And besides, she's the consummate pro. She'd never get mad at a guest. And you're a pro at this social thing, too," he said. "You really know how to charm a guy's family."

Olivia sucked in a breath and tried to look like she deserved credit for that, but Cole went still, and then cocked his head. "Tell me you've done this before, met a guy's mom."

Actually, no. No, she hadn't. Not once.

"Olivia? Am I the first guy who's ever brought you home?"

Her throat was tight again. Damn it. She decided to ignore the embarrassing and far too revealing fact that yeah, he was her first…whatever he was. "What's important here is that I think your mother actually likes me. I'm not going to get caught in the pantry with her favorite son and jeopardize that."

"I'm her *only* son," he said. "But you're right, she does like you."

The knowledge made Olivia glow a little bit, even as she squirmed with…discomfort. His family cared about each other, and it was genuine. Even the thing between Cole and his sister wasn't dysfunctional. They didn't throw booze bottles at each other, light each other's bedrooms on fire, sleep with each other's boyfriends, steal money…

Instead, they fought. And then hugged and made up.

"I like you, too," he said, and this only served to give her more warm fuzzies. And more terror.

"Olivia," Cole said, voice low.

Kind.

Warm.

She met his gaze and he crooked a finger at her, the universal sign for *come here*.

And though she wanted to resist, wanted to walk away, her feet took over, bringing her right to him.

Chapter 22

♥

Cole had wondered if Olivia would relax enough to have a good time. When he'd caught a glimpse of her tears, his heart had stopped. But he'd quickly realized that she'd been deeply touched by his family, and possibly missing hers. "Come here, little mermaid," he murmured, wrapping her in his arms when she stepped into him.

"You going to pillage and plunder?" she asked softly.

"Yeah." Actually, what he was going to do was his damnedest to erase the sorrow from her eyes. Spreading his legs, he pulled her into the V until they were snug against each other.

"Your sisters are—"

"Crazy?" he asked. "Yeah. I know."

"I was going to say nice," she said.

"Huh." He laughed a little. "That's a word I haven't heard associated with them before."

Smiling, she shook her head. "You love them. You're close."

He blew out a sigh. "For better or worse. That surprises you." He held her gaze, trying to see inside her, to the secrets she held so close to her heart. "Tell me about your family, Olivia."

She pressed her face into his throat. He could feel her lips on him. Since this threatened to derail his thought process, he urged her head up so that he could see her face again.

Her eyes remained on where she'd nipped him on the Adam's apple. "Olivia," he called.

She pressed her hips to his, rocking the softest part of her against what was now the hardest part of him. With a groan, he tightened his grip on her, holding her still. "Were you close to your family?" he asked.

"It's been a long time."

He heard the pain in her voice and he softened his hold, cuddling her into him. "Kiss me, Supergirl."

She didn't hesitate, lifting her mouth to his, opening when he gently nipped her lower lip, sucking her tongue into his mouth with a soft moan that had him insta-hard.

And that's when the door opened.

A three-and-a-half-foot-tall minion stood there. Jonathan, Clare's mini-me, stared at them, taking in the way Cole was gripping Olivia close with one hand, his other cupped the nape of her neck. "Uncle Cole?"

"Yeah, buddy," Cole said, hearing the residual huskiness in his voice.

"Why were you swallowing the Little Mermaid's tongue?"

"I wasn't," Cole said. "I was…" You were what, genius? "Checking her tonsils."

Jonathan turned his gaze on Olivia, awe in his eyes.

"When I get to be big like you," he said to Cole, "I wanna check the Little Mermaid's tonsils, too." And then he slammed the pantry door shut, the sound of his little feet running out of the kitchen echoing around them.

Cole grinned and pulled Olivia back in. "Where were we?"

"We can't," she said a little breathlessly, which was damn good for his ego. "We can't do it here."

No, regrettably, they couldn't. But he intended to chase away the last of her sadness. And he knew a really great way to do that, too. Nuzzling her throat, he opened his mouth, sucking on a patch of her soft skin.

She melted into him like her knees had liquefied.

Also gratifying.

"But someone might come," she whispered.

Yeah, he'd like that. He'd like it to be *her*, coming all over him. "We're not going to do it now."

"Oh," she said, sounding so disappointed he laughed against her soft skin.

"*We're* not going to do it," he said again. "Just *you*."

Her eyes flew to his. "What? No, I—"

He cupped a breast in his left hand, letting his thumb rasp lightly over her nipple, back and forth.

"Oh," she breathed softly into his mouth. "Oh, that feels good."

His other hand slid down her back to squeeze her sweet ass. "What's beneath this skirt?"

A soft huff escaped her, and she dropped her forehead to his shoulder. "I had to be careful of VPL."

He had sisters. He knew what VPL meant—visible panty lines. "Are you telling me you went commando?" he asked, his voice as rough as sandpaper. *If there is a God…*

"No!" Another soft huff of laughter. "I didn't go entirely without…"

Taking that as a challenge, he slid his hand into the skirt's waistband and cupped her backside.

Oh Christ, yeah. She was wearing the teeny-tiniest G-string he'd ever had the pleasure of exploring. He let his fingers do the talking, tracing the narrow strip of barely there silk south until she gasped.

"Spread your legs, Little Mermaid," he whispered.

The skirt didn't give her much room, but he got an inch or two when she did as he'd asked and shifted. He stroked her until she fisted her hands in his shirt at his pecs and was breathing in hot, short pants against his throat, her hips pressing into him with every stroke of his fingers.

"Cole," she whispered, voice tight and a little desperate.

He slid his hand around to her front, letting the tips of his fingers glide beneath the little triangle of silk.

Thankfully the waistband of her skirt had loosened even more, and with her quickening breath, it gaped at every inhale.

"Cole," she choked out. "I need—"

"This?" His fingertips slid south.

She moaned.

And more south, until he was letting out a shaky breath of his own. The silk was drenched.

Scraping it to the side, the pads of his fingers rasped over her bare flesh now. Soft, wet, heated flesh.

She said his name again, her fingers tightening on him when he stroked her. "Oh, please," she whispered, straining against him. "We've got to stop, I'm going to—"

"Come, Supergirl. I want you to come for me."

"Oh, my God. I—" Her head fell back, her eyes at half mast, her mouth in a surprised *O*. Her thighs clamped his hand as if she was worried he'd do as she'd said and stop.

No chance in hell.

Leaning in closer, he kept his fingers busy with her rhythm as he took a little tour of her throat, working his way down to her collarbone. Still cupping her breast, he lifted it from the corset and sucked her into his mouth.

When she came, he surged up and ate her soft, delicious little cries with his mouth. He brought her down gently.

"Holy cow," she breathed, finally sagging back. "I can't believe how fast you can do that to me." She let out a low laugh, and then shocked him by dropping to her knees and reaching for the zipper on his pants.

He caught her wrists and she tipped her head up to his, face still flushed from her orgasm. "Turnabout's fair play," she said softly.

The eroticism of having her on her knees, her mouth level with an erection he could have hammered nails with, was nearly enough to tip him over the edge, but he controlled himself.

Barely.

With a rough groan, he pulled her up to her feet.

"No?" she asked.

"Yes," he said. *God, please, yes*. "Trust me, I need to get you naked in the worst possible way. But it isn't going to happen in my mother's pantry. And it's not going to happen with you in costume. I love it, but this time I want just you. No costume, nothing but Olivia beneath me."

She stared at him, looking utterly dumbstruck.

"What?" he asked her.

"Nothing," she whispered.

It was more than nothing, but there was little he could do to press her here in the closet. "We've got to get out of here. I have a feeling our time is just about up."

And sure enough, right on cue, they heard footsteps.

"Cole?" Clare called from the kitchen. "Cole, where the hell are you? Mom wants a Cosmo, and you're the only one who can ever make them to her satisfaction, you suck-up."

Cole helped Olivia straighten out her skirt, though there was little he could do about the just-had-an-orgasm glow to her cheeks.

"I owe you," she said softly, her voice low and throaty and full of promise.

"I like the sound of that," he said, and caught her just before she escaped to give her a quick, hard kiss. "A pirate always collects on his debts."

Fifteen minutes later, Olivia was standing at the edge of the makeshift dance floor in the courtyard, watching Cole behind the bar mixing drinks on demand, when someone tugged at her skirt.

The Lorax.

He had two fingers in his mouth and was drooling down his chin. With his other hand, he tugged on Olivia's skirt again. "Up!"

"Uh…" Olivia looked around for Cindy. She found her not two feet over, arguing with Thing One and someone else who might or might not have been the Cookie Monster.

"Up!"

"Okay, okay." Sheesh. Were all the Donovan men demanding? Olivia obeyed the imperious command and scooped up the Lorax, looking into a pair of eyes the color of the ocean. "Hi," she said as she felt her phone vibrate again from within her tiny gold purse.

It'd been doing so with annoying regularity tonight, a flurry of texts from her mother and sister, which she'd been ignoring.

The Lorax looked at Olivia's wig, said "Da!" reverently, and put both fists in the red strands.

"You like the hair, huh?"

He pressed his face into it.

"Kyle's going to be a hair man," Cindy said, coming over to rescue her. She took her son and expertly shifted him to a hip. "You're good with kids."

"I've no idea, to be honest," Olivia said. "I'm new to kids."

"You've got the touch."

"How do you know?"

"'Cause you picked him up without worrying about your gorgeous costume," Cindy said. "And that just bought you the seal of approval from this mom."

Olivia was still glowing when she went back to the bar. Cole had shoved up the sleeves of his pirate shirt past his sinewy forearms. The hat had been tossed aside, leaving just the bandana and beaded dreads, and damn.

Damn if he didn't look hot as hell.

When her phone vibrated again, she took a quick peek at it just to make sure there wasn't a life-or-death situation.

Jolyn had gotten right to the point.

Mom says TV Land doubled their offer. Don't make me come up there and drag you back to LA.

Oh hell no was her sister going to come here. Except…
Olivia closed her eyes. She would. For money, Jolyn
would do just about anything. She'd show her face here in
Lucky Harbor, smell Olivia's happiness, and ruin it somehow.

Panic, unreasonable as it might be, clutched at Olivia's
heart. Cole joked about Clare, Cindy, and Cara being a
coven, but he had no idea. None. She looked up and found
his eyes on her, narrowed in concern. He said something
to Iron Man, and then he was drying his hands on a towel
and walking toward her.

She forced a smile onto her face and started to take
a step back, knowing she needed a moment to gather
herself. But she got an unexpected helping hand when
Amelia stepped in front of Cole, looking animated.

Cole's gaze shifted from his mom to Olivia as he
spoke. His mom put her hands on his arms and he cut his
eyes back to her. He spoke softly, and with what looked
like a great gentleness, and then he hugged her. Amelia
cupped her son's face, kissed both cheeks, and let him go.

Olivia realized she'd lost her chance to bolt when Cole
came right to her. "Hey," he said. "You okay?"

"Yep."

"Because you just looked at your phone like you had
bad news."

He was far too observant, not that this surprised her.
Most men didn't notice the little stuff, but Cole never
missed a thing. "What's up with your mom?" she asked.
"She seemed upset."

His jaw tightened. "She's got a problem that is now my
problem."

"Can I help?"

He pulled her in and brushed his mouth over her temple. "Look at you, being all sweet."

"Don't get used to it."

He huffed out a warm laugh against her. "It's one of my sisters. She had something to talk to my mom about tonight, and some decisions were made. She needs me. Or rather, my mom needs me to butt into her life."

She pulled back and looked into his face. There was regret there, but no anger. He wasn't doing this to impress anyone, or to gain favor. "You really do love all of them."

"Sometimes I have to really reach for it, but yeah, I do. Warts and all. That's a family, right?"

"Right," she said as if she knew, when really she had no idea. "It's Cara?" she guessed.

"Almost always," he said. "She needs me to help her move out of her husband's apartment and back into this house."

It didn't escape Olivia that both of them had family who wanted something from them, and that only Cole was going to jump in and do whatever was needed, without hesitation. "And what do *you* need?" she asked.

He stroked a finger over her jaw. "A rain check from you."

Chapter 23

The next day, the bell above the shop door rang and Olivia looked up to see Cindy Donovan. She was carrying Kyle, who gurgled in pleasure at the sight of Olivia.

Cindy looked around. "Nice place."

Kyle said something, too. "Yabbayabbayabba." Then he grinned at Olivia with pride, and her ovaries actually ached.

Closing the laptop she'd been working on, she came around the counter. "Looking for anything special?" she asked Cindy.

Cindy shook her head. "Not really."

Olivia took a deep breath. "You're not here to shop."

Cindy's smile was real enough, but her eyes were bluntly honest. "No. I'm not."

Olivia forced herself to stay still, not to fidget or shove her hands in her pockets and give away her nerves.

Kyle cooed again, trying to get her attention. She

smiled at him and he flashed her a toothless grin that had so much charm in it she couldn't help but melt.

"I know," Cindy said. "He's already a total lady-killer."

"It's not his fault, it runs in his family." Olivia picked a teddy bear from a bin of stuffed animals and held it out to Kyle.

His eyes went wide and he snatched the bear, clutching it to his chest as he bounced up and down in Cindy's arms.

"Treat it nice," Cindy told him, and looked at Olivia. "I know who you are."

Olivia's heart skipped a beat. "Do you?"

"I watched every episode of *Not Again, Hailey!* fifteen times. I could recite the entire boxed set. I know it's you."

Olivia inhaled a deep breath and confessed to nothing.

Kyle waved the teddy bear at Olivia and yelled some adorable baby gibberish that she figured meant "thank you."

"Look, I'm sure you've got your reasons for keeping this a secret," Cindy said, patting Kyle on the back. "And you know what? I don't blame you. I wouldn't want to be associated with your crazy past, either."

Now Olivia's heart outright sank into her boots, but she shouldn't have been surprised. Her wild and crazy days had been well documented. People loved to watch child star meltdowns.

YouTube was the bane of her existence.

But Cindy wasn't done. "Word to the wise," she said. "My brother's a very honest sort of guy. To the core." She paused and gave Olivia a long look. "And he expects the same out of the people he lets in. Trust me, I know first-hand how difficult it can be to live up to his expectations."

"I know you mean well," Olivia said as gently as she could with panic rolling like a greasy wave in her gut. "But your brother and I aren't—"

"Don't," Cindy said. "Please don't even try to tell me you don't have feelings for him. I saw you watching him from the dance floor when he was making drinks behind the bar, like he was the puppy you always wanted for Christmas but never got."

True story.

Cindy pulled out her wallet. "How much for the teddy bear?"

Kyle had set the bear on his mom's shoulder, and then his head on the bear, his gorgeous baby-blue eyes drooping.

"It's a gift," Olivia said softly.

"That's very sweet, thank you." Cindy moved to the door, gave Olivia one last knowing look, and left.

Olivia stood still a long moment, then let out a shaky breath. Sweet baby Jesus, she was in over her head and going down for the count.

Cindy was right, of course. She had to tell Cole the truth.

That night Cole boarded the boat, but not for work. Tanner and Sam were right behind him, each of them holding a bottle of their poison of choice.

None of them prepared the boat to leave the harbor.

Tonight it wouldn't be safe sailing. Not because of the weather—it was actually a hauntingly beautiful night. Crisp sky so clear that the stars looked like scattered diamonds on black velvet. No wind. Barely a swell on the water.

The three of them sat on deck, sprawling in various positions. Tanner knees up, leaning back against the bolster. Sam on the bow.

Cole at the helm.

In silence, they lifted their bottles to each other.

"To Gil," Cole said.

"To Gil," Sam said.

"To Gil," Tanner said.

Then they each took a long pull, the first of many. Paused to swallow.

And then repeat.

And…repeat again.

It was their second annual Get Shit-Faced in Gil's Memory drunk fest.

They didn't speak at all through the next few shots, which left too much time to think. There was a dull ache in Cole's chest. For Gil.

For his dad.

For Cara, who'd decided that her cheating husband needed to get the hell out instead of her leaving, and who'd needed Cole to help enforce her decision last night.

Which meant he'd never gotten back to Olivia's…

He drank some more and enjoyed the burn down his esophagus. It matched the one in his gut.

And heart. "Gil would've liked it here," he said. "Lucky Harbor."

Sam blew out a breath. "He would've liked anywhere that wasn't on a rig."

Tanner's mouth quirked in a barely there smile. "He did hate the rigs."

And he'd never gotten to leave them…

They all drank again. Pleasantly numb, Cole leaned

back and studied the starry night. "Remember that time he set all the toilets to blow at two in the morning?"

Both Sam and Tanner laughed. This was the tradition.

Remembering.

Never forgetting.

"You went apeshit," Tanner said to Sam.

"Yeah, because two guys were on the pot at the time. Luckily no real injuries, but it took me days to sort that shit out. Literally."

"He always loved a good prank," Tanner said fondly. "Remember when he put laxative in the meatloaf?" He pointed his bottle at Cole. "You're the one who went apeshit."

"Because it was my guys who ate three servings and couldn't work for two days. The shit really hit the fan then."

They all laughed and drank again.

"How about when he left us fake messages from our girlfriends, moms, and sisters," Sam said, "saying that they knew what we were up to in our free time."

"Now *that* was fun," Tanner said. "Getting hounded by the moms."

"Yeah," Cole said. "Mine said my mom had heard that I was getting serious with Susan, that she knew I'd been online ring shopping and wanted to give me diamond-buying advice." He took another long swig. In hindsight, when the shit had once again hit the fan and he'd had time to think, it'd bothered the hell out of him.

Because he had been getting serious about Susan. So serious that he'd asked her to marry him. After a lifetime of not particularly seeing himself with kids and a family, something deep inside had shifted, and he'd changed his mind. He'd wanted his own unit to belong to. To belong to him.

But Susan had said no, that she wasn't ready for that.

What she hadn't said was that she'd fallen in love with Gil. Nope, she'd saved that little tidbit until the day of Gil's funeral.

Cole didn't register the long, heavy silence around him until Tanner sighed and set down his bottle. "He shouldn't have pulled that prank on you," he said to Cole. "He thought he was being funny, but he regretted it, big time."

Cole stared at Tanner, a sudden sinking in his gut. "Why would he regret it?"

Tanner got a sort of oh-shit-I-fucked-up look on his face and said nothing, which did not help Cole's gut.

Or his brain, as the organ helpfully rushed to come up with a few explanations, not a single one of which he liked. Cole set down his bottle as well. "Susan and I had talked about marriage, so he was right there." He stilled as his brain finally settled on what was bugging him. He hadn't told anyone he'd asked Susan to marry him, but clearly she had. Shit. Fuck. "Goddamn. Susan told Gil."

Sam and Tanner exchanged a look that Cole had no problem interpreting. They knew something. And yeah, he was halfway crocked, maybe more than half, but he could still think.

At least a little bit. "What?" he demanded.

Tanner picked his bottle back up and tipped it to his lips.

Sam did the same.

"*What?*" Cole said again. Even though he knew. Yeah, he knew, and it wasn't sitting well. In fact, he was thinking about throwing up.

"Nothing, man," Tanner said.

"Let it go," Sam said.

Cole nodded. But then he shook his head because he wasn't much good at letting anything go, and now didn't seem like the time to start. Hell no. Plus the room was spinning just a little bit.

Or a lot.

As he looked around the interior of the boat he loved nearly as much as he did Sam and Tanner, the effects of the alcohol made it seem as if they were on the high seas. Except maybe it was him moving. "Susan told Gil, and he told you two."

Another look passed between his supposed best friends. He stood up and pointed at Sam and Tanner. "Someone better fucking start talking."

"Let it go," Sam repeated, standing up too.

Cole narrowed his eyes and got up in Sam's space. "And what exactly am I letting go?"

Sam's jaw bunched. "You're pissed. I get that. But you want to back the fuck up."

"No, I don't."

Tanner sighed and stood up, too, pushing his way between them. "We're fucking up the celebration of Gil's life."

Staring at the two guys he'd loved for so long he couldn't remember being without them, Cole shook his head. "I can't believe it. Susan told Gil she'd turned me down." He shook his head again. "But I'm getting the feeling you both already knew that, too. Yeah?"

Sam's gaze never left Cole's.

"Yeah," Cole said. "I'm right." He stared at them both. "Jesus." He shoved his fingers into his hair. "For two years I've sucked that bullshit down like a serving of cut glass. Thought that was the worst of it. Guess I was wrong there, huh? You two knowing all along and not telling me? That's worse by far."

Tanner had the good grace to grimace.

"How long have you known?" Sam asked Cole.

"I found out at the funeral. When she fell to a thousand pieces in my arms over the real love of her life being dead," Cole said. "I think the real question here is, how long have *you* known?"

The looks on their faces had him closing his eyes and dropping his head into his hands. "Longer than me," he muttered. "Doesn't matter how or when, you've known longer than me." He lifted his head again. "And you kept it from me. Jesus, was there some sort of memo on how to fuck me over?" He grabbed his bottle. "I need another drink. I need…" *To throw up.* "I need to get the fuck out of here."

Sam reached for him but he shoved free and also nearly planted his fist in Sam's face. When both friends started to follow him, Cole pointed at them. "Don't."

Sam opened his mouth.

"Don't talk, either. Don't…" He turned away. "Don't *anything*."

"Come on, man," Tanner said. "Don't leave. Not like this. It's not what you think—"

"It's exactly what I think," he said, and left. He was only halfway up the dock when Tanner's first text hit.

Get your moody bitch-ass back here.

Delete.

He was at the warehouse when Sam's text arrived.

We thought you were over her. We didn't want to stir it
up. Come back.

Cole stopped in the lot, momentarily stymied. Definitely too toasted to drive. He could hitch a ride home—if
he'd remembered to grab his house keys from the boat.

Since going back wasn't an option, he hit the beach
and started walking. His heart was pounding and so was
his head.

Old memories.

Old hurts.

We thought you were over her.

He was. He'd also thought he was past the fact that his
woman and his best friend had sneaked around behind his
back.

He'd really thought that. After all, Gil was dead, Susan
had moved on. There was no reason to harbor the resentment and bad blood.

So he hadn't.

He'd been a grown-up and done as Susan had. He'd
moved on. And in the brilliance of twenty-twenty hindsight, he'd come to realize that he and Susan wouldn't
have made a good pair anyway.

He hadn't been the one for her.

He'd taken that unforeseen blow to his heart and soul,
to his ability to love and trust in a woman, blah blah. And
he'd gone on, choosing to believe that there was someone
else out there for him, someone better suited.

Not that he'd gone looking. No, he hadn't been all that
eager to possibly get screwed up again. He'd figured if it

was meant to be, it would happen. Someone would walk into his life, past his walls, and right into his heart.

Olivia.

Her face came into his head. Her dark, deep eyes always held just a little bit of pain, no matter whether she was laughing or working or just standing still.

Always.

A kindred spirit, she'd walked right past his barriers. Not willingly. No, she was just as reluctant as he was to let herself feel.

And somehow that made her even more trustworthy.

His phone buzzed again, a call this time. From Sam, one of the two people he'd trusted to have his back no matter what.

And he, like Tanner, had known about Susan and Gil, and hadn't told him.

What if Cole had never found out? What if he and Susan had stayed together?

Would Sam and Tanner have let Cole continue to love someone who didn't, couldn't, love him back? *Ignore.*

Again his cell buzzed.

Tanner this time.

Cole resisted the urge to chuck his phone into the churning water and turned it off instead. He shoved his hands into his pockets. Hunching his shoulders against the chill, he kept walking.

When he got to the end of the harbor, the rocky terrain cut him off. He could go for a hike straight up the rock bluffs, or he could go for a swim in the choppy water.

Or he could head back.

It took him a good long time to decide, but he was pissed off, not suicidal. So he headed back. All too quickly he was staring up at the dock. At their boat. At the two guys sitting at the top of the stairs from the beach to the dock waiting for him.

Suddenly Cole was glad it was so damn cold. He hoped they'd frozen their balls off. Taking every other stair, he walked past them without a word.

"Ah, come on," Tanner said to his back. "You're the level-headed one. You know why we didn't tell you."

"Because you're assholes?" he asked.

"Yeah," Sam said. "I know that's how it looks, but— Christ, will you stop walking?"

No. No, he wouldn't. And when he heard their footsteps signaling they were following him, he spun around.

And nearly fell over.

Note to self: Getting too old for a bottle of Jameson.

"We need to talk," Sam said.

"That time came and went." Cole held their gazes hard, and he knew his message was received when they both took on a frustrated expression.

And worried.

And guilty.

Not giving a shit, Cole turned—more carefully this time—and hightailed it out of there.

He had no idea where he was going, of course. None. Used to be when he was a train wreck, he'd go to Sam and Tanner.

Not tonight.

The cold night coupled with the alcohol had his chest tightening painfully. Or maybe that was because the numbness had worn off. He wanted oblivion. He wanted warmth.

He wanted…to be wanted.

And suddenly he knew exactly where he was going.

Chapter 24

Olivia was locked in a dream, one she hadn't had in a very long time. She was sitting on the set of *Not Again, Hailey!*, her hair being brushed by a grumpy hairdresser, listening to the director and producer argue over her clothing.

"She's getting fat," the producer whispered, except that the people in China could've heard him. "Someone needs to cut her off from the craft services."

"Shh!" the director hissed. "Don't let anyone hear you say that; we'll get sued. Jesus. Just dress her in layers or something, and I'll work the lighting and angles."

I'm not fat! Olivia tried to yell this, but her mouth wouldn't open. She looked down at herself. She was what, turning sixteen? She'd just gotten boobs and okay, so her belly wasn't concave any longer and she'd developed hips. It was hard for her to deal with it; she didn't need it spelled out.

It'd been bad enough when she'd gotten her period that

last summer. Everyone on the entire set had been privy to the information, all of them panicked because now that she wasn't a petite little girl anymore, the show would change.

How was she to possibly have avoided puberty?

The director knocked on the producer's forehead. "Hello? You in there?"

"Hey," Olivia said, and...sat up.

She'd been dreaming.

She knew why, too. It was because she needed to face Cole and be honest. She looked at the clock on her nightstand. One a.m.

The knock came again, and she realized that someone was really at her door. She slipped out of bed, bent low to grab the baseball bat she kept under her mattress, and padded to the door. One look out the peephole had her sucking in a breath and undoing the chain, dead bolt, and lock to pull open the door.

Cole was arms up, hands flat on the doorjamb above him. He didn't speak, didn't move except to lift his head and look at her.

His eyes were hollow, his mouth grim.

"Are you...okay?" she asked.

He gave one slow shake of his head, put a hand low on her belly, and nudged her backward so that he could take a step inside.

Then he shut and relocked the door.

Guess he was staying.

He turned back to her and took in her appearance, the corners of his mouth tipping up very slightly. Maybe it was her hair, which probably resembled a squirrel's tail. But it could've just as easily been the baseball bat or her

Superman PJs—a blue tank top with a red-and-yellow *S* on the chest and red boxers. She'd seen them at Target and knew she had to have them.

"Supergirl," he said, but there was something off in his voice.

She cupped his rough jaw, frowning at the expression on his face.

Or the utter lack thereof. He was blank, like he was feeling too much to let it out. Her heart cracked for him, this man she hadn't meant to care for but did.

So very much. "What's wrong, Cole?"

Reaching out, he took the bat from her and tossed it aside. Then he put his hands on her hips and backed her up again, until she bumped into the couch.

And then fell onto it.

"Feeling frisky?" she asked breathlessly.

He dropped to his knees, spread her legs, and pulled her flush to him.

Well, he was feeling something. "Cole—"

He shook his head, his body tension-filled, hard as rock.

Everywhere.

He was also warm, almost too hot. And then there was the scent of alcohol. "Are you…drunk?" she asked.

"Not as much as I'd like to be."

"But—"

Planting his hands on either side of her hips, caging her in, he leaned close and covered her mouth with his.

The kiss was different than his other kisses. No warm-up, no soft coaxing, no preamble, nothing but tongue and teeth and desperation.

And it felt more real than any kiss she'd ever had. But

something was wrong. "What is it, Cole? What's happened?"

Again he shook his head, his eyes stark. Hollow. He pulled something from his pocket and slapped it down on the coffee table.

A condom.

She stared at it and then met his gaze.

He closed his eyes. "I shouldn't be here. I shouldn't need you. But I do."

He was strong of body and mind. He was self-sufficient, independent, and a stubborn male to boot. He didn't do the need thing; she knew this. And even if he did, he had family. He had incredibly close friends that might as well be his brothers. In other words, he had options.

And he'd come to her.

"It's just in case," he said about the condom. "It's your call."

"Yes," she said, and enveloped him in her arms.

Cole waited a beat as if giving her time to kick his ass out. When she didn't, he slid his hands beneath her tank top and lifted it up and over her head.

And then it was gone.

Next his thumbs hooked into the sides of the red satin boxers and tugged. He looked down at what he'd revealed and growled.

"There," he said roughly. "Finally. You. Just you."

For a minute she thought he was going to skip all the preliminaries and sink right into her body. But then he kissed his way down her throat to a breast. He took his time, drawing out a response that had her arching up into him.

With a groan, he kissed his way to her other breast, his big body trembling with the effort to hold back.

"It's okay," she said, threading her fingers in his hair. "Whatever it is, I'm here, right here. And I want you."

At that, he closed his eyes and dropped his forehead to hers. "So fucking sweet," he murmured.

She wasn't. Sweet. Not even close.

But then again, he didn't know the real her. If he did, he wouldn't be here. Not wanting to go there, not wanting to imagine being without him, she tugged up his shirt. "Off."

He rose to his feet and began to strip, kicking off his shoes, tearing off his shirt and then his cargoes, his eyes on her the whole time.

She reached out and grabbed the condom, but with a shake of his head, he dropped back to his knees, manacled her wrists at her sides with his hands, and bent his head to kiss an inner thigh.

And then the other.

And then...in between.

She bit her lip hard as she rocked up into him, and when his tongue flicked over her, she cried out.

He slid his hands beneath her. "Watch," he said, and lifted her to his mouth.

She watched. She watched his broad shoulders wedge her legs open, watched the muscles in his sleek back flex and ripple with every movement, watched his eyes drift shut in pleasure as he moaned at the taste of her.

And then she couldn't watch because he sucked her into his mouth and her eyes rolled back in her head as she came.

Hard.

And then, because he didn't let her go, again.

When she was boneless, he took the condom from her limp fingers. Her breath was still coming out in erratic gasps when he used his hips to nudge her legs farther apart and thrust inside her.

They both stilled with wondrous pleasure, and then she dug her nails into his back as he rocked her through two more orgasms before he reset his grip on her hips and let himself go, his head falling back as he hit his own release.

Eventually, their sensuous movements slowed and their heart rates reduced from stroke level to something resembling normal. She felt the touch of his mouth brushing against her damp temple.

"You okay?" he asked, his voice a barely there rasp.

She nodded; it was all she had. After another year or so, she tried to speak. "I'm starting to think that's how it's going to feel every time."

"And how does it feel?"

Like the best thing to ever happen to her. Like something she wanted to have happen again, and again. "Like I was just hit by a Mack truck."

He lifted his face from where he'd planted it in her throat and searched her expression. "I hurt you?"

"Yes," she said, and pulled him back to her. "In the very best possible way."

He relaxed and nuzzled at her for a moment, then rolled off her and onto his back on the couch, bringing her with him. He gathered her in and she draped herself across his magnificent abs, linking her leg through his.

"So," she said on a satisfied sigh. "To what do I owe this pleasure?"

He didn't answer, and she lifted her head to search his gaze.

He blew out a sigh and covered his eyes with his arm. "Had a rough night, that's all."

And he'd come here, to her…"Weren't you with Sam and Tanner?"

His pause was so brief she was sure she imagined it before he possessively cupped her butt with two hands, squeezing, rocking his hips to hers.

He was hard again, making her moan. "Okay," she said shakily. "You don't want to talk."

Chapter 25

Half an hour later, Cole found himself flat on the floor. Olivia was at his side, sprawled out like she didn't have a bone left in her body, her chest rising and falling as fast as his.

"Holy cow," she gasped.

That about covered it, Cole thought.

"You're pretty lethal when you're avoiding talking," she said.

He discovered he had just enough left in the tank to haul her in against him. "You should know."

She set her hands on his chest and then rested her head on them, gazing up into his face. "Sometimes talking's overrated."

He let out a long exhale. He didn't want her to feel that way. "They knew," he said. "Sam and Tanner. They knew all along."

She stroked the hair from his forehead and ran a finger along his jawline. "Knew what?"

"That Gil and Susan were…"

When he didn't finish, she blinked and then stilled. "Your best friend and your girlfriend were…?"

"In love."

"Oh, Cole." She stroked her hand down to his chest, directly over his heart, as if she could hold it safe for him. "I'm so sorry."

Sitting here with her like this, buck-ass naked both physically and mentally, wasn't as easy as he'd thought. Sliding out from beneath her, he rose and pulled on his jeans. Leaving them unbuttoned, he turned to her kitchen, hoping to see a bottle of anything out on the counter.

Olivia came up behind him, stroked a hand over his back, and then moved past him to her stove.

In nothing but his shirt.

Barefoot, hair a gorgeous cloud of silk, her beautiful body looking better in his shirt than he ever had, she started water to boil and set out two mugs.

"I'm not feeling tea right now, Olivia."

She dropped a tea bag into each mug, and then some honey. And lemon. "Trust me."

He wasn't much for trust at the moment, either.

Trust. Such a deceptively simple word.

He'd grown up with parents who'd given their all to their kids and sisters who maybe had enjoyed torturing him, but were always the first to stand up for him.

He'd had good, solid relationships in his life, of all kinds. Family, friends, lovers. And he'd never had a problem with trust.

Ever.

But he was feeling a little shaky on the concept after Susan.

Still, he didn't say a word as she poured the boiling water, didn't know how to tell her that while she looked hot as hell with that orgasmic glow on her face, tea wasn't what he wanted from her.

Then she removed the tea bags, turned away from him, and reached up high into a cupboard. His shirt rose on her thighs, giving him a heart-stopping quick peek of heaven before she faced him again.

With, God love her, a bottle of brandy.

She liberally laced the tea, stirred it with a primness that made him smile, and then brought him a mug.

Trust me, she'd said. Demanded, really, in her quiet but steely voice.

It wasn't the voice that had gotten to him, though. It had been her dark, warm eyes. Trust her? Damn if his heart hadn't decided to do just that.

His fingers brushed hers as he took the mug, and he held her gaze as he drank deeply.

"There's more to the story, isn't there?" she asked.

Oh yeah. So much more.

"Did you just find out about them tonight, then? Susan and Gil?" she asked.

"No. I found out the day of Gil's funeral."

She stared at him, then shook her head as if she couldn't imagine. "That must have been quite a blow. How did it come out?"

"Susan fell apart," he said. "Just completely fell apart." He remembered holding her trembling, crying, devastated form in his arms. "It didn't make sense to me because she and Gil bickered," he said. "All the time. It drove me nuts. I thought they hated each other. So when she lost it, I pushed her for why. And that's when it came out. She loved him. And he apparently loved her." He paused. "They'd hidden it out of respect for me. She told me that and a bunch more crap, like they hadn't meant to, they were terrified of hurting me, blah blah. And then she dumped me."

Her eyes softened. "And you what, kept it to yourself?"

"Yeah," he said. "Not exactly the sort of thing you want to share. I didn't tell anyone."

"Not even Sam and Tanner?"

"No," he said. "Not even Sam and Tanner. But as it turns out, they knew."

"So that's what you meant." She covered his hand with hers. "You just found out tonight that they've known all this time, same as you."

"Yeah." He stared down at her fingers on his. "I didn't know how to process that bullshit, so I left."

"Why is it bullshit?"

He jerked his head up to meet her guileless gaze. "Are you kidding me?"

"Cole." She squeezed his fingers. "How were they supposed to tell you that the two people you cared about so much had had this happen to them?"

"To *them*?" He let out a mirthless laugh. "I'm pretty sure I was the one bent over a barrel." He pulled his hand free and pushed his tea away, reaching for the bottle of brandy.

Olivia got it first and added a second shot to his mug, which she handed to him.

"I'd rather have it straight up," he said.

"The honey and lemon will help you when you hit the hangover at full bore."

"If I stay drunk, I'll never hit the hangover."

"Cole." She stepped into him and then went up on tip-toe, brushing her body to his as she slid her arms around his neck. "Being angry at what happened to you, at what happened between Gil and Susan, that's understandable. Required even, in the grief process."

"Good to know," he said. "Thanks for your approval."

She slid her fingers into his hair. "I've seen Sam and Tanner," she said. "I've seen them with you. There's no doubt in my mind how much you mean to them and the lengths they'd go to for you."

"Then why didn't they tell me?" he asked.

"I don't know, but I'm betting they had your best interests at heart." She paused, cupped his jaw, and looked directly into his eyes. "But what happened between Gil and Susan wasn't Sam's or Tanner's doing. You know that."

"They knew and didn't tell me. That's a betrayal as sure as Gil and Susan's."

She stilled and then slowly dropped back to the balls of her feet, her hands falling to her sides. "We're going to have to agree to disagree here," she said slowly.

"Is that right?"

"Yeah."

"Why?" he asked.

Her smile didn't quite make it to her eyes as she turned away. "Because we have two very different definitions of betrayal."

"What the hell does that mean?"

"I don't think now's a good time to get into it," she said.

"Because?"

"You're pissed off."

"Damn right," he said. "I expected more out of the people who claimed to love me."

"You expect a hell of a lot," she said, which immediately put him on the defensive because Christ, he was so over hearing about him and his unrealistic expectations. "What's so wrong about expecting honesty?" he demanded.

She didn't say anything to this. Of course she didn't. God forbid she tell him a damn thing. "You don't have the relationships in your life that I do, with Sam and Tanner and my family." He regretted the words the moment they left his mouth, but anger leapt into her eyes before he could take the words back.

"You're right," she said stiffly. "But this isn't about me." She moved to a chest of drawers and hopped into a pair of jeans. And then pulled on a sweatshirt. And then, before he could formulate a thought or catch her, she stormed out of her own place.

That was the second time now. He looked around, at the bed they'd decimated after the couch, at the clothes all over the floor. "What the fuck just happened?"

Her apartment had no answer.

Chapter 26

Olivia went for a very long walk, and when she got back to her place, it was empty.

She ignored the little pang of disappointment.

After all, she'd been the one to walk out. Again.

She'd work on it. But she wasn't used to being in this position, which was falling for a guy. It was damned uncomfortable.

And so not smart, because it meant letting him inside her carefully protected heart after a long period of disuse, never mind the fact that she'd jumped the gun, and instead of waiting for *him* to walk out on *her*, she'd done the walking.

God. She was such an idiot.

She tried to get another hour of sleep, but it was a lost cause. She got into the shower, scrubbing her hands over her face, wishing she could take last night back. She refused to let herself cry. But the good thing about a shower was that she could tell herself the drops on her face were just hot water.

Not tears.

Never tears. She didn't cry over people anymore. This was just exhaustion from spending her night staring up at her ceiling wishing she'd done things differently.

So differently.

As in maybe told Cole the truth about her past. The problem wasn't him.

It was her.

She was afraid. That was the bottom line. She was a coward.

Lots of people had shitty childhoods and had managed to overcome them. She'd thought she'd done exactly that. After all, she'd picked herself up, dusted herself off, and gone on, creating her own story, giving herself her fantasy identity. It'd meant freedom.

She'd been happy. Or she'd thought so. But for the first time, she was regretting what she'd done, how she'd chosen to escape her past.

Other people faced their demons by accepting them and moving on. Not making shit up. That she'd done just that suddenly felt…childish. Like maybe she hadn't grown up at all.

She dressed, grabbed her purse, and headed out with no real destination in mind, just knowing she needed a change of scenery.

"Hey. Right on time."

Olivia turned in the hallway and came face-to-face with Becca and Callie, clearly on their way to breakfast.

"You're joining us, right?" Becca asked.

"If there's a short stack of pancakes in my immediate future," Olivia said.

Becca looked at her for a long moment. "Whatever you want," she finally said. "You okay?"

As okay as she could be. "Just hungry."

Becca nodded. "Me too. Have you seen Cole, by any chance?"

Seen. Touched. Kissed. Hurt…But he'd given as good as he'd gotten, hadn't he? "Yes, I saw him last night."

"Is he okay?" Becca asked. "I guess there was some sort of misunderstanding between the guys, and he took off."

There'd been a lot of misunderstandings last night, as it turned out. But Olivia wasn't about to air Cole's dirty laundry, no matter how much she liked Becca, who was watching her with care and concern.

"Sam felt really bad about what happened," Becca went on. "He thought maybe the best thing to do was give Cole some space. Which is of course the opposite of how women would've handled the situation. We'd have talked it out."

Olivia would have liked to help the guys reconcile, but she didn't know how to do that without betraying Cole's confidence, which was just about the last thing he needed at this point. "In this case," she said carefully, "maybe a little space and *then* talk."

Becca nodded. "Good advice. I'll pass it on."

Olivia just wished that same advice would apply to her. But in her experience, people who walked out stayed out, burning bridges while they were at it. Cole wouldn't welcome her back.

And damn, there went that pain in her chest again.

The three women hit the diner, and while they were

waiting for their order, Becca slapped her own forehead. "Forgot to tell you, someone came looking for you yesterday afternoon. Knocked on your door and seemed pissed off that you weren't around."

"Who?" Olivia asked.

Becca shrugged. "She wouldn't say. I offered to leave you a message, and she refused."

A bad feeling curled through Olivia's gut. "She?"

"Mid-twenties. Long blond weave, but going by her roots, she was born a dark brunette. Dark eyes." Becca blinked. "And actually, come to think of it, she kinda looked like you."

Yep. There was a damn good reason for the bad feeling in her gut.

Her sister had shown up in Lucky Harbor. "What did you tell her?"

"Nothing," Becca said firmly. "She kinda stormed off before I could find out who she was. I hope she's not a crazy person. Maybe we should get a security camera in that hallway."

"It's okay," Olivia said. "I've got a feeling I know who she is."

"Who?" Callie asked.

Olivia stood up, dropped some money on the table, and gave a short shake of her head. "Nobody to worry about. I've gotta get to the shop. See you guys later."

Becca caught her wrist and met her gaze, her own very serious. "You know I'm your wingman, right?"

Olivia laughed. "You're not single."

"I'm talking about in life." Becca tugged until Olivia sat back down. "I'm your wingman in *life*."

Olivia had spent most of her adult life excelling at controlling her emotions. Or better yet, not having any. She'd done this by going solo. No expectations. No one to fail or disappoint.

And in return, no one to stand at her back and fail or disappoint her.

But Lucky Harbor, and the people in it, had sneaked in past her boundaries. With shocking difficulty, she swallowed the lump in her throat. "That's sweet," she said. "But unnecessary. I've got my own back."

"Well, duh," Becca said. "But it's so much nicer to have backup. Besides, I'm cute and hard to resist. And while Cole's much more hot than cute, he's also hard to resist. And Callie here, she seems like the solid sort, too. I bet she'd take a place at our backs."

Callie nodded. "Absolutely. I'm really good at having people's backs."

"But you only just met us," Olivia said.

"Some things don't take long to figure out," Callie told her. "Like recognizing a really good person when you see her."

"But you don't know me," Olivia said. Whispered. Because her throat had gone tight again. Damn it. "You don't know anything about me."

"Not true," Callie said. "I know you cry at those Humane Society commercials late at night and then call and donate money. I know that you trash-talk other bidders when you're on eBay—which I love about you—and that in spite of being white on white, you can really rap in the shower." She shrugged at Olivia's surprise. "No insulation, remember?"

"Now me," Becca said, grinning. "What do you know about me?"

"Waaaay too much," Callie said. "Did you ever stuff the pipes near your bed? 'Cause last night you and Sam—"

"That wasn't me," Becca said on a laugh. "Not last night, I swear."

Crap, Olivia thought, and grimaced. "That might've been me. Sorry."

"Are you kidding? Don't be sorry," Callie said. "I'm jealous as hell. Everyone's getting some except me."

Becca hadn't taken her eyes off Olivia. "You're getting some? It's gone that far?"

There was no good answer to that question, but apparently one wasn't required.

Becca grinned. "Yeah, you are. You're getting some."

"It's not like you and Sam," Olivia said quickly. "It was just…well, I don't know exactly. But it's over now."

"Because of last night and what happened on the boat with the guys?" Becca asked.

"No, it's because of me," Olivia admitted. She stood again. "Listen, I'm sorry. But I can't talk about this, and also, I really do have to go."

She'd screwed up with Cole and that was done. But now she had to get ahold of her sister before Jolyn opened her big mouth and ruined her life even more. She left the diner and walked to the shop, calling Jolyn as she did.

But being perverse by nature, her sister didn't answer.

Heaven forbid she ever do anything helpful. "Call me," Olivia said to Jolyn's voice mail. "Call me back as soon as you get this and tell me you are not here in Lucky Harbor asking about me."

Then, to distract herself, she went through new stock. She had two boxes that had come in the day before, and was deep in them when she nearly jumped out of her skin at the sound of a low, unbearably familiar voice.

"Hey, Supergirl."

Cole stood on her office doorstep, one shoulder propping up the jamb, arms casually crossed over his chest, baseball hat low on his face.

It was so cold out that she was still shivering in her boots from her walk over here, but Cole wore nothing but a long-sleeved T-shirt tight over his broad shoulders, loose over his flat abs, half tucked into his low-riding cargoes. Also, it must have started to rain, because he was dotted with raindrops.

And she ached at the sight of him.

Chapter 27

Cole took one look at Olivia's face and straightened in concern. She looked absolutely stunned to see him, so much so that she nearly fell on her face.

He reached out to grab her arm. She was trembling. "Hey," he said. "Hey, come here."

As he pulled her in, she gripped him like she'd never expected to see him again. "I'm so sorry about last night. I shouldn't have butted in with my opinion and then walked out, I—"

He shook his head and cuddled her into him. "Don't ever be sorry for your opinions," he said.

"But I walked out—"

"Honey, that's called a regular night at my house. Tempers ebb and flow, it's okay."

She stared up at him like he was speaking Greek. Had no one ever had a fight with her and then forgiven her before? "Olivia," he said quietly. "I'm the sorry one. I got

my world rocked last night, and you took the brunt of it."
Then he lowered his head and kissed her.

He'd meant to keep it short and sweet, comforting. But
it was one hell of a hot, hard kiss.

"So…" She blinked up at him when he lifted his mouth
from hers. "Does that mean we're okay?"

She slayed him. "So okay." Dropping his forehead to
hers, he cupped her face and kissed her again.

"And that?" she asked. "What was that for?"

"For being the real deal," he said. "For the utter lack
of pretense, always." He slid his thumb over her still wet
lower lip, watching the movement before meeting her
gaze. "I could fall for you, Olivia." He let that sink in before letting out a low laugh.

"That's funny?" she asked, looking confused.

"No. What's funny is that it's a lie." He dipped down a
little to look right into her eyes. "I *am* falling for you."

Olivia stared at him, heart in her throat. She couldn't
breathe, she couldn't do anything but gape at him like a
fish out of water.

Yay! the devil on her left shoulder said. *Oh yay! He's
falling for us!*

The angel on her right shoulder wasn't nearly so happy
and warm. In fact, she was terrified. *No. No, no, no, this
isn't good. What will we do when he finds out the truth
about us and he changes his mind?*

So many things were hitting her at once. Happiness.
Warmth.

Terror. "You mean that?"

"I'm not in the habit of saying things I don't mean."
Cole checked the lock on the front door and picked her

up. "Wrap your legs around me," he said. "Yeah, like that." And then he turned and headed for her desk.

"What are we doing?"

He set her down on the wood surface. "Lose the clothes, Olivia." And when she didn't move fast enough, he lent his hands to the cause and had her down to skin in three seconds. He dropped to his knees between hers.

"You're so beautiful," he said quietly, kissing his way up the inside of her leg, a big hand on her ankle, holding her open for him.

She felt incredibly naked. And she was. One hundred percent naked while he was fully dressed.

Intimacy had always been a problem for her. Relaxing into it. Allowing it. But here, now, with Cole like this, it felt...freeing. "I don't think—"

"Good. Don't think," he said gruffly. "Just give. Give me you."

And then he put his mouth on her, and in less than five minutes, she'd have given him anything he asked for. Her worries began to slide away. Even her angels went silent. Her bones were liquid; her body sagged against the desk like a limp doll when he rose up and kissed her. His mouth was hot and hungry, and he growled when she pulled him closer.

But then he let go of her, and she gasped at the lack of contact.

"Don't move," he ordered as he tugged off his shirt and unbuttoned his cargoes, stripping to skin. God. She knew she needed to stop this, but she couldn't. Nor could she take her eyes off him.

He rolled a condom down his length, and then his

hands were back on her, hard and deliciously possessive. He leaned over her, looking deep into her eyes.

She squirmed beneath him, desperate for him to push inside her, but he just looked at her, his gaze touching over her face, his bluer-than-blue eyes communicating more than she knew how to process.

And then a slow, warm heat filled her that had more to do with the things she saw there in those eyes than what his body was making her feel, and that was saying something. "Cole," she whispered, and cupped his face.

He smiled at her as if he'd won a prize, and finally, God, finally, he sank into her body.

Neither of them said much after that, but she didn't need any words. His eyes said it all. So did his hands as they trailed over her body. She lost herself in the sensations as he heated her from the inside out, completely lost herself, and she realized she was saying his name again, over and over.

Oh yes, she thought; in spite of herself, in spite of her secrets and her fears about what was going to happen when he found out the truth about her, in spite of *everything*, she was most definitely falling...

And then all the air left her body and she pulled at him, digging her nails into flesh and muscles as he pounded into her.

His mouth was against her ear. "Come for me."

As if she could do anything but. And as she did indeed come for him, something in her heart shattered along with her body. Pulsing, throbbing, she tightened around him again and again.

And knew she loved him.

She opened her mouth, but blessedly before the words

could escape, he kissed her, and as he raced to his own orgasm, she met his every thrust with an almost frightening
level of passion.

Afterward, they didn't move for a long time. His hands
were tangled in her hair, his body still deep inside hers,
his breathing ragged, his heart pounding against her, and
she knew she didn't want to let go of him.

Ever.

"Maybe we should fight every day," he said on a low
laugh that she could feel reverberate through her.

Ducking her head low, she nodded and surreptitiously
wiped her cheeks, not wanting to share how much he'd
moved her. Cuddling into him, she took what she desperately needed—just one more minute in his arms.

"Hey," he said softly, bending his head, speaking low
in her ear, his voice tender. "Hey, look at me. You okay?"

She slowly raised her head and met his gaze. He
cupped her face and kissed her. Warm. Slow. Sweet.

"Yes," she said. "*Very* okay." At least in the moment.
Later she would go back to how absolutely wrong this
was, how she shouldn't have gone there without being up
front with him. But for now, right now, she wanted this
moment with him.

He held her gaze for a long beat, as if making sure
he believed her. Then, not five minutes later, she watched
him dress, his body language relaxed. Confident.

Not second-guessing anything.

She wished for half of his self-assuredness. Hell, she'd
have settled for a quarter.

He moved to the door and looked back, smiling when
he found her staring at him. "I'm going to pull my truck
around back," he said. "You'll hear me going in and out."

"For what?"

"I got some plywood. I'm going to make you that hanging dress display in the other room."

Tell him, she ordered herself. *It's time. It's past time. You've got to tell him that you're not the real deal. After all, he was honest with you, so be brave and return the favor.*

But he was gone, and she…she was a chickenshit.

Over the next half hour, she heard him go in and out numerous times—he was out now. About ten minutes ago he'd said he was running to the hardware store. She was just lighting a few candles and getting herself organized to open when someone knocked on the front door.

She glanced at the clock. Only nine thirty, still a half hour before official opening time. She turned to the door expecting Cole.

Not Cole.

She opened up to Jolyn. Her sister walked into the store and turned in a slow circle. "Wow, look at you, store proprietor. Long way from Hollywood, huh, Sharlyn? You enjoying slumming out here in the sticks?"

Olivia hadn't forgotten how to act, and she spoke smoothly in spite of the fact that her stomach had hit her toes. "You know I go by Olivia here. And there's nothing wrong with working for a living. You should try it sometime."

Jolyn snorted. "What did you think I did as your servant for all those years when you were the princess of Nickelodeon?"

"You were my personal assistant," Olivia corrected. "And highly paid."

Another snort. "I was your bitch and we both knew

it." She picked up an antique frame, turned it over in her hand, rolled her eyes at the price, and set it back down. "And for the record? I do work. I work my ass off. I take care of Mom. And speaking of which, I could really use some help in that area, dear sister mine."

"I think I've helped plenty."

"Is that what you tell people here in Lucky Harbor? Jesus, have you looked around? It's like a damn postcard. What does everyone think about the fact that they're housing the original Miley Cyrus in their midst?"

"No one knows."

Jolyn turned back to her in surprise. It had always been beyond her why Olivia wouldn't want the world to know who she was. "Don't tell me you're still going with the bullshit bio—that you grew up on a Kentucky horse farm." She took in Olivia's expression and laughed again. "Unbelievable. You're standing right in the middle of a windfall, and you haven't even tried to capitalize on it." She gestured to the things in the store around her. "Do you have any idea how much more you'd sell if you told people that you starred in the most popular kids' show to ever hit the air?"

"I'm not telling anyone that, and neither are you."

Jolyn shook her head. "You're crazy, you know that, right? But whatever. Just come back to Hollywood with me. It's where you belong. The best years of our lives were spent there, even with the ups and downs."

Olivia nearly laughed at just how wrong every word in that sentence was. "I'm not going anywhere."

"Why?"

"I like my life here."

"You don't have a life here, *Sharlyn*, you have lies here."

"I'm not leaving." She was surprised at how easy it was to say. "I've met someone."

"Uh-huh. And does this guy know you're just playing your latest role?" Jolyn asked. Her gaze suddenly shifted to something behind Olivia, her face brightening as she straightened. "Well, hello," she purred.

Olivia went stock-still and then whipped around. Oh, God. *Cole*.

He had a hammer in one hand, a two-by-four in the other. He'd shoved up the sleeves of his shirt and was covered in sawdust, and still he looked like the best thing that had ever happened to her.

Had he meant what he'd said? That people got mad, and then they got over it? Hope slammed her heart into her ribs painfully. Maybe her happy marker didn't have to come up.

But then he met her gaze, and the hope died so fast her chest felt like it had caved in on itself.

With one last long look at her, he turned and walked out.

Chapter 28

Cole couldn't remember walking out of Unique Boutique, but when he blinked, he was standing outside in a very light mist. He actually had to look down at himself and make sure he was still upright, he'd gone that numb.

Reeling, he shook his head. She wasn't Olivia Bentley. That was just someone she'd made up. Her entire life was a lie. No, scratch that. She hadn't told him enough about herself to equal an entire life. Just bits and pieces.

But those bits and pieces had all been lies.

His brain was stuck on that. He'd opened himself up and revealed himself to her. And she'd lied about…everything.

"Cole."

As if from a distance, he saw himself shoving his hand into his pocket for his keys and heading for his truck. He was on autopilot, which worked for him. Numb.

"Cole, please stop."

He didn't until he was at his truck and she put a hand on his arm.

"How much did you hear?" Olivia asked.

He stared at her. "Seriously? Is that the concern here?"

"I can explain," she said.

Yeah, he'd heard that one before. From Susan's lips on the day of Gil's funeral. And hell if he was going to be made a fool of for a second time in a row.

Too late, asshole.

Shrugging her off, he hauled open the door of his truck and slid behind the wheel.

Olivia stepped into the space between the cab of the truck and the door so that he couldn't close it.

"We need to talk," she said.

He let out a harsh laugh and tilted his head back to stare up at the roof of the truck. "Now she wants to talk."

"Please," she whispered.

He closed his eyes and his heart to the pain in her voice. "It's too late for that."

"No," she said. "When I walked out last night, you said it was okay, that I was just mad. That's what this is, right? It's your turn to walk out mad, and later it will be okay. Right?"

"Wrong." So very wrong. "Olivia, you let me think you didn't have any family. You stood in my mother's house, moved by my relationship with my family, and let me console you because you were alone. I wanted to make things better for you."

She was pale and wide-eyed. "It's...hard to explain."

"No," he said. "It's one word. Lies." He turned the key. His truck engine roared to life, which was a relief. Something was working.

She reached for him but he caught her hand in his, and put his other hand to her stomach to hold her back.

But touching her was a mistake, a big one. His brain

hadn't yet gotten the message that he'd been screwed over yet again. And plus she was shaking.

Apparently he could feel something after all.

"You don't understand," Olivia said softly, hoping to reach him. Desperate to reach him. "All my life, it's been me playing someone else, so that I didn't even know who I really was. I stopped being honest with people a long time ago."

"That was your choice," he said.

"Yeah, a hard-learned choice. The last person I told the truth to was my college boyfriend. He had a film fest and charged admission to the party without warning me. I showed up and it was…" She shook her head. "Humiliating, to say the least."

"Jesus." He scrubbed a hand down his face. "That was a real asshole move, but I'd never have done that to you, and you damn well knew it."

"I just wanted to start over," she said. "So I came here and erased my past."

"You can't erase your past," he said. "It's a part of you. You have to accept it before you can move on."

She met his gaze. "Is that what you did after Gil and Susan? You accepted it and moved on?"

He stared back for a long beat. "I actually thought I was doing just that. And I thought I was doing it with you."

She searched desperately for some softening in him and saw nothing but cool, calm resolve. He'd made up his mind about her. She hadn't met his expectations, and it was over. Done. The thought made her shiver.

"Go inside," he said, sounding as weary as she'd ever heard him. "It's too cold and wet out here."

"No. I—"

"I don't want to hear it, Sharlyn."

"Olivia," she whispered. "I'm Olivia now."

He just looked at her like she was a stranger.

Yeah, she was cold. Cold to the bone, and it had nothing to do with the mist. Staring into his closed-off face, she slowly shook her head. "I knew it'd come to this. I've been counting down."

"What does that mean?"

"It means we had a shelf life, and we're expired. It was only a matter of time, and I knew it going in."

His jaw tightened. "Fuck that, Olivia. You can't hold me accountable for the way this has gone down." He shoved his fingers through his hair. "You kept secrets. You can't build a relationship on secrets."

"I didn't keep anything from you that mattered to the here and now."

"Are you kidding?" he asked incredulously. "You kept *everything* from me, including the fact that you do have family, and your real name. Jesus."

"It wasn't like that—"

"What was real?" he asked. "Any of it?"

Her throat got so tight that she couldn't talk, which was just as well, really. Because the one thing that had been unequivocally true had been her feelings for him.

Which she wasn't about to admit now.

And besides, maybe after acting and faking emotions all her life, she couldn't trust those feelings anyway. "You're not listening," she said.

He shook his head slowly. "Actually, I'm listening to every word, especially the ones you're not saying."

When she didn't respond, didn't know how to respond,

Cole nudged her back, shut the driver's door, and hit the gas.

She was still standing on the sidewalk trying to figure out how her life had just imploded when she heard someone come up behind her.

"Do I even want to know?" Jolyn asked.

Olivia drew in a deep breath, doing her best not to completely lose it.

"Let me guess," her sister said, propping an elbow on Olivia's shoulder as she gazed down the street after Cole. "You messed something up."

"I messed everything up."

"It's a Peterson trait," Jolyn said. "How did you land him anyway? 'Cause nothing personal, but that guy? Out of your league."

Wasn't that the bleak truth.

And worse, she realized she had an audience of more than just her sister. Lucille was standing under the bakery's awning kitty-corner from her shop, eating some sort of pastry out of a white bag.

"Hi honey," she called out, waving. "You want me to post to Twitter, ask him to come back?"

Olivia blinked and tried to change gears, but couldn't.

I'm listening to every word, especially the ones you're not saying...

"Because I can do that," Lucille said. "People love it when I tweet."

A few more elderly ladies came out of the bakery, each with her own small white bag.

"Honey, are you listening to me?" Lucille asked.

This wasn't happening. This really wasn't—

"What's doing?" one of the bluehairs asked.

"She chased off Cole Donovan," Lucille told her. "Right before my very eyes."

"That charter captain hottie?" another one of them asked, and then tsked, like maybe Olivia wasn't the sharpest tool in the shed. "How did she do that?"

"I'm not sure, I turned my hearing aid all the way up and still missed some of it. Something about her not being Olivia but Sharlyn," Lucille said. "But I don't know what that means."

"It means she's Sharlyn Peterson, that little girl TV star who put the crazy in crazy. Went off the deep end about a decade ago and vanished."

"Get out," Lucille said. She cupped her hands around her mouth and called out to Olivia again. "Honey, is that true?"

"Well, of course it's true," the other bluehair said. "I watch episodes of *Not Again, Hailey!* when my Xanax wears off. It reruns at two in the morning on Nick at Night. Cheaper than watching the shopping network. I had to cut up my credit cards after I realized I'd ordered twelve sets of paring knives. And I don't even like to cook."

Next to Olivia, Jolyn snorted. "This place isn't so bad after all," she murmured.

"So is that it?" Lucille asked. "You lied to us? Because if that's what happened, well then shame on you, honey. Unless you had a really good reason. Did you? Why don't you run it by us, and we'll vote on it."

Olivia turned on her heel and walked back into her shop.

Of course, Jolyn followed.

"I should've locked the door," Olivia muttered.

Jolyn was grinning. "Shame on you," she said, imitating Lucille's ancient, smoked-three-packs-a-day voice.

Olivia ground her back teeth. "You enjoying the show?"

"Oh, yeah. This is better than anything you ever acted on."

Olivia wanted to scream, she wanted to throw something. She wanted...

To figure out how to go back in time and strangle Jolyn before she'd come to Lucky Harbor.

God, she was tired. Tired of pretending to have it all together. Tired of the fiction. She just wanted to be herself.

Whoever that was.

"So do tell about the charter captain hottie," Jolyn said. "He loaded?"

She could feel her blood pressure rising. "Out," she said, pointing to the door. "Go."

"Where?"

"Anywhere other than Lucky Harbor."

Jolyn got the same look that a pit bull did just before he sank his teeth into you. "I like Lucky Harbor."

Great. Frigging great. "You don't belong here," Olivia told her.

"Neither do you. But hey, if you want to implode your life the way you always do, who am I to stop you?" Jolyn said.

"What will get you to leave?" Olivia asked.

"Do the show and get Mom off both our backs."

Olivia turned to face her sister. "The doctors said she was fine, you know. I talked to them myself."

"Fine is relative. The accident took a lot out of her."

Yes, that's what happened when one got drunk off one's ass and drove into a pole.

"She gave up doing hair," Jolyn said. "She says it hurt to stand on her feet all day."

"She owns the hair salon," Olivia said. Which she ought to know, as Olivia had purchased it for her. "When it's managed properly, she doesn't have to work a day in her life if she doesn't want."

"Define managed properly," Jolyn said.

Olivia stared at her. "You are kidding me."

"You made a tactical error by believing she could manage anything properly. Which is your own fault, seeing as she handled your career. You should've known better."

This was undoubtedly true, but at the time, Olivia had been thinking only of how to be free. Buying her mother her own salon and walking away seemed like the best thing.

For Olivia.

Which made her selfish. A new and unsettling thought.

"She's in trouble, and I need your damn help," Jolyn said. "We're in this together, you and I. We're all she has."

"Contrary to what you think, I don't have any hidden pockets of money," Olivia said. "We spent my royalties, all of them."

"Which, hello, is why you need to green-light this TV Land special. They're going to pay you out the ass to sit there and look pretty. I don't see what the BFD is."

"The big effing deal is that I don't belong in that world anymore," Olivia said.

"One day," Jolyn said. "You smile and make nice for the camera, and then hold out your hand for a big, fat paycheck like in the old days."

"And then?" Olivia asked tightly. "I suppose I sign it all over to you and Mom?"

"Well, why not?" Jolyn asked. "This was never about just you. Mom moved all three of us across the country to Los Angeles. We gave up everything for you, everything. We earned your paycheck every bit as much as you did."

The only thing she'd ever really done of worth was make money for her family. "Fine," she said. "I'll do the show." But she'd do it her way. "Now you've got to go, and so do I. I've got somewhere to be."

"Now? Captain Hottie must've been pretty important, huh?"

"Yeah." Heartsick, Olivia pulled out her keys. She needed to find Cole and make him understand that the past didn't matter.

Jolyn stared at her for a long beat. "I'll watch the shop for you."

"What? Why would you do that?"

"Because you look like a puppy who's just been kicked. Consider it my good deed for the month."

"I'm not leaving you in charge of my livelihood," Olivia said.

"Hey," Jolyn said. "My petty thieving days are long over. I'm auditioning and shit. If I get arrested now, I'll blow my chances when you do this show."

Olivia blew out a breath. "Ironic, isn't it?" she asked. "Last time you wanted my show to fail. Now you want me to succeed."

"It's not exactly a bad deal for you, either," Jolyn said. "I'm getting you closure, a reunion with your beloved *Not Again, Hailey!* community, not to mention the undying love of your family."

That love was pretty damn expensive. She'd always just accepted that was how it worked, but now she'd seen the Donovans. She'd seen Cole do whatever was in his power to be there for his family, no matter what. No price. Their love didn't cost a damn thing except unconditional acceptance. And the only way to get that was with complete honesty.

The exact thing she'd withheld from Cole.

Maybe instead of wishing she could go back in time to strangle Jolyn before she could spill the beans, Olivia should go back in time and…never have lied in the first place.

The phone rang, and she picked up. "Unique Boutique."

"Honey, it's Lucille. Listen, I'm getting ready to announce what you did at our weekly tea, but it occurs to me that you might want to speak out on your behalf about why you lied to our very own Cole Donovan."

Olivia pulled the phone away, stared at it, and then brought it back to her ear. "You only heard this about five minutes ago, and you've already got a tea organized?"

"Oh, lucky for us, this tea was a preplanned event. So…your reason?"

"No comment," Olivia said, and hung up. "Good Lord. And I used to think the paparazzi were bad."

Jolyn walked over to the cash register. "Okay, so how do you work this baby?"

"Not happening."

"Oh, come on," Jolyn said. "You can argue with me, during which time your hottie is getting farther and farther away, or you can give in and let me help you out. And honestly…" She looked around the shop. "It's a nice place, I'll give you that. Warm and homey. Sweet. But let's face it, it's not exactly my style. Not emo or dark enough."

Real family. *Sometimes I have to really reach for it. But yeah, I do love them. Warts and all. That's a family, right?* She stared at Jolyn. "I'll be back in one hour. Don't screw up."

Jolyn lifted her hands like she was surrendering. "I'll be an angel. Promise."

Uh-huh. Olivia didn't believe that for a second, but she wanted—needed—to believe in something. In family. In love. She needed that as much as she needed to go after Cole.

Chapter 29

Olivia hit Lucky Harbor Charters first. The hut was closed, with a sign letting people know that the fall season schedule was now by appointment only, with a phone number listed to call.

Olivia ran down the dock and stopped at the boat moored there, hoping to find Cole on board.

"He's not here."

Olivia turned, but saw no one. Then two hands appeared on the dock, and a man propelled himself out of the water, lithely landing on his feet in front of her.

Tanner.

He was in a full wetsuit that delineated his extremely fit body, which was dripping onto the dock. "You were swimming?" she asked. "It's freezing out."

He ran a hand over his short, dark hair. His equally dark eyes gave nothing away. "It's not that bad."

She eyed the water, which was choppy with at least two-foot swells.

Tanner followed her line of sight and shrugged. "Compared to some of the places I've been, it's downright balmy. And it's actually calmer around the bend."

Around the bend had to mean the far end of the harbor, past the bluffs and rocky cliffs into the open water—at least a two-mile swim.

Each way.

Holy cow. The guy wasn't even breathing hard. "Do you know where I could find him?"

"I'm guessing in hell," Tanner said.

"He told you," she breathed.

"No," Tanner said. "He's not speaking to me, either."

"Then how do you know he's not speaking to me?" she asked.

"Just guessing by the slightly panicked look on your face. And no, I don't know where he is, but I saw him just tear out of the lot. Burned some good rubber on his new tires, which is unlike him. He tends to baby his truck."

"Oh, God." Weak-kneed, Olivia sat right there on the dock. "I blew this so bad. I thought I was doing the right thing, but it was the right thing for me, not him, and I hurt him. The one person I didn't want to hurt." She shook her head. "So stupid."

Two long legs came into view, and then Tanner crouched in front of her. "Hey," he said, surprisingly gentle. "Hey, it's okay."

"No, it's not!" She grabbed him by his very broad shoulders and tried to give him a shake.

He didn't budge.

Instead, he took her hands in his and squeezed. "Tell me what's going on, Olivia. I'll help."

"Why? Why would you help me?"

"Because Cole's been happier with you around than at any other point in the past two years. Because you two are good for each other. And because you're looking crazy right now and scaring me a little bit."

She let out a low laugh and wiped her nose.

"Cole could use a little crazy," he said. "His sisters notwithstanding."

She choked out another laugh. "You might not feel that way when I tell you what I did. I lied to him about who I was and where I came from. I lied to everyone here, actually."

His gaze was empty of judgment. "Why?"

She stared at him and realized that she'd not yet said the truth out loud. "Because Lucky Harbor was a new start for me. I wanted that. I wanted that so badly."

Tanner frowned. "And Cole didn't get that?"

"He might have," she said, "if I'd told him. But he found out from my sister, not me."

"Ah," Tanner said. "He's had a lot of that happen to him lately. He's a straight shooter, our Cole. You got his back, or you don't. He doesn't deal with hidden agendas, subterfuge, or bullshit very well, never has. He doesn't get it, just isn't wired for it."

"Because he's real," she whispered.

"Yeah. He is."

She covered her face. "I can't believe I've screwed up the first real, good thing to ever happen to me."

"You love him," Tanner said.

Her heart squeezed.

Tanner pulled her hands from her face and stared her down. "Yes?"

She opened her mouth, then closed it. Her throat closed along with it. Just refused to allow air through.

Tanner's eyes softened, as did his voice. "You aren't the only one," he said quietly.

"I want to make things right," she said. "I *need* to make things right."

"Then do it. He deserves that." He paused and looked her over. "And maybe you do, too." A smile curved his lips. "I'm rooting for you."

She took strength from that, and as she headed to Cole's house, she thought about what Tanner had said. Without a doubt, Cole deserved a shot at happiness again.

But the problem was, she did not.

Olivia didn't find Cole at his place, or anywhere. She ended up back at her own apartment, where Becca was pacing the hallway.

Becca whipped around, spotted Olivia, and said, "About damn time. Is it true?"

"What?"

"That you're some child star from Nickelodeon?"

Unbelievable. Though she shouldn't have been surprised, not with Lucille on the scent. And this was, after all, Lucky Harbor, where crime was rare but gossip spread like wildfire. "It's true," she said.

Becca stared at her. "Wow," she finally said. "Cool."

"Not cool," Olivia said, and gave her the CliffsNotes version of the situation with her family and Cole. "And also, I'm pretty sure the geriatric gang is busy putting out a hit on me."

"They do move fast," Becca said, and hugged Olivia. "Tough day. My sympathies."

"You're not pissed off at me?"

"Honey, no one understands self-protection as much as I do," Becca said quietly.

Olivia remembered sitting with Becca in a rehab waiting room, clutching hands as Becca watched her brother check himself in.

Yeah. Becca knew all about it.

"You'll explain it to him," Becca said. "It'll be okay."

"Hello, have you met him? Once he gets a thought in his head, it's in cement."

Becca grinned. "Okay, so you go to him and make him listen to you. After you knock some sense into him, you tell him you love him and—"

"I didn't say I love him."

"Didn't have to," Becca said.

Olivia stared at her as her phone rang. She didn't recognize the number, and answered cautiously. "Hello?"

"He's at the Love Shack," Tanner said without preamble. "Talking to Sam, finally. Go do your best. And I mean your *best*. Our boy put ornery into the dictionary. You got a frying pan to hit him over the head with?"

Olivia slid a look at Becca. "I'll work on that. Thanks."

"I'm not kidding about the frying pan," Tanner said. "You've got your work cut out for you, but I'm still rooting for you."

Her throat tightened. "Thanks for your help." She disconnected and turned to Becca. "I've gotta go."

Becca locked her door. "Where we headed?"

"We?"

"I'm your wingman, remember?"

Olivia stared at her. "I don't deserve you as a wingman."

"Now you're going to piss me off," Becca said mildly, and squeezed her hand. "Let's go."

Sure enough, Cole was in the Love Shack with Sam. The bar was filled. In one corner were the bluehairs. Olivia looked at Lucille. "I thought you were having tea."

"Yep." Lucille lifted a glass. "I've got a little bit of tea right here in my brandy." She gestured to a table across the way where Cole sat with Sam. "You here to make it right?"

Olivia looked over at Cole and felt her heart catch. "Yes."

Lucille smiled. "Attagirl."

Olivia took a deep breath and headed toward the guys' table. She could feel eyes on her, and she realized she'd just come up against her first real negative of living in a small town.

News traveled fast. And she was news, of that she was positive. It was in the curious gazes as she waded through the bar and grill. And for the first time in a very long time, she felt judged.

Vulnerable.

She drew a deep, steady breath and pretended she was on a sound set. A closed sound set. Everyone around her was just doing a job. Their job was protecting their own, and their own was Cole.

She understood that.

"You've got this," Becca said in her ear, reminding Olivia she wasn't as alone as she'd thought.

"Thanks," she whispered to her wingman, and strode straight up to the guys.

Sam looked surprised as hell.

Not Cole. He met her gaze slowly, giving nothing away.

"You were right," she said. "I was keeping secrets, but it wasn't just you. I was keeping secrets from everyone. See, the very nature of a secret is that you don't want it revealed. And that gives it power over you. Terrible power."

"Everyone has secrets," he said. "I get that. I'm not angry at that. I'm angry that I trusted you with mine; I opened up and gave you a part of me. I told you about my failures, and you withheld yours."

"You loved someone," she said. "It didn't work out. There's no failure or shame in that. But you have to understand, my whole life was a failure. You try dealing with that, Cole. For years I was successful, until I wasn't, and it felt like the world watched me fail. Everyone knew me as Sharlyn, the loser child star."

"Not me," he said. "I knew you as…you." He paused. "So what was real?" he asked. "Any of it? Or was it all a fiction you created?"

"We all create a fiction," she said, aware that the whole damn place had gone quiet, but she couldn't pay attention to that without losing her nerve. "But it was all real for me," she said, and oh, God, how his look of disbelief hurt. "Yes, I should've told you who I was. I know that. But the truth is, I'm ashamed of Sharlyn Peterson, a spoiled child star who ended her career with a public meltdown. I'm not ashamed of Olivia Bentley, a hardworking woman who just wanted to be herself and live her life." Just saying it out loud made her mad, and maybe it was unreasonable since she'd brought this whole thing on herself, but she found she was revving up to a good temper.

Cole opened his mouth, and she pointed at him. "I'm not done. You asked me why I ended up here in Lucky Harbor. My on-set tutor was from here. Mrs. Henderson."

"Oh!" Lucille stood up on her chair and waved her arm to catch their attention. "A wonderful woman, and a dear friend. You were lucky to have her, honey."

"I was," Olivia agreed, not taking her eyes off Cole. "Lucky Harbor was her favorite subject. She told me all about it: the gorgeous Olympic Mountains, the pier, the Ferris wheel, the arcade, the people…especially the people, how you all loved each other, looked out for each other, always. Living here became a fantasy of mine," she admitted softly. "One that got me through some pretty hard times."

Cole started to stand up, and she pointed at him again. "Don't," she said. "I'm not done. You're the guy who's known for fixing whatever's broken, and I admire that skill. I was just trying to do the same—to myself. I didn't mean to hurt anyone in the process. I'm sorry about that, so sorry. And I get that regrets are a dime a dozen, and hindsight's twenty-twenty, but I can't undo it, Cole. And if I'm being honest, I should tell you…I'm not even sure I would if I could. Because when I first arrived, I promised myself a clean start. At first, I thought of it as creating a person, a character to play, because that was all I knew how to do. But you know what? This person I made up?" She pressed a hand to her chest. "She's actually me. The *real* me. So you either like that person, or you don't. I'm never going to be Sharlyn again, not even for you, Cole."

And with that, she turned on her heel and headed out.

The next day matched Cole's mood. According to his phone, Lucky Harbor was on storm watch, expecting the storm of the year later that night.

He pulled on his running gear and hit the pavement

for a long, punishing run through town, past the pier, the diner, the bar, the firehouse...the art gallery.

Lucille was out front, struggling with a string of lights that she was trying to remove from her mailbox.

"You're going to pretend not to see me, aren't you?" she said, her voice easily carrying on the damp, salty air.

"Thinking about it," he admitted.

She smiled. She was wearing bright red lipstick and a neon yellow tracksuit that said PINK across her sunken-in chest. She was barely taller than the mailbox and she was going to kill herself unstringing those lights. "Want to bring them in before the storm hits," she said.

Shit.

He stopped.

"Aw, you're a sweet boy," she said, and had to reach up to pat him on the shoulder. "A little slow, but sweet."

He narrowed his eyes at her.

"The sweet part's a compliment," she said innocently.

"Uh-huh."

"In fact, maybe you're sweet enough to help some of my friends, who'd love to have their chores handled by Captain Hottie as well?" She took in his expression and grimaced. "I don't have that much power, huh?"

"God doesn't have that much power," he said.

"Hey, it was worth a shot. Listen, honey, I don't mean to pry, but—" She broke off when he snorted, and she smiled. "Okay, so I do mean to pry, and we all know it. But about you and Olivia—"

His smile faded. "I'm not going to discuss it," he said. "She had her reasons for what she did to me."

"Actually, I wanted to discuss what you did to her."

He blinked. "Excuse me?"

"Well, you didn't listen very well when she tried to talk to you, and also, you let her put it all on the line and then you didn't reel her in. And here I thought you were the fisherman." She tsked.

"She lied to me."

Lucille laughed. *Laughed.* And then she patted him on the arm as if to say *You poor, stupid, penis-carrying idiot.*

"Can I make a suggestion?" she asked.

"Could I stop you?"

She flashed another smile. "Why don't you make use of the World Wide Web on the matter?"

"The World Wide Web."

"Yes," she said. "Or as you youngsters call it these days, the 'Internet.'" She added air quotes.

And when he just stared at her, she sighed. "You know," she said, "for research?"

"And what might I be researching?"

"Why, Olivia's illustrious past, silly. The one that made you so upset." She gave him a light smack on the chest. "Listen, I don't want to be presumptuous, but you should consider taking some vitamins to keep your mind sharp. You're losing your edge, boy."

And with that sage advice, she gave him one last teacher-to-errant-pupil look and then turned and walked inside her gallery.

Leaving him standing there wondering, *What the fuck?* Shaking his head, he headed back to his place, where he showered and got into his truck.

He needed to get the hell out of the Twilight Zone.

He needed answers.

And he wasn't going to find them on the "World Wide Web," either.

Chapter 30

Cole headed south. It was four hours to Salem, Oregon, but that suited him just fine. He needed to think.

Halfway there, the weather turned to shit as promised. According to the insanely cheerful weatherman on the radio, Cole was heading directly into a nasty, temperamental weather system that was sporting for a fight.

That suited him, too.

Dark, tumultuous clouds were churning the sky as he parked outside the address he'd used Google Maps to find. He took in the house.

Susan's house.

It was a small blue-and-white Craftsman-style. The yard was neat and trimmed, matching the rest of the street. There were oak trees lining the sidewalk and bikes and toys in the yards, with inexpensive cars that suggested a young but hardworking neighborhood.

There was lace hanging in the windows, a stroller on the front step, and a swing hanging from the tree in her yard.

Cole closed his eyes, let out a long, ragged breath, and thunked his head on the steering wheel a few times.

"Gonna knock something loose in there."

Cole turned to the familiar female voice.

Susan, standing just outside his truck, gave him a small smile as he cursed. "Hey," she said.

She looked the same, and the two years fell away. Willowy, serene, her pretty hazel eyes warm.

"You're a surprise," she said, and opened his truck door. She got a look at his expression. "Oh," she said. "Were you planning on just sitting here and staring at my house, then?"

He gave her a rueful smile. "Actually, I hadn't decided yet."

"Fair enough." She leaned against the truck and studied the sky.

"What are you doing?" he asked.

"Waiting for you to decide."

"Shit." He got out of the truck and leaned against it next to her. He could see that she was holding a baby monitor and he had to laugh. "I have no idea why I'm here."

"I do."

When he met her gaze, she gave him a small smile.

"Shit," he said again. "Who called you, Tanner or Sam?"

"Both. They tracked you on your Find Your Friends app and figured out where you were headed."

"Christ, it's like they've joined Lucille's geriatric gang," he muttered.

She lifted the small monitor. "Listen, the baby's still sleeping, but I'd really rather be inside where I can be closer. Coming with?"

"Yeah." What the hell. He wanted answers, and she had them. "Sure."

They sat in her small but cozy kitchen while she poured some coffee and he tried not to stare at the wedding ring blinding him from her finger.

She set a mug down in front of him, ruffled his hair like she always used to do, and sat across from him. She held out her hand with the ring and they both stared at it. "A year," she said.

"I didn't ask."

"You wanted to," she said. "The baby's two months old." She smiled with so much love it made his heart squeeze. "Sierra's the best thing that ever happened to me."

"So you're happy," he said.

"Very." She paused, studying him. "And you want to know how I possibly can be."

He blew out a breath. "I'm not judging."

"Yes, you are. And that's okay, I get it. I told you I loved you. And while I loved you I fell in love with another man."

"My best friend."

"Yes," she said, voice even, only her eyes revealing a past pain. "And now, two years later, I'm in love again. When the real thing comes along, there's nothing like it. And," she said, "you don't, or can't, understand."

"I don't," he said honestly. "I want to, but I don't."

"Some people have to learn how to love by going through it multiple times. That was me." She paused. "And some people love so completely with their entire heart, every single time."

He closed his eyes. "Me."

"You," she said softly. "Why are you here, Cole?"

"I don't know," he said honestly. "There's a woman."

She nodded. "And you…aren't sure?"

No, he was sure. Or he had been. Now he had no clue.

Susan drew a breath and then spoke carefully. "I know you're angry at me about my feelings for Gil. You've got a right to be. But Cole, don't be angry at Sam and Tanner. It wasn't their doing. And it wasn't their place to tell you about it, either."

"No, it was yours," he said. "Yours and Gil's."

"Yes," she agreed easily. "It was. And now I'm going to say something really important to you, so I need you to hear me." She reached across the table and squeezed his fingers until he met her gaze. "And I need you to believe me."

"Just say it."

"At the funeral, when my feelings for Gil came out, you left. You left and you wouldn't speak to me about any of it."

"You broke up with me right then and there," he reminded her. "While I was spinning and heartsick. Can you blame me?"

"Yes," she said. "Because there were things you needed to know." She drew a deep breath. "Gil and I—"

He closed his eyes. "Susan, don't—"

"—never slept together."

He opened his eyes. "What?"

"What was between us was never acted on, Cole. Gil didn't want to be that guy," she said quietly. "He refused to be that guy." She hesitated. "I'm not saying that we were innocent, because we weren't. After we realized our feelings, we tried to avoid each other for months, couldn't even look at each other, but eventually we couldn't do it anymore. It was wrong, it wasn't planned, it wasn't fun, and we never felt good about it. We fought it."

"Out of guilt," Cole said.

"Out of respect and love for you," she said. "I've always hoped you would forgive me. But honestly, Cole? That's your choice, not mine. And as it's out of my control, I've let go of it."

He had to be impressed by that, and how she'd gone on with her life. "I just don't get it," he said. "I can fix just about anything—except myself and my own relationships."

"Not true," she said. "You've got some of the best relationships of anyone I know. You've got Sam and Tanner, who would lay down their lives for you. Your sisters, who worship the ground you walk on. Your mom, who can and does depend so much on you. And last, but so definitely not least, Gil. I know you feel betrayed by him, and by, well, everyone else. But whatever your feelings are on how we handled things, Cole, please don't let it ruin the relationship you and Gil had. Or what you and Sam and Tanner have."

"But they knew," he said. "They knew and didn't tell me. I don't know how to get past that."

"Cole," she said slowly, gently, "everyone knew. It wasn't that hard to see. Everyone saw it except you."

He stared at her. "That…can't be true."

She let out a long breath, and he saw it in her eyes. Well, damn. Olivia wasn't the only one who could create a fiction all around her. Apparently he was good at it as well.

"I know there's someone new," she said. "And I know she wasn't completely honest with you about her past."

"Seriously," he muttered. "Going to kill Tanner and Sam."

"Just don't judge her from my actions," Susan said.

He shook his head. He wasn't sure how to do anything but.

"What she did probably had nothing to do with you, Cole. Do you get what I'm saying? She probably didn't mean to hurt you, but sometimes shit happens."

"That's it?" he asked in disbelief. "That's your big piece of advice—shit happens?"

"We're all different," she said. "We're not all good, or all bad for that matter. The world isn't black or white; you know that. Everyone's their own complicated puzzle, with a bunch of mismatched pieces. You put the pieces together the best you can and accept the flaws. Even learn to love the flaws."

"Easier said than done," he said.

"I know," she said, smiling when he swore. "You can be a little…rigid and unbending once you get an idea in your head of what you expect from a person."

"I always thought I was so easygoing."

She laughed, which he didn't give a lot of thought to as they said their good-byes and he made his way back to his truck.

Bullshit he was rigid and unbending.

Right?

Okay, so he hadn't exactly been a good listener when Olivia had tried to talk to him, but he'd been…

An ass.

A rigid, unbending ass.

Chapter 31

Olivia called the TV Land producer. "I'm in."

"Making my day, sweetcheeks."

"On one condition," she said. "Well, make it two."

"Name 'em," he said without hesitation.

"Call me sweetcheeks again, and I kick *you* in your sweet cheeks. And two, you film my part of the retro special here in Lucky Harbor."

"You don't want to come to the studio? We were going to re-create the set of *Not Again, Hailey!* for you."

"No." She shuddered. God, no. "I want to do it here, where my life is now. Just a quick interview, and if you need an audience, we'll use locals." She wasn't hiding here in Lucky Harbor, she was living the way she wanted to. No shame in that. Time to prove it to both herself and her world. "In my shop."

"Done," he said. "People will love the current look-see into your life. Can you do something wild and crazy to help ratings?"

"No! And I want to do this in the next few days."
She wanted this over with. An incoming call beeped. She
looked at her screen.

Cole.

Surprise, anxiety, and hope hit her. Along with a good
amount of anger. God, she was mad at herself, but she
was mad at him, too. "I have to go," she said.

"Just hold on a second. I'm working my mind around
trying to get up there that fast," he said. "I don't know."

"Take it or leave it; I have another call."

"Jesus, you're as difficult as they say."

"Yeah, I am. You've been in a hurry for this for a long
time," she said. "And now I'm in a hurry to be done."

"Killing me, Sharlyn."

"Olivia," she said. "My name's Olivia. Yes or no?"

"Yes."

God help her, but it was done. "Fine. Gotta go." She
clicked over to Cole, but he was gone.

About an hour into Cole's return trip to Lucky Harbor, it
began to rain. It came down in long, steady slashes that
made seeing out the windshield a challenge.

This didn't bother him any. Hell, he could remember
being five years old and sitting on his dad's lap in the
family truck, hands on the wheel, steering while his dad
worked the accelerator and brake.

And then being ten and driving his dad's truck better
than any of his sisters. Or his dad, for that matter. The old
man had gotten a big kick out of that, and had let Cole
drive on the back roads whenever they were out there together.

By the time Cole had turned fifteen, he could drive

anything, with wheels or without. Hell, he could've parked a semi in an asscrack. Backward.

He'd been given free rein with the family boat two years before he was legal, and that had cemented his love for all things with an engine.

His mom had worried that they'd bred a daredevil, but Cole had never felt compelled to be stupid.

Just fast. Smart.

And good.

He was still those things, or so he liked to believe. On and off the road. And on and off the water.

But as for real life?

Not so much, apparently.

In matters of the heart, for instance, he was slow as a fucking turtle in peanut butter.

And stupid to boot.

What was real? he'd asked Olivia. *Any of it?*

She'd actually taken a step back, as if he'd physically slapped her.

All of it...

It'd certainly felt real. Before her, he'd been just floating through life. Living but not experiencing. And then she'd jumped off that dock and nearly drowned him, and he'd thought of little but her ever since.

He had people in his life, good people, and he'd always been loved, accepted. Wanted.

She hadn't been so lucky.

And yet she instinctively knew how to love, how to give back, and in fact, she was better at it than he was. She'd jumped into the water after a perfect stranger to try to help. She'd given a piece of her past so a little girl in need could have the costume she wanted for Halloween.

She'd braved his entire family with a smile and no visible fear—and only now was he realizing just how hard that must have been for her.

Had he accused her of acting her way through life? Jesus, what a complete idiot he was. Her emotions were always there for him to see, whether she was facing him down, laughing with him, or simply making him ache like a son of a bitch as she lay beneath him by moonlight, rocking up into him, eyes locked on his, hiding none of her feelings...

We all create a fiction.

Yeah, she'd been as honest with him as she could. He knew that now.

Could he say the same? Had he given her everything he had or held back out of his own damn fears?

When the real thing comes along, there's nothing like it.

Until recently, he wouldn't have recognized the real thing if it'd hit him in the face.

Or jumped onto his head in the water...

But he knew it now. The real thing was back in Lucky Harbor, and he'd let it go.

Let her go.

Two hours into the drive, the rain turned to sleet. And then thirty minutes later, snow. Visibility went down to zip. Cole shifted into four-wheel drive and slowed accordingly to meet the road conditions.

He was one of the lonely few in that regard. Over the next five minutes he watched cars playing Slip 'N Slide across the road.

Damn. He knew what came next, and sure enough, not ten minutes later—during which time he'd gone a whopping half a mile—Oregon Department of Transportation shut the highway down.

He exited into no-man's-land and found a tiny hole-in-the-wall inn on a stretch of highway across the street from a McDonald's. No WiFi. The bathroom sink dripped in an uneven rhythm that made him want to crawl beneath it and fix it. The toilet ran. The bedside lamp kept flickering. And there was a low-level hum coming out of the smoke alarm that made him wish for a BB gun to shoot the fucker.

Or himself.

With nothing else to do, he lay in bed and stared at the lights from the McDonald's arches dancing across the ceiling.

It was six thirty at night, and he was alone with his own stupidity. He played the images on repeat through his mind. Like walking away from Tanner and Sam in anger…The three of them had fought plenty over the years, sometimes quietly, sometimes not so much, and yet they'd never stayed mad. They threw words, and occasionally a shove or two, and they got over it.

No one had ever walked away.

He regretted doing that, hugely.

Drip, drip, drip.

The bathroom sink was going to give him an embolism. That is, if the flickering light of the lamp didn't give him an aneurism first…

Shit. He rolled out of the bed, pulled a few tools from his cargo pants, and took the lamp apart.

And then put it back together.

And then, because he'd lost all self-control, he fixed the bathroom sink.

He was looking around for something else to fix—or toss through the window—when the power went out. On the bright side, he no longer had to worry about the lamp. And hey, a side benefit—no more slashing yellow light from the McDonald's across the way, either.

Six forty-five.

He had two bars of battery left on his phone. Nope, make that one bar. Since he was going to die in this god-forsaken hellhole, he blew through some time checking email. His mom wanted to get a Christmas list together early this year because she liked to shop on the Internet. Cindy's laptop was still not working. Sam wanted to know if Cole was over himself yet.

Tanner hadn't been so politically correct. *You're an asshole* was all his email said.

Right. He'd just make a note of that.

There in the dark, he began a fun little game called Torture Yourself by Replaying Your Most Idiotic Moments.

Such as acting like a first-class asshole with Tanner and Sam.

Such as acting like a first-class asshole with Olivia.

And then he pictured Lucille, standing out there by her mailbox in her bright red lipstick and rheumy blue eyes, suggesting he get on the Internet.

He looked at his phone and decided what the hell. Why not waste his last bar doing something productive?

He looked up *Not Again, Hailey!*

He vaguely remembered the show, though he'd never seen it. He hit Wikipedia first. Holy shit, Wikipedia was a veritable cornucopia of…shit. The pictures and YouTube clips he found numbered in the tens of thousands, and he just started at the beginning, working his way through some of the interviews and clips of the cast and crew.

As he flipped through hundreds of pics and articles, watching clips of Olivia singing and dancing and acting her little heart out, he got grim, and more grim.

She'd been plucked out of obscurity by a pushy stage mom. She'd carried an entire show from the age of seven until she'd hit sixteen. With that birthday had come a maturity that could no longer be hidden. And then it'd come to an end. Everything and everyone she'd known had scattered.

She hadn't handled it like an adult, but she hadn't been an adult. And ouch on the DUI, but he forced himself to keep watching and reading. It was like a train wreck, and he couldn't look away. In the pictures and clips from after the show had ended, her smile was all wrong.

No one had seemed to notice. How had no one noticed? She'd had all those people around, but they'd been looking out for numero uno—themselves. Who'd had her back? Who'd protected her?

She'd been forced to do that herself, and she had—by burying her past. Her right, he realized.

He wished he could kick his own ass.

He tried calling her again, and just as it rang once, his phone shut off and went dead as a doornail, whatever the fuck that meant. Dead as he'd felt after Gil's death, after his dad's death...

But there was something that was no longer dead.

His heart.

And he knew who to thank for that. The person he'd walked away from, and God, he couldn't believe he'd done that to her, when all her life, people had walked away from her.

He didn't deserve a second chance with her, he knew this, but he was going to ask for one anyway, and spend the rest of his life trying to make it up to her.

Chapter 32

♥

Unfortunately for Cole, the "storm of the year" blew in and made itself at home along the entire Pacific Coast, socking in fifteen hundred miles of the west.

It carried on the drama for two days, during which time he—holed up in the motel room—ground his back teeth into powder, ate a whole lot of Mickey D's, and stalked the unstocked, trampled aisles of a convenience store.

When he finally got back into Lucky Harbor two days later, it was six in the morning and so cold he had no choice but to be thinking painfully and clearly.

There was no doubt he'd screwed things up. He was hoping that could be fixed. After all, he was good at fixing things.

Almost always.

With that one silver lining in mind, he drove straight to Olivia's.

She didn't answer.

Probably she didn't want to get out of her warm bed and answer the door. And because he knew that about her, knew too that her heater was probably not even on so she could save money, he didn't hesitate to take out a slim tool from a pocket and help himself by picking her lock.

Her place was empty.

Shit. He slid behind the wheel of his truck and picked up his cell phone, which was finally charged and going off.

Nothing from Olivia, but he had twenty-five texts from Cindy. With a sigh, he headed over to her house and found his sister trying to feed the baby with one hand and working her tablet and her cell phone with the other.

"Where the hell have you been?" she demanded, trying to shove a spoonful of applesauce into Kyle's mouth.

Kyle tightened his mouth and shook his head back and forth, sending a happy, drooling coo in Cole's direction.

Cole smiled at him. "Hey, tiger."

Kyle bounced up and down in his seat and blew raspberries, trying to entice Cole to scoop him up.

Cole bent low, lifted the kid's shirt, and blew an answering raspberry on the baby's belly, eliciting a gut laugh and some serious leg kicking.

"Both of you cool it," Cindy said. "Trying to feed him here."

Cole took the spoon from her and promptly made like a plane with it for Kyle, complete with sound effects.

Kyle opened his mouth like a bird and swallowed the whole bite. Then he smiled like an angel at his mama.

Cindy rolled her eyes.

"So what's the emergency?" Cole asked.

"I screwed up my laptop."

"And?"

"And," she said, frowning at him, "you always fix it when I screw it up. And also you told me last time that I shouldn't dare attempt to fix it myself, or ever let anyone else touch it, or you'd toss it into the harbor."

"I shouldn't have said that," he said. "That was…rigid of me."

She narrowed her eyes. "What's the matter with you today?"

"Nothing."

"Uh-huh," she said. "So can you fix it or not?"

He stared down at the offending piece of technology. "You didn't deny the rigid thing."

Craning her head, she blew a strand of hair from her harried face. "Huh?"

"Do you think of me as rigid?"

She paused. "Define rigid."

"Doesn't stray from a routine," he said. "Unbending. *Rigid.*"

She blinked, then clearly bit back a smile. "And you want me to tell you that you're not those things?"

"Shit." He stood up and headed to the door.

"Hey," she called after him. "My laptop!"

"I'm straying from routine," he said.

He'd no sooner slid behind the wheel of his truck than Sam pulled up behind him.

Then Tanner in front, the two of them blocking him in.

"Been looking for you," Sam said as he opened Cole's passenger door and got in. Tanner helped himself at the driver's door, forcing Cole over so that he was sandwiched between them, coming into such a close and personal relationship with the gearshift that the two of them should have gotten a marriage license first.

Tanner hit the autolock, as if Cole could possibly even move to escape without climbing out over the top of one of them.

"You know," Tanner said conversationally, "when you're alive, you answer your phone."

"There are at least six ways to get ahold of me that don't involve me having to speak to you," Cole said. "Try one of them next time."

Sam and Tanner exchanged a look, and Cole ignored it. And them. A mean feat given that they were practically in each other's laps. Cole tipped his head back and stared up at the ceiling of the truck. "Am I...rigid?"

"I don't know, man," Tanner said. "But I'm really hoping not."

"In *general*," Cole said with a clenched jaw. "Am I rigid, as in unbending. Unforgiving."

"Okay, that question makes a lot more sense," Tanner said, relieved.

"Am I?"

Sam started coughing to hide a laugh.

Tanner didn't try to hide anything, he just grinned.

"Shit," Cole said. "Somebody let me the fuck out."

"Not yet," Sam said. "First things first. We give you shit about being rigid and unbending, but it's just that. Shit. Your sister lied to your mom, and you helped her anyway. Tanner and I kept this from you, and you're here speaking to us."

"Barely," Cole said.

"My point," Sam said, "is that you're not *completely* rigid and unbending."

"Gee," Cole said. "Thanks."

"And secondly," Sam went on, much more seriously. "There wasn't a memo to fuck you over."

Cole squeezed his eyes shut. "I know."

"We only found out by sheer dumb luck about a week before the fire," Tanner said. "Gil was at the bottom of a bottle. It was killing him. He was going to tell you. He didn't because I stopped him."

Cole looked over at the guy who he believed would always have his back, no matter what, to the end. "I'm trying to imagine under what circumstances you could have possibly believed I was better off not knowing," he said with what he felt was admirable calm. Especially because he was imagining rearranging Tanner's teeth.

"We were in the gulf," Tanner said. "And in case you don't remember, you were in the middle of upgrading the entire safety system and having a rough go of it. I told Gil that while we were on the rig wasn't the time to tell you. That only a selfish asshole would assuage his own guilt right then."

Cole tried to absorb that.

"Telling you would have cleared his conscience," Sam said, "but it'd have wrecked you. And that was bullshit. Tanner convinced him that waiting was best."

Cole took in Tanner's hard expression and wondered exactly what the "convincing" had consisted of. "The week before the fire," Cole said, remembering. "He showed up one morning with a black eye and fat lip."

Tanner didn't move, didn't blink.

"That was you," Cole said.

Tanner lifted a shoulder, the only confirmation Cole was going to get.

"We told Gil that he could damn well wait another two weeks until we were all on a three-day break," Sam said.

Only that break had never come because there'd been the fire...

And then Gil had been gone.

Christ.

He let his head fall back. Two years and it still didn't feel real. "I've been an asshole."

"No worries," Sam said. "It was your turn."

"Maybe it can be my turn next," Tanner noted almost wistfully.

"You are due," Sam noted.

"I went to Olivia's," Cole said. "She wasn't there. I need to find her."

"She came looking for you after you left," Tanner said. "I told her that even ass-hats deserve second chances after detonating the best relationship to ever happen to them."

Sam snorted.

"You need to fix it with her," Tanner said. "She's good for your rigid ass."

"Says the guy who avoids relationships like the plague," Cole said.

"At least I know a good thing when it hits."

Cole thought of how he felt when he was with Olivia. He called her Supergirl, but the truth was, she made him feel like Superman. With her he wasn't just the guy who could fix anything, navigate, repair, referee, or mitigate.

With her, he was a better version of himself. "I need to find her," he repeated.

"Maybe if you said please," Sam said.

Cole stared at him. "You know where she's at."

Sam cupped a hand around his ear. "Did you hear 'please,' Tanner?"

"Nope," Tanner said.

Jesus. "Tell me where she is and I won't kill you both with my bare hands," Cole said.

Sam and Tanner grinned, the asses. But finally they got the hell out of his truck.

Tanner leaned into the driver's window. "The answer you seek is readily available."

"What are you, a fortune cookie?" Cole snapped. "Just tell me."

"She's at her store," Sam said, giving Tanner a shove with a laugh. "Genius here is referring to the fact that it's all over Tumblr."

"What's all over Tumblr?" Cole asked, but they were walking to their respective vehicles.

"Oh, and I'd practice your groveling on the way," Tanner called back.

Chapter 33

♥

Cole drove straight to Unique Boutique. Normally he wouldn't have been surprised to find the lot behind the shop full. Olivia usually had a lot of people coming in and out; she was good at drawing steady business.

But it was...he checked his phone. Eight thirty. She didn't open until ten.

The back door was locked. Good girl, he thought, and headed around to the front.

That door was locked, too, and the CLOSED sign was still up. He peeked in the window and went still. The front room had been transformed. In the corner where she normally held Drama Days, everything had been cleared except for an antique bar stool smack in the center of the rug like it was on a stage.

Olivia sat on the bar stool wearing a gauzy top and tight, dark jeans with boots, all of which showed off her gorgeous body, looking beautiful and aloof.

She was facing the other side of the room, where chairs

had been lined up and were filled by…people. Lots of them. There was Becca, Sam, and Tanner— *Sam and Tanner?* Cole squinted and stepped closer. His sisters were there, too. And so was his mom. And Lucille and her merry band of stealth geriatrics. All of them glued to a camera crew and a man standing before Olivia with a microphone.

Cole caught Sam's gaze and jabbed a finger at the door.

Sam shook his head.

Oh hell to the no. Cole narrowed his eyes.

Sam gestured for him to go around back. Cole took another look at Olivia. She was sitting there, showing the world her I'm-tough-as-hell face, but something in her eyes reminded him of how she'd looked a decade earlier in all the videos he'd watched just the other day.

Alone.

So damn alone.

He'd been alone, too. Surrounded by people and yet utterly alone—until she'd jumped on his head.

He met Sam at the back door. "What the fuck?"

Sam shrugged. "You went the highway route, we took the streets."

"I meant what the fuck, as in what the fuck are you doing here at all?"

"Becca asked us to come. Said they needed bodies for some sort of shoot. That's all I know."

"You didn't ask questions?"

"When you have a hot fiancée who asks you for a favor in a voice that promises reward later, trust me, you don't stop to ask questions."

Cole pushed past him, strode through the back room,

and came to a stop in the doorway to the main room. There were lights and cameras set up, centered around Olivia. And in that moment, he knew.

She'd agreed to the retro show for TV Land he'd overheard her and her sister discussing.

"Let's have some questions from the audience to warm us up," the guy with the mic was saying to Olivia in front of the cameras.

She smiled. It was the same smile from her past, the one that didn't reach her eyes or come anywhere close to touching her heart.

And his own heart sank. "Goddamn it."

Several audience members were vying for the microphone, wanting to ask Olivia a question. And unbelievably, first up was Cindy, his own sister.

"Do you have fond memories of the show?" she asked Olivia.

"Some," Olivia said. "It was my childhood, after all. But a lot of bad things happened to me as a result of the years in Hollywood. Which is why I changed my name and…vanished."

Cindy nodded solemnly, her eyes filled with understanding. "If I'd been in that show and gone through all you did, I'd want to change my name, too. By the way, thanks so much for the donation of that Dior dress for the after-school kids' programs fund-raiser next week. You saved the day there. We have the bid up to twelve hundred dollars already. I can't express enough how much that'll mean to the rec center."

Cole stared at Olivia, though he shouldn't have been surprised. She was one of the most generous people he'd ever met. She gave her best, always.

He'd had a chance to give her his very best, to forgive her for a mistake she apologized for and regretted, and he'd failed her.

He wanted another chance. He wanted that badly.

Lucille hopped up. "Me next!" Her head came up at least a foot below the microphone. This didn't faze her. "I have a question," she yelled up at it.

"You don't have to yell," the interviewer told her. "Just speak in your normal voice."

Lucille nodded. Then she proceeded to yell some more up at the microphone. "Why stop acting? Why not stay and continue on with another show?"

Olivia hesitated. "The people in my life at the time had all moved on. My agent, my manager, the show's producers. But even without them, I wasn't young enough or cute enough for the kid roles, and the only other roles I was offered were for adult film. I was going through a wild stage, but not that wild."

The interviewer reached for the mic, but Lucille held on to it and took a step away from him. "For the record," she told Olivia, "we're all very glad you ended up here in Lucky Harbor."

The interviewer finally wrested the mic from Lucille. "Time for someone else to ask a question," he said, jerking down the hem of his suit jacket.

Cole strode to the front of the line to grab the mic, cutting off several people, including his own mother.

"Hey," the interviewer started, only to swallow hard when he caught a good look at Cole's expression. He lifted his hands in surrender and backed off.

"The people who left you," Cole said to Olivia. "They were a bunch of idiots. Anyone who's ever left you is an idiot." He didn't break eye contact. "Including myself."

"That's not really a question," the interviewer said, but backed off when Cole gave him another hard look.

Lucille pumped a fist in the air. "Yes! I knew this was going to get good. Hang on, honey, stop talking a second." She shoved a hand into the pocket of her neon green tracksuit and pulled out her phone. "I want to catch this on tape for my YouTube channel." She paused, then turned to Cole. "Do they still call it 'tape' even though it's not tape?"

He ignored her and stepped onto the carpet to take Olivia's hand in his.

"What are you doing?" she asked, eyes wide.

"You came into the Love Shack, willing to be public about our feelings in order to talk to me. I wronged you that day, and I'm hoping to fix it. Fix us."

"Speak up," Lucille demanded, holding up her phone.

"Us?" Olivia asked Cole, looking like she was afraid to hope.

"Us," he said firmly, and hauled her off the bar stool and into his arms.

Olivia was having trouble tracking this whole conversation because her heart was smacking up against her ribs with every single beat. *BOOM, BOOM, BOOM.* It was all she could hear.

Well, that, and the voice of the angel on her right shoulder saying, *Oh my God, he's back! He's here! He's looking at you like you're more important than his next breath!*

But the devil on her left shoulder was standing firm, shaking her head. *Don't believe…*

"Is it hot in here?" Olivia asked the interviewer as she pulled free from Cole. Because she was sweating in impolite places, and yet her teeth were chattering a little bit as well. Worse, her brain had gone on an island vacay without a forwarding address. "Maybe we should take a little break." Or better yet, cancel—

"I was wrong to walk away from you," Cole said. "I was wrong to let you think that you didn't matter to me. If you'll let me prove it, I'll never walk away from you again."

A new sensation fluttered in Olivia's chest, and she was desperately afraid it was hope, that cruel bitch.

Cole took in her expression and frowned. His arms banded around her tight, and then there were his eyes. Fierce. Protective. Determined.

Her heart squeezed. She knew that look; he was going to kiss her. Here? In front of everyone? No, she thought, he wouldn't. As he'd mentioned, their last public appearance hadn't gone so well—

But he hauled her up to her toes and laid one on her, the kind of kiss that had her coming alive, the kind of kiss that was both too fast and yet somehow also in slow motion so she could remember every detail of it, from the feel of the warm touch of his mouth to hers to the way his arms were so tight that maybe he was never going to let go.

When he finally pulled back an inch and met her gaze, she barely heard the applause of the room over the thundering of her own heart. She could hardly draw a breath for all the terrible, burning hope flickering to life within her.

Cupping her face, Cole tilted it to his. "I'm sorry. I let you think I was furious with you. I was angry at myself that I fell for you and then didn't know if it was real or not. I used a previous hurt and betrayal as a reason to not trust you. I shouldn't have walked out like that without giving you a chance to explain. Let me make it up to you, and I'll start by telling you this—you're so precious to me, Olivia. And worth fighting for."

Lucille sighed dreamily and turned to Amelia. "You did good with this one, honey."

Amelia nodded. "I sure did."

Olivia couldn't pay attention to their audience or she'd lose it. "Cole, don't. I can't— Not unless you mean it—"

"I've never meant anything more," he said.

She wanted to ask if that could be true, if the promises he was making were real, if she could trust how he was making her feel. But she didn't, because Cole never did anything he didn't mean. He meant this; he meant every second of it.

"I love the way you're always willing to jump in feetfirst," he said, "whether that's into the water on top of my head—"

She choked out a half laugh, half sob.

"—Or into a party with me to meet the insanity that is my family—"

"Your family is amazing," she said.

"It's true," Cara said to Lucille. "We're all pretty amazing."

Cole ignored this and turned back to Olivia. "You're the amazing one," he told her. "I wish you could see yourself the way I do. See yourself telling stories to the kids at Drama Days, or how you handle Lucky Harbor's crazy geriatric gang—"

"Hey," Lucille said.

"You change the chemistry in a room, Olivia," he said, ignoring Lucille. "You make it good. And then there's the way you have of taking the path that works for you. Even when you're half convinced you're going to get hurt along the way, you still go for it."

"It's called being ornery."

"Yeah," he said. "We're a good match there." He pointed to their audience, mostly his family and Lucille, as if to say *Don't you dare comment*.

Olivia snorted and he smiled. "And I love that you don't put up with my shit." He cupped her face. "And God, I especially love the way you look at me."

"Like you're crazy?"

He flashed a grin. "Yeah. That. You tried to save me, remember?"

Like she could forget. "But you didn't need saving," she reminded him.

"Yeah, I did. I just didn't know it. But that's not the point."

"It's not?"

"No. It's that you went for it. You gave me you."

Their audience gave a collective sigh and Olivia's eyes filled. It was too much, so much. Everything. "Cole—"

"I love you, Olivia. I love who you were, and I love who you are. I love everything about you."

She blinked. "Everything, except…"

"No exceptions," he said, voice low but fierce. "I just want to be the man you can be yourself with."

"That's a lot for me."

"Too much?"

She thought about how she'd felt when she'd thought they were over, how her heart had cracked into pieces. "I've recently learned that it's never too much, not with you."

He brought their joined hands up to brush a kiss over her knuckles. "You only need to tell me when you need space."

"What if I want you in my space?"

He smiled. "I like the sound of that. A whole hell of a lot. My world doesn't work without you in it, Olivia. I missed you." He pulled her into him from head to toe, and every glorious thing in between, and she became aware of one particular part that missed her more than the others.

She lifted her gaze and met his. "What am I going to do with you?"

He dipped his head and brushed his mouth to her ear. "I have a few suggestions," he whispered.

She laughed and then dropped her head to his chest. "No, seriously. *What am I going to do with you?*"

"Keep me?" He tilted her head up, and his grin was gone. "Listen, I know I'm not very good at this, keeping the right woman in my life. That's because I've never had her before. But that woman is you, Olivia. I'm willing to work on it, even beg you for a learning curve if I have to."

She felt her throat tighten. "Oh, you're most definitely better at this than you think."

His thumbs stroked her jaw. "Is that a yes?"

"I didn't hear a question."

"Neither did I!" Lucille turned to the audience. "Did any of you hear a question?"

A resounding "no" went through the crowd, but Cole had eyes only for Olivia. "Will you give me another shot at your heart, Olivia Bentley?"

She smiled. "Not necessary. You already own it."

Callie runs a one-stop wedding website, even though she doesn't believe in love.

Tanner knows love exists, but he can do without it.

So what are the odds that they're right for each other?

Please turn this page for a preview of

ONE IN A MILLION.

Chapter 1

♥

I want a hoedown wedding."

Callie Sharpe, wedding site designer and planner, was professional enough to not blink at this news. "A hoedown wedding."

"Yes," her client said via Skype. "The bridesmaids want to wear cowboy boots, and Jimmy wants to eat pigs in a blanket at the reception. Can the wedding site you're creating for me reflect all that?"

"Sure," Callie said to her laptop. After all, she loved pigs in a blanket, so who was she to judge? "It's your day, whatever you want."

Her bride-to-be smiled. "You really know your wedding stuff. And you always look so wonderful. I love your clothes. Can I see what shoes you're wearing? I bet they're fab, too."

Callie didn't let her easy smile slip. "Oh, but this is about your wedding, not my shoes. Let's talk about your invitations—"

"Please?"

Callie sighed. For the camera, she wore a silky cami and blazer. Out of camera range, she wore capri yoga pants, which doubled as PJs, and...bunny slippers. "Whoops," she said. "I've got another call. I'll get back to you when your site is up and running."

"But—"

She disconnected and grimaced. "Sorry," she said to the client who could no longer hear her. She went back to work, clicking through page after page of the season's new wedding dresses, uploading the ones she liked best. She switched to the latest invitation designs next. And then unique party favors and stylish accessories.

You really know your wedding stuff.

Unfortunately, this was true. She'd been a bride once, the most silly, hopeful, eager bride ever. Well, an *almost* bride. She'd gotten all the way to the church before getting stood up, and since that memory still stung, she shoved it aside. She'd married something else instead— she'd united her strong IT skills with her secret, deeply buried love of all things romantic and had created TyingTheKnot.com. On a daily basis, she dealt with demanding, temperamental, and, in lots of cases, batshit-crazy brides, all looking for their happily-ever-after. She'd made it her job to give them the dream.

It was exhausting. Standing, Callie stretched and moved to the wall of windows. Her apartment was one of three in a battered old warehouse that had once been a cannery, then a saltwater taffy manufacturer, and then, in the fifties, a carnival boardinghouse. The building wasn't much to write home about, but the view made the lack of insulation and heat worth it.

Mostly.

Today the waters of Lucky Harbor were a gorgeous azure blue, dotted with whitecaps thanks to a brutal mid-November wind that was whistling through the tangle of steel rafters, metal joists, and worthless heating ducts above her.

Callie had grown up here in this small, quirky coastal Washington town sandwiched between the Pacific and the Olympic Mountains, and once upon a time, she hadn't been able to get out of here fast enough.

She was back now, and not exactly because she wanted to be.

There was a man in the water swimming parallel to the shore. Passing the pier, he moved toward the north end and the row of warehouses, including the one she stood in.

Transfixed, she watched the steady strokes and marveled at his speed. He might as well have been a machine, given how efficiently and effectively he cut through the water.

Callie had been in those waters, although only in the summertime. She couldn't even swim to the end of the pier and back without needing life support.

But the man kept going.

And going.

After a long time, he finally turned and headed in, standing up in the water when he got close enough. After the incredible strength he'd shown swimming in the choppy surf, she was surprised when he limped from it to the sand. Especially since she couldn't see anything wrong with him, at least from this distance.

He was in a full wetsuit, including something covering

his head and most of his face. He peeled this off as he dropped to his knees in the sand, and she gasped.

Military-short dark hair and dark eyes. And a hardness to his jaw that said he'd had the dark life to go with it.

He looked just like…oh, God, it was.

Tanner Riggs.

While she was standing there staring, her cell phone started ringing with the *I Love Lucy* theme song, signaling that her grandma was calling. Eyes still glued to the beach—and the very hot man now unzipping his wetsuit—she reached for her phone. "Did you know Tanner Riggs was home?" she asked in lieu of a greeting.

"Well, hello to you too, my favorite nerd-techie grand-daughter."

"I'm your only granddaughter," Callie said.

"Well, you're still my favorite," Lucille said. "And yes, of course I know Tanner's in town. He lives here now. Honey, you're not following my Instagram or you'd already know this and much, much more."

She didn't touch this one. The sole reason she was back in Lucky Harbor and not in San Francisco was because of her grandma.

Callie's dad—Lucille's only son—had been an attorney. Actually both of her parents had, and even retired, they still liked things neat and logical.

Grandma Lucille was neither, and Callie's parents were pretty sure her grandma was no longer playing with a full set of marbles. Callie had drawn the short stick to come back and find out what needed to be done. She'd been here several weeks, staying in the rental because she needed to be able to work in peace. Her grandma had loaned her the car since Lucille had recently been soundly rejected by the DMV for a license renewal. The two of them had daily meals together—mostly lunches, as Lucille's social calendar made the queen of England look like a slacker. But there'd been no sign of crazy yet.

Not that Callie could give this any thought at the moment, because Tanner shoved the wetsuit down to his hips.

Holy.

Sweet.

Baby.

Jesus.

Back in her high school days, a quiet brainiac like Callie had been invisible to him. Which had never gotten in the way of her fantasies, as the teenage Tanner Riggs had been rangy, tough, and as wild as they came.

He'd filled in and out, going from a lanky teen to a man who looked like every inch of him was solid muscle, not a spare ounce in sight.

Was he still tough and wild and a whole lot of trouble?

Oblivious to both her musings and the fact that she was drooling over him, Tanner moved to the fifty-foot sport boat moored at the dock, where he came face-to-face with a teenager who looked so much like him that Callie actually blinked in shock. Unless time travel was involved and Tanner had come back as his fifteen-year-old self, she was looking at his son.

The two males spoke for a moment, the teen's body language sullen and tense, Tanner's calm, stoic, and unreadable. Then, still shirtless, his wetsuit low on his hips, Tanner hopped lithely onto the boat and shimmied his way up the mast, moving seemingly effortlessly on the strength of his arms and legs. He had something between his teeth, a rope, she saw, and damn if her heart didn't sigh just a little bit at watching him climb with heart-stopping, badass grace.

"He's certainly romance-hero-material," her grandma said in her ear, nearly making Callie jump. She'd forgotten she was on the phone.

"Tall, dark, and a bit of attitude written on the outside," her grandma went on, "but on the inside, he's really just a big softie."

Callie couldn't help it, she laughed. From her view, there was nothing soft about Tanner Riggs.

Nothing.

Not his body, not his mind, and certainly not his heart. "I remember him," she said softly. And what she remembered was getting her teenage heart crushed. "I need to go, Grandma."

"You coming for lunch?" Lucille asked. "I want to introduce you to the guy I think I'm going to take on as my new boyfriend."

Callie tore her gaze off Tanner and looked at her phone. "Wait— What? You haven't mentioned this."

"Yes, well, sometimes you can be a little prudish about these things."

"I'm not prudish. And what do you mean, 'taking on a boyfriend'?"

"Well, I'll need your definition of boyfriend first," her grandma said.

Callie stared at the phone. "Okay, we really need to have your hormone levels checked."

Lucille laughed. "I didn't tell you about the boyfriend because my sweetie and I like to keep things on the down-low. And plus, it was a test. A test to see if you've got skills to sniff out the dirt like I do. You failed, by the way."

"You mean because I'm not a snoop?" Callie asked, trying not to picture her eighty-plus grandma having a "sweetie." "And you do realize you have a reputation as the town's unofficial media relations director, right?"

"Yep. Although I'm lobbying to make it official—as in a paid position." She laughed when Callie snorted. "I swear, honey, it's like you're not even related to me. And anyway, how is it that you're the one who taught me how to work a computer and what social media was, and yet you don't utilize them to your favor?"

"You mean manipulate them?" Callie asked. "And I taught you all that because I thought you were getting elderly and bored and your mind would go to rot. I didn't know you were going to terrorize people with it!"

Lucille laughed. "I've got a bunch of good years left before I'll even consider getting elderly and bored. And no worries, my elevator still goes to the top floor. Come on over, honey. I've got to put the new registration sticker on the car; it just came in the mail. Nice that the state allows me to pay them for the car they won't license me to drive, huh? To sweeten the deal, I've got dessert from Leah at the bakery. She makes the best stuff on the planet."

Callie blew out a breath. "Okay, I'll bring the main course, something from the diner."

"I could make my famous fried chicken."

Last week, Lucille had set her fried chicken on fire and had nearly burned her house to the ground. Hence the "famous." Which was really more like infamous. "I'm on a diet," Callie fibbed.

"That's ridiculous," Lucille said, obviously outraged. "You don't need to go on a diet to catch a man. You look fantastic! I mean, you're a little short, but your curves are all the rage right now. And sure, you can come off as a little standoffish, but I blame your parents and their inability to love anyone other than themselves for that, not you."

Callie choked back her laugh. It was true; she was the product of two college sweethearts who'd been so crazy in love with each other that nothing had ever really penetrated their inner circle—including their own child. They'd raised her kindly and warmly enough, but her quiet upbringing had left her introverted and preferring the company of a computer to that of people. "I'm not trying to catch a man," she said.

"Well, that's a shame. And not to add any pressure, but you do know Eric's around too, right?"

Eric. Damn. Just the sound of her ex's name made her stomach cramp. "Eric who?" she asked casually.

Lucille cackled. "Attagirl. Perfectly normal tone. But next time, no hesitation. That was a dead giveaway. Just be forewarned that your ex-fiancé—may his soul turn black—has married and has a kid on the way."

Callie told herself she didn't care that the man who'd left her at the altar due to a sudden severe allergy to commitment had apparently managed to overcome said allergy.

"And I'm not sure how long you're planning on staying in Lucky Harbor," her grandma went on, "but I doubt you'll be fortunate enough to avoid him. He's the only dentist in town. So the question is, how are your teeth? In good condition? You flossing daily? You might want to make sure you are."

Callie thunked her head against the window, and when she looked up again, she was startled to realize that Tanner was back on the dock and looking right at her.

For a minute, her heart stopped. "I've got to go, Grandma." She needed to be alone to process things. Like the fact that Eric was in town. And also that her very first, very painful, very humiliating crush was as well, and he'd grown into the poster child for Hottest Guy Ever.

"Wait," Lucille said. "Bring salads, because you might be right about a diet. The one of us who is going to get lucky needs to stay hot and all that."

Oh, boy. "Salads it is." Since there was no sign of recognition in Tanner's gaze, she forced herself away from the window, heading directly to her refrigerator. More accurately, her freezer, where she had two choices.

Ice cream.

Or vodka.

It was a tough decision, but as it was still early and she wasn't the one trying to look hot, she passed over the vodka and reached for the ice cream. Breakfast of champions, right? She had a spoon out of the drawer and the lid off the ice cream when she remembered. Ice cream was sugar. Sugar was bad for her teeth. And bad teeth required a dentist. "Crap."

"What?" Lucille asked.

Screw it, she needed this ice cream. "Nothing."

"Did you hear what I said about Eric?"

"Yeah." Callie took her first bite. "I'll floss." She was older and wiser now. No big deal. And her hefty armor of indifference and cynicism toward romance and happily-ever-after would help. "I'll be fine."

"Do you want me to set you up with another hottie?

'Cause no offense, honey, but you could do a lot better than Eric anyway. Listen, I'll start a poll for you on my Tumblr asking who people want to see you with—"

"No!" Callie nearly went back to the freezer for the vodka. "No," she said again, firmly. "No men."

"A woman, then?" Lucille asked. "Being a bisexual is in style."

Forget the vodka. She needed a new life. Maybe on Mars. "Grandma, I love you," Callie said. "I love you madly, but I don't want to discuss my love life with you."

"You mean your lack of?"

She sighed. "Or that."

"Fair enough," Lucille said. "But for the record, we can discuss mine anytime you want."

"Noted."

"I mean, it's amazing what those little blue pills can do to a man, let me tell you. He can just keep going and going like the Energizer Bunny—"

"*Really* gotta go," Callie said quickly. "I'll see you later." She disconnected, and she and the ice cream made their way back to the window.

Tanner was gone.

Chapter 2

♥

The ice cream didn't cut it. Needing caffeine, Callie went back to her kitchen before remembering her coffee-maker had died and gone to heaven the day before.

Damn. This was going to require a trip into town. And possibly seeing people. Which in turn meant kicking off her slippers and shoving her feet into her fake Uggs. Quite the look, but she wasn't planning on socializing; this was purely a medicinal trip.

In light of that, she skipped the diner and hit the bakery, thinking she'd get in and out faster. What she hadn't planned on was the amazing, mouthwatering scent of the place and the way it drew her straight to the dough-nut display. A pretty brunette was serving behind the counter. "How can I help you?"

"You Leah?" Callie asked.

"Yep."

"Perfect. It's rumored you make the best desserts on the planet."

"True story," Leah said.

"I'll take two of those powdered sugar doughnuts, then," Callie said, pointing to the display.

"Excellent choice. They solve all problems."

"Yeah?" Callie asked.

"Well, no. But they taste amazing."

"Good enough," Callie said.

Two minutes later, lost in a doughnut-lust haze, she'd forgotten her resolve to get in and get out. Instead, in a hurry to ingest the sugar, she looked for a seat in the crowded place. She finally snagged the last table and tried to look busy so that no one would ask to share it. But given the long line, the odds were against her. Which in turn meant she was going to have to be social.

Damn.

That should be in her game plan, she decided. Help out her grandma and also learn to be social with something other than her laptop and vibrator while she was at it. Shaking her head at herself, she dug in, taking a huge first bite and maybe, possibly moaning as the delicious goodness burst onto her tongue. Oh, yeah. Definitely the best powdered sugar doughnuts on the planet.

She took another bite, eyeballed the place, and then nearly did a spit-take across the room when she caught sight of the man at the front of the line. His back was to her, but there was no mistaking those broad shoulders.

Tanner had changed out of his wetsuit and now wore dark, sexy guy jeans and a light windbreaker that said LUCKY HARBOR CHARTERS across his back. He was talking to Leah, but he was also scanning the place as if by old military habit.

Don't look at me, she thought. *Don't look—*

He looked. In fact, those dark eyes lasered in and locked unerringly right on hers.

Her first reaction was a rush of heat. Odd, as she hadn't had one of those in relation to a man in a while—but not completely surprising, as Tanner was hotter than sin. An ice cube would've had a reaction to him.

Self-awareness hit her, as did reality. She looked down at herself. Yep, still wearing capri yoga pants and fake Uggs. Perfect. She was dressed like she didn't own a mirror. Even worse, she wore no makeup, and her hair...well, mostly the long, strawberry-blond waves had a serious mind of their own. The best that could be said this morning was that she'd piled them up on top of her head and they'd stayed. Thank God the messy topknot was in this year.

Not that this knowledge helped, because when a woman faced her first crush, that woman wanted to look hot—not like a hot mess.

"Is this chair taken?" Tanner asked.

Callie promptly swallowed too fast. Sugar went down the wrong pipe and closed off her air passage. When had he left the line and moved to her side? And damn it, why couldn't she breathe? Hiding this fact, she desperately went for a cool, unaffected look—difficult to pull off while suffocating.

His dark eyes were warm and filled with amusement. "Yes?" he asked. "No chance in hell?"

That's when she realized there was something worse than asphyxiation in public—he didn't recognize her.

Damn. In a single heartbeat, she was reduced to that shy, quiet, socially inept girl she'd once been. Talk, she ordered herself. Say something. But when she opened her mouth, the only thing that came out was a squeak.

And a puff of powdered sugar.

"It's okay," he said, and started to turn away.

This surprised her. The cocky, wild-man teenager she'd once known would've sent her a lazy smile and talked her into whatever he needed.

But it'd been a long time, and she supposed people changed. She'd certainly changed. For one thing, she was no longer that quiet, studious dork with the foolishly romantic heart. Nope, now she was a suave, immaculately dressed professional...She kept her legs hidden and decided this could be a good thing. His not recognizing her meant that she could make a *new* first impression. She didn't have to be a nerd. She could be whatever she wanted. Or more correctly, whatever she could manage to pull off. "Wait!" she called out to him. Maybe a little too loudly.

Or a lot too loudly.

Half the bakery startled and stared at her. And then in the next beat, everyone seemed to find their manners and scurried to look busy. Lowering her voice, Callie gestured to the free chair. "Sit," she told Tanner. "It's all yours."

He kicked the chair out for himself and sprawled into it. Sipping his coffee, he eyed her over the steam rising out of his cup, all cool, easy, masculine grace.

She tried to look half as cool, but she wasn't. Not even close. And she had a problem. A twofold problem.

One, the table was tiny. Or maybe it was just that Tanner's legs were long, but no matter how she shifted, she kept bumping into a warm, powerful thigh beneath the table.

And two, his eyes. They were the color of rich, dark melted chocolate.

God, she loved dark melted chocolate.

But he had no recollection of her. A definite blow to her already fragile, powdered-sugar-coated self-esteem. She wished she didn't care.

But it was the damn decade-old crush.

How did one get over a crush, anyway? Surely the statute of limitations was up by now. After all, he'd devastated her and hadn't even noticed.

To be fair, he'd had other things on his mind back then. She'd been a quiet, odd freshman, and he'd been a senior and the town's football star. She'd loved him from afar until he'd graduated and left town. She knew his story was far more complicated than that, but her poor, romantic heart had remained devastated by his absence for nearly two years. Then, in her last year of high school, Eric had moved in across the street. He and Callie had become a thing. They'd stuck, and by their last year of college, she'd had their wedding completely planned out—and she did mean *completely*, from the exact color of the bridesmaids' dresses, to the secluded beach where they'd say their vows, to the doves that would be released as they did...

Yeah, there was a reason she understood her client brides as well as she did. She'd once been a batshit-crazy bride, too. But she'd honestly believed that Eric would be the perfect groom and the perfect husband. After all, he'd spent years making her happy.

Up until the moment he'd stood her up at the altar.

"You okay?" Tanner asked.

"Sure." Just lost in the past. But she was done with

the past and took a bite to prove just how okay she really was. Bad move. Turned out it was hard to swallow correctly once she'd already choked. She then promptly compounded her error by gulping down some hot coffee on top of the sore throat and lump of doughnut that wouldn't go down and commenced nearly coughing up a lung.

She felt the doughnut being removed from her hand, and then the coffee. Tanner had stood up and was at her side, patting her back as she coughed.

And coughed.

Yep, she was going to die right here, in yoga capris and fake Uggs.

"Hang on," Tanner said, and strode to the front counter of the bakery.

From the dim recesses of her mind, she saw that he didn't bother with the line, just spoke directly to Leah behind the counter, who quickly handed him a cup of water.

Then he was back, pushing it into Callie's hands.

Nice and mortified, she took a sip of water, wiped her nose and streaming eyes with a napkin, and finally sat back. "I'm okay."

Tanner eyed her for a long moment, as if making sure she wasn't about to stroke out on him, before finally dropping back in his chair.

She opened her mouth, but he shook his head. "Don't try to talk," he said. "Every time you do, you nearly die."

"But—"

He raised an eyebrow and pointed at her, and she obediently shut her mouth. And sighed. She wanted to ask him about his limp, but he was right; she probably couldn't manage talking without choking again.

Way to wow him with a new first impression.

A woman came into the bakery and eyed Tanner with interest and intent, and unbelievably he leaned in closer to Callie, as if they were in the midst of the most fascinating of conversations.

"You settling into town okay at your new place?" he asked.

"My new place?"

"I see you watching me from your window."

Damn if she didn't choke again.

Seriously? She lifted a hand when he started to rise out of his chair, chased down the crumbs stuck in her throat with some more water, and signaled she was okay. "Sorry, rough morning."

"Let's go back to the not-talking thing," he said.

Yeah, she thought. Good idea.

A few minutes went by, during which Callie was incredibly aware of his leg still casually brushing hers. And also, a new panic. Because now she realized she was trapped, forced to wait until he left first so that he wouldn't catch sight of her wardrobe.

But he looked pretty damn comfortable and didn't appear to be in a rush to go anywhere.

She drew out her coffee as long as she dared and eyed her second doughnut. She wanted it more than she wanted her next breath, but she didn't trust herself. And what did he mean he'd seen her watching him? She didn't watch him. At least not all the time. "I don't watch you," she said.

He gave her a long look.

"I don't. I can't even see you from my window." She waited a beat to be struck by lightning for the lie. "I watch the *water*," she clarified. "It calms me."

"Whatever you say." He looked amused as he drank the last of his coffee. "So if I get up and go, are you going to choke again?"

Funny. "I think it's safe now," she said stiffly. "And anyway, I'm going to be good and give up doughnuts." Forever.

Or until he left.

"Good luck with that," he said, still amused, damn him. "But as you know by now, Leah's stuff is addicting." He cast his gaze around the room, watchful. He caught sight of the perky brunette hovering near the door. "Can I walk you out?" he asked.

Absolutely not. If he was afraid of the perky brunette, he was on his own. No way was Callie going to reveal her bottom half. With what she hoped was a polite, disinterested smile, she shook her head. She wasn't moving again until he was gone, baby, gone.

Just then, the little toddler at the table behind her dropped his pacifier. It rolled beneath her boots.

He began to wail.

Pushing her chair back, Callie picked it up and handed it to the mom with a smile before realizing she'd moved out enough for her body to be seen. With a mental grimace, she quickly scooted close to her table again and stole a glance at Tanner.

He was smiling. "Cute," he said.

She blew out a breath. "I was in a hurry."

"No, I mean it," he said. "Cute."

Cute? Puppies and rainbows were cute. Once upon a time she'd spent far too many hours dreaming about him finding her so irresistibly sexy that he'd press her up against the wall and kiss her senseless.

And he found her cute.

"Maybe you should steer clear of the dangerous powdered sugar doughnuts next time," he said. "In case there's no one around to rescue you."

"I like to live dangerously," she said, and because this was such a ridiculous statement, not to mention wildly untrue—she lived the opposite of dangerously and always had—she laughed a little.

He smiled at her, and it was such a great smile it rendered her stupid and unable to control her mouth. "You don't remember me."

"Sure I do," he said, and pushed away from the table as he stood. His gaze met hers. "Seriously now. Be careful."

And then he headed to the door.

Nope. He really didn't remember her. Still, she watched him go.

Okay, so she watched his fantastic butt go. After all, she was mortified and maybe a little bit pissy to boot, but she wasn't dead.

VISIT US ONLINE AT

WWW.HACHETTEBOOKGROUP.COM

FEATURES:

**OPENBOOK BROWSE AND
SEARCH EXCERPTS**

•

AUDIOBOOK EXCERPTS AND PODCASTS

•

AUTHOR ARTICLES AND INTERVIEWS

•

**BESTSELLER AND PUBLISHING
GROUP NEWS**

•

SIGN UP FOR E-NEWSLETTERS

•

**AUTHOR APPEARANCES AND TOUR
INFORMATION**

•

SOCIAL MEDIA FEEDS AND WIDGETS

•

DOWNLOAD FREE APPS

BOOKMARK HACHETTE BOOK GROUP
@ WWW.HACHETTEBOOKGROUP.COM

Find out more about Forever Romance!

Visit us at
www.hachettebookgroup.com/publishing_forever.aspx

Find us on Facebook
http://www.facebook.com/ForeverRomance

Follow us on Twitter
http://twitter.com/ForeverRomance

NEW AND UPCOMING TITLES

Each month we feature our new titles
and reader favorites.

CONTESTS AND GIVEAWAYS

We give away galleys, autographed copies,
and all kinds of exclusive items.

AUTHOR INFO

You'll find bios, articles, and links to personal websites
for all your favorite authors—and so much more.

GET SOCIAL

Connect with your favorite authors, editors, and
other Forever fans, and share what's important to you.

THE BUZZ

Sign up for our monthly romance newsletter,
and be the first to read all about it.